CRITICS RAVE ABOUT MELANIE JACKSON!

THE NIGHT SIDE

"*The Night Side* delivers in spades. . . . A seasoned storyteller, Jackson delivers another entertaining story."

—Fresh Fiction

DIVINE FANTASY

[Jackson] "has a wonderful way with descriptive language. There are some great connections with previous books and a surprise at the end."

—*RT Book Reviews*

A CURIOUS AFFAIR

"For a very different type of murder mystery and some very quirky characters and a twist at the end you won't see coming, pick up *A Curious Affair*, because in this tale, curiosity does not kill the cat!"

—Romance Reviews Today

DIVINE NIGHT

"Not to be read quickly, Jackson's latest is closely connected to the two previous Divine stories. . . . This is an excellent addition to this series."

—*RT Book Reviews*

WRIT ON WATER

"An intriguing mix of mystery and romance, with shadings of the paranormal, this is a story that pulls you in."

—*RT Book Reviews*

DIVINE MADNESS

"This tale isn't your everyday, lighthearted romance. . . . Melanie Jackson takes an interesting approach to this tale, using historical figures with mysterious lives."

—Romance Reviews Today

"Jackson pens a ⸻ of solid love stories like ⸻ enjoy Jackson's tale, wh⸻, then wait hungrily for ⸻

Booklist

THE SAINT

"This visit to the 'wild side' is wonderfully imaginative and action-packed. . . . [A] fascinating tale."

—*RT Book Reviews*

THE MASTER

"Readers . . . will not be disappointed. Her ability to create a complicated world is astounding with this installment, which includes heartwarming moments, suspense and mystery sprinkled with humor. An excellent read."

—*RT Book Reviews*

STILL LIFE

"The latest walk on the 'Wildside' is a wonderful romantic fantasy that adds new elements that brilliantly fit and enhance the existing Jackson mythos. . . . Action-packed."

—*Midwest Book Review*

THE COURIER

"The author's imagination and untouchable world building continue to shine. . . . [An] outstanding and involved novel."

—*RT Book Reviews*

OUTSIDERS

"Melanie Jackson is a talent to watch. She deftly combines romance with fantasy and paranormal elements to create a spellbinding adventure."

—*WritersWrite.com*

TRAVELER

"Jackson often pushes the boundaries of paranormal romance, and this . . . is no exception."

—*Booklist*

THE SELKIE

"Part fantasy, part dream and wholly bewitching, *The Selkie* . . . [blends] whimsy and folklore into a sensual tale of love and magic."

—*RT Book Reviews*

THE ARRIVAL

Thunder crashed outside. The rain had grown ferocious while I read, and the wind all but screamed. It was a fit night out for neither man nor beast, so nothing could have surprised me more than to have my late reading interrupted by a pounding on the ancient cottage door. The blows were heavy and spaced evenly, like the tolling of a funeral bell. This was the sound of doom calling, and it demanded I answer.

I had a welcoming if insincere smile pasted in place when I pulled back the heavy bar and opened the door, but it faded quickly as I surveyed the creature on my doorstep. He was male—oh, definitely male—and quite the most beautiful being I had ever seen. But there was also something about him that seemed sinister and made me feel weak and insignificant as I stood before him. Perhaps it was the fierce black eyes or the alabaster skin, or the long hair that fell in a sleek cascade to below his shoulders. Or perhaps, most alarming of all, it was how not a drop of rain seemed to cling to him—not to his hair, not to his skin, not to his old fashioned sark and kilt.

Other books by Melanie Jackson:

MELANIE JACKSON

THE SELKIE BRIDE

LOVE SPELL

NEW YORK CITY

For Auntie Nell and Uncle Ernie
and all the happy childhood memories they gave me.

LOVE SPELL®

February 2010

Published by

Dorchester Publishing Co., Inc.
200 Madison Avenue
New York, NY 10016

ISBN 10: 0-505-52834-7
ISBN 13: 978-0-505-52834-6
E-ISBN: 978-1-4285-0810-1

Visit us online at www.dorchesterpub.com.

THE
SELKIE
BRIDE

Editor's Note

By all accounts my great-aunt, Megan Culbin, was always an eccentric woman. I never met her, so I can offer no firsthand impressions of the soundness of her mind. Certainly she had no high regard for my grandmother (an opinion for which I forgive her, since I also had no great liking for the woman; sorry, Mom). As for the truth of this narrative, I must confess to having some doubt. I am, in fact, all doubt. The story is a compelling one, though, so fictitious or not I present it here with only marginal editing and compiling and leave readers to decide what is or is not true, and whether Megan Culbin was deliberately misleading or simply insane.

The following collection of documents was purportedly received by Mr. Alexander Waverly of the firm of Waverly and Woolencott of Edinburgh in December of 1923. The solicitor claimed it came with an attached affidavit that it is in my aunt's hand. Mr. Waverly's grandson forwarded it to me on his death because I am my aunt's only living female relative, and it took some decades to find me. Since there is no other money or property involved, I suspect the firm has been less than diligent in seeking me out and

Mr. Waverly may **have felt that** he was protecting my aunt's reputation.

I present the whole collection now with no further comment.

Melanie Jackson

The Selkie Bride
An American Woman's Adventure in Scotland
by Megan Culbin

Memory is faulty on its own, and mine has been interfered with to some degree, but I have rendered this account of the events of fall 1923 as honestly and accurately as possible. Any omissions are not intentional. Believe or don't, but I've done all I can to make a record of my actions before I leave Findloss forever. Enclosed is a copy of my will, drawn in my own hand but not witnessed. We shall not meet again.

Many thanks, and all best wishes.

—Megan Culbin

From the journal of Megan Culbin
Somewhere in the Atlantic, aboard the good ship
Morgana
July 2, 1923

Where do dreams go when they die? In my case, they are headed for Scotland and I have high hopes of giving the nightmares a decent burial there. Maybe then the dead will rest in peace and I will live in the same.

To begin with, you must know that I did not love my husband. I hadn't much liked Duncan when he was alive—not once we married and he revealed himself fully for the crazed fiend he was—and I liked him only slightly better once he was dead and buried as far underground as the sexton could decently place him. The man made my life a bewildering nightmare of humiliation from the time we were married, but he did do one thing for which I was grateful: He actually got around to making a will in my favor before surrendering himself to complete drunkenness and debauchery. So, along with inheriting all his debts to angry tradesmen, I also gained title to his late Uncle Fergus Culbin's cottage in Scotland, the mysterious and unmentioned old man having the consideration and forethought to die the week before my husband overdosed on absinthe and a seven-percent solution of cocaine while visiting a prostitute.

Thus I am on my way to Scotland, a widow of extremely modest means, and no kin to turn to except a puritanical aunt and uncle in Charleston and perhaps some distant relations of my late husband, who would doubtless prefer not to know me. My prospects are bleak enough, but I still count myself as the most fortunate of women. After all, I have escaped the worst possible marriage and will yet have a roof, however modest, over my head this winter. I am young and able-bodied. Whatever may yet come, not all widows—or wives—are so lucky.

Moan ye winds that never sleep,
Howl ye spirits of the deep . . .
— "The Maiden of Morven"

Chapter One

October 31, 1923

"Did nowt scare you yonder noo?" a gruff voice asked, around the stump of a long pipe held clenched in yellowing teeth that I could see even at a distance.

"Weel, 'tis a feart place but I feel nae venom here. Nae ghosts. And still . . ." I heard the younger of the fishermen answer slowly.

It was a trick of the shifting wind that parts of their conversation would occasionally be blown to where I was sitting some yards away with my sketchbook, half hidden by the swaying marron grass. I was resting on what used to be the banks of an old river, whose course was marked by a thin line of aquatic grasses and gaunt, distorted trees where noisy bitterns lived. The water began at what once was Loch Findloss, a winter lake that dried up almost every summer but returned again in fall. Its course now remains forever dry, surrounded by the remains of a wildwood that was prostrated by the wind during a horrific tempest and then fossilized in its surrendered posture. The village is likewise frozen. It has been this way since the Storm.

"Naeone ever carried the deid away for burial. They are either beneath the sand or taken by the sea. Either way, I doubt they rest easy here."

The older fisherman spat and quickly looked about him. The nineteenth century lingers here, and the local custom is to never speak of those lost to the Storm if a bird or seal is near, lest they carry word back to the ocean and summon something unholy. He was safe that day; it was only me, the silent American, and a few fat hares eavesdropping on the conversation.

The fisherman's opinion was a popular one, but I sincerely hoped that he was wrong about the ghosts, because this was now where I lived: Findloss, the cursed village. What I didn't need were thoughts of the restless dead struggling out of the sand to keep me up nights; the restive winds and often nervous living were quite trial enough now that days were growing short and cold and the tide called uproariously night and day, temporarily thwarted from taking back the earth that had thrust itself out of the oceans, but never giving up entirely.

"Be it ever so humble," I muttered, shaking sand from my skirts, an action that had grown so customary, I rarely marked it. The dunes around me were constantly shifting, and if one sat still for too long when the breeze was blowing the sand would bury one. All towns have their quirks and charms; ours was an ever-changing landscape—though I have to admit that our whispering dunes possessed none of the appeal of the more famous singing sands of Eigg, and were in fact a great deal more sinister.

Findloss was and is a fishing village, granted official charter in 1411, though people lived here long before that in crude, windowless huts, and perhaps in caves before that. This is a fact listed in many books and also proved by the tax rolls the solicitor showed me while trying to dissuade me from moving here. It is also a well-documented reality that the village disappeared one Beltane night in 1845, buried under thirty feet of storm-driven sand, and for fifty years no taxes were collected because the village was missing. The rest of the stories about what happened here—and why, and caused by whom—are both conjecture and a source of endless discussion by the local fishermen and their brave spouses, the few souls who have reluctantly re-populated the area.

Everyone in the village and surrounding environs agrees that the original inhabitants of the cursed village did something terrible to bring tragedy on themselves. Most say that the villagers were greedy and made some deal with a pagan demon-god for rich fishing grounds and no storms, and that the annihilation of the village was God's judgment upon them for their blasphemy. Another story says the villagers kidnapped some sea god's daughter and held her hostage in exchange for fish and good weather. On the day that she escaped—or died—it is believed that her enraged father retaliated and sent the storm as punishment. Yet another story is that the secretly pagan villagers made annual human sacrifices to appease some sea monster, and that one year the virgin tribute ran away rather than doing her duty, having predictable nasty consequences.

Whatever the case, much like the more famous Pompeii, Findloss was buried, destroyed in this instance by an angry storm driven by venomous west winds that washed over the village and smothered it in sand, where it was eerily preserved for five decades. Only two villagers survived this holocaust. Terrified by the inundation, most inhabitants fled to the church for sanctuary, but two men took flight in their boats and braved the gale. They alone lived to tell the tale, and spoke in a whisper about the Biblical-strength tempest that claimed their town. One of the men was Uncle Fergus's father, a man called Iain Dubh, which is "Black John" in English.

I wonder sometimes why the wider world knows nothing of this terrible inundation, particularly when all of the British Isles are so proud to tell tales of their lost and sunken cities to gullible visitors. The damage must have been far-flung and economically devastating, not to mention the whole horrible fairy-tale quality to the event that made the story appealing; so why no legends about Findloss? I asked this of the solicitor after arriving in Scotland, and received a startling answer from a man I took to be educated and reasonably truthful. Fear, he said; atavistic dread so strong that people still won't speak of it except in a whisper, because this storm was uncanny in ways that cannot be explained, even in terms of divine retribution. Couple that with the fact that it happened within the living memory of many local people, and you find an extreme reluctance to speak of the shameful and terrifying matter.

Also, Findloss is "different." It always has been. I soon discovered what the solicitor meant: peopled by witches and other wicked beings, who tend to be insular, keeping the outside world and its religious persecutions at bay. All murder was local.

I am not superstitious, but see the solicitor's point now that I have lived here for a while. Six miles south of Findloss lies the town of Glen Ard, and four miles north is the village of Keil. Neither was disturbed by the wind or rain, or molested by the ocean on that fateful Beltane Eve. The inhabitants felt nothing and heard nothing of the storm that took their neighbors. Their skies were clear, the seas calm, and their celebration bonfires burned brightly. The wild-eyed survivors who arrived by boat at dawn were not at first believed when they appeared in Keil, relating their impossible tale of tempest and destruction, but investigation soon proved that they were right. Findloss had indeed disappeared in the night and been replaced with a desert wasteland where it would be found that almost nothing could grow. Of other survivors, if there were any, nothing was ever heard.

This is fairly standard fare as tales of disappearing cities go, and if the story ended there, it would be a site worthy of a visit by any intrepid visitor interested in exploring auld haunted Scotland. But that isn't where the tale terminates. For fifty years Findloss lay buried, and the rocky waters nearby remained as shunned as the village's shores, but on another Beltane Eve a half century later, a wind arose, this time from the east, and in the morning the village reappeared. Houses, the kirk and churchyard, a small dead orchard and fishing boats—all were unburied, if apparently lifeless. It was a town for ghosts.

This was as disconcerting to the village's neighbors as its disappearance had been. In many ways, even more so. If it was God's wrath that took the village, shouldn't that be a final judgment? Why had the town been returned to the light of day? Was it haunted?

Immediately following the resurrection, a party of intrepid and perhaps slightly inebriated fishermen armed with holy icons put in on the shore and went to investigate. Knowing the story of Findloss well, they walked first to the kirk, reasonably expecting it to still be filled with sand and many skeletons in need of burial. Instead they discovered the place scoured, swept clean by some supernatural broom that had carried away every last grain of sand and human bone. Every pew was in place. The water-damaged Bible was on the altar, open to Revelation.

There was more talk of curses and the influence of the Devil, but the alarmed fishermen bravely pressed on and found the entire village the same as the church: pristine and vacant, a ghostly place waiting for life to return. Since both nature and humanity abhor a vacuum, eventually it was re-inhabited. After all, as it says in Genesis: *If therefore any son of Adam comes and finds a place empty, he hath liberty to come and fill it and subdue the earth.* The kirk, however, was never re-consecrated, and so the sons of Adam in this locale are on their own when it comes to spiritual guidance. The village is stuck in uneasy status quo. Nothing old is ever taken down; nor are the stones recycled for other purposes, lest the gods be offended. And nothing new is ever built, either. The town might as well still be imprisoned in sand, for all that it has changed since its rebirth.

I rather liked hearing the suggested stories of supernatural agency. I even began to collect them in my journal with an eye toward perhaps someday having them published. These dark fairy tales (I thought smugly on my arrival) were reassuring explanations for God-fearing folk who know that they will never personally have dealings with the Devil and therefore have nothing to dread from the Lord's wrathful vengeance. I wasn't able to believe in them myself, at least not at first. I think that I must be forgiven for this, in spite of all the warnings I received, both from the solicitor and from the villagers who would speak with me, for it is far easier for someone not raised with superstitious beliefs to suppose that the village disappeared due to some natural though freakish phenomenon rather than blaming it on magic and monsters.

Of course, because I did not believe the event happened due to some long-ago curse by a sea monster, I had the constant worry that another tempest might overtake the village at any time. The solicitor did nothing to reassure me on this score, and I found myself understandably fearful every time a storm arrived.

Findloss is only barely a village. It has taken decades to lure people back to it, and they come only because the fish are so abundant and the cottages there for the taking by any brave enough to dare the curse. There are no small children. Men with young families do not come. Get the older fishermen drunk and they'll claim the superior fishing is because the local sea god has relented on his curse or gone off to plague Norway. I myself suspected it due to the fact that the waters were unfished for fifty years and the creatures had a chance to breed unmolested and forgot to fear men. Not that I've said this out loud. I say very little out loud, just take notes on what I hear and smile politely. My late husband's Uncle Fergus had not been liked, and was even suspected of sorcery by some of the weaker minds. I was viewed with a certain amount of superstitious awe for my willingness (as a defenseless female) to live in his cottage alone. Apparently Fergus Culbin was the last of the local line of Culbins, and it was widely believed that it was one of his godless ancestors, living in a now-ruined keep, that brought the curse down upon the village.

Twaddle, all of it. Nonetheless, Fergus was rumored able to dispense with his shadow when desired, a sure sign of diablerie—or a sign of a cloudy day, but that was less exciting to talk about late at night around the peat fires. And if the subject of Fergus's wicked ways failed them, they could always talk about me. I had thought that I was leaving notoriety behind in the States, but such was not the case. However, the pity that had followed me after Duncan's death had not made it here, so pride insisted the situation was an improvement. Better by far to be notorious than pitiful.

Though the idea of Fergus being a wizard was preposterous, there was enough anecdotal evidence of his moral turpitude in Findloss and Keil, especially in regard to women, that I can readily believe he was a bad man who gave himself over, without reserve, to all forms of sin and vice. What a family I married into! My own husband had been given to nightmares and hallucinations, which I always blamed on drink but was now inclined to attribute in part to his upbringing. Who knew what memories and horrible ancestral tales pursued him even across the ocean and made him take refuge in opiates and strong spirits? It was enough to make one believe that the sins of the fathers really were visited on the children in the form of bad blood.

Need I say that if I had any other alternative—any chance of selling the cottage—I would have moved elsewhere? But I had no real options. Returning home to the scandal brought on by my husband's death by overdose in a whore's house was not to be borne, especially since I would be a poor relation suffered by my pious aunt and uncle only in the name of familial charity. And I hadn't enough money to start over somewhere else. My meager inheritance from my parents had gone to pay Duncan's gaming debts and my ticket for Scotland. My marketable skills were few: Before my marriage, I'd served as an unofficial amanuensis for an elderly lawyer, but he was dead and could not vouch for me. I had some proficiency at French and Latin and a smattering of Gaelic, a mild talent for drawing and storytelling, and minimal competence in the kitchen and with a needle, but that was it.

Of course I could remarry. As more than one person had put it, my face was my fortune. But I had turned my mind against this idea. Marriage had not suited me the first time; I would not willingly enter into it again. That would be quite unfair to whomever I wedded. My corroded heart was still filled with uncharitableness and general distrust of men. Actually, of people in general. The undertaker, a longtime friend of my late father, didn't know whether to send condolences or congratulations when Duncan died. Neither did my minister or my friends.

The latter hurt worst of all, though I understand what they were feeling. I was the first of my contemporaries to discover that eternal love could actually be perishable under the right, or wrong, circumstances. My situation frightened them and made them question—at least in a small way—the security of their own lives. They saw Duncan as a malignancy growing in the societal body and were relieved when he was excised. I, the shamed widow, became the living version of the cautionary tales told to young girls by their mothers. Who would wish to be reminded of such a thing, to live next door to it? Of course I became a pariah. At the end of the day, it was difficult to say which of my problems was most pressing, the financial or the emotional.

Sand hit my face and I felt myself grimace. Men—it was they and not the love of money that were the root of all evil, at least in my life. Not content with the boring but upstanding young men in my hometown, who I knew all too well, and sure some other romantic destiny awaited me, I had searched diligently for my great love in someone more exotic, and fate had cursed me for my desire by giving me what I thought I wanted. For that reason, I had lost everything but my life. I would not search again. More than that, I told myself that I would run away if love came around once more to plague me. It seemed most unlikely that it would find me in Findloss, and that suited me, even if the village and the weather did not.

As I thought of these unpleasant things, I touched the charm that I wore on a silk cord beneath my dress. My late husband had given it to me in the early days of our courtship and I had worn it to please him though I did not like it. Later, after his unprovoked hatred of me surfaced, and there began the constant accusations of my failure to help him—though help him with *what* he would never say—I had put the token away. It was an ugly and disturbing charm that resembled a Celtic knot, but one made of tentacles or perhaps serpents. But on the day after his funeral, when it began to rain with a strange and unseasonable ferocity, I found myself disturbed by the idea that the wet was falling on his defenseless body buried in the churchyard while I was at home, safe from the flood. I had taken the charm back out and begun wearing it again. It was my hair shirt, my penance for not finding any love left in my heart for the man I married. The minister had even said to me, "Carry rancor to the grave but no further," but I could not let my anger go. *Wouldn't* let it go.

A cloud passed over the sun as I brooded on old wrongs committed half a world away. The disappearance of light happened frequently now that autumn had arrived and the land was in full sear. Fall in Findloss does not look like autumn at home. For one thing, there are no living trees to turn fiery colors and lose their cheerful leaves. What we do have are frequent gales and the almost daily punishment of the wind that throws about the white stinging sand and drains the world of color. Heeding the warning of rain, I gathered my charcoal and paper and made haste for my cottage and the reassuring light of the paraffin lamps I kept by the door. I knew that I was now visible to the men on the beach and was being studied as I fled. I usually wore a bright red scarf of unusual length and width, and it made me what the drabber locals call *kenspeckled*. The fishermen would have had to be blind not to see me. There would be more gossip that night about Fergus Culbin's odd relation.

The wind was cold, an assault, but I was still grateful for it. When the breeze dies the midges emerge, tenacious and even suicidal in their quest for human blood—usually mine—and there is no getting rid of them. On the way home I passed the kirk and the cemetery, my skirts flapping loudly enough to scare away a fearful swift fluttering deep into the dying heather as it tried unsuccessfully to shelter from the approaching storm. The churchyard was intact, no headstones disturbed by the town's sandy burial, though I found myself wondering whether the bodies were still in their graves or if they had disappeared like all the lost souls in the church. At least one body was here. Fergus Culbin had been buried in the section for strangers, a fact I found vaguely disturbing since the cemetery was no longer consecrated and local custom had it that a soul could not rest if its body was buried there. I did not hasten past the uncanny place since I was already traveling at just below a trot, but I kept my eyes averted and made every effort to push my morbid thoughts away so they would not follow me home.

My new house was surprisingly generous-sized. The four rooms were large, even if they had low ceilings and were rather dark because there were few windows whose glass was badly pitted. I knew that I might regret them in the spring, but for the time being I was grateful for the stout walls and strong shutters that could be closed against the winter storms and the bleak autumn sea view.

The cottage lay beyond the reach of the highest tide—highest *normal* tide—but not beyond the reach of wind and sand. I had swept the path that morning, but it was again covered in grit and I had to clear this away from the sill with my shoe before opening the door. As the cottage has settled over the years, the floor's paving stones are slightly slanted toward the heavy fireplace, and the pavings are worn down by the passage of countless feet around the perimeter of the all but immovable dining table, whose marble surface actually rather resembled a cathedral altar. If furnishings reflect the hands that tend them, then this monstrous table had known a hard and unloving touch. I could not imagine a family sitting down to dine at it. Certainly I never did.

I have no records of when the cottage (Clachan Cottage it was once called, though now known as Culbin's Cottage) was built, and architecturally there is nothing to distinguish it from others built in the last five centuries, but it is safe to say that it is old and erected in the days when one might actually need a home that could survive cannon fire. That cannon fire had happened precisely once, according to the book lent to me by the solicitor Mr. Waverley. In September of 1588, the village was actually attacked by a stray galleon, a member of the Spanish armada blown off course and stranded in the small port of Findloss. Chased by Sir Francis Drake—supposedly because this ship carried a generous store of gold—the *Fidencia* was trying to escape by sailing around the very top of the isle or perhaps lose her pursuers in the Hebrides. In unfamiliar and often violent water, they miscalculated and came too close to the shore. Run aground and fearing attack by land and by sea, they opened fire on the village, perhaps hoping to scare the inhabitants into fleeing in panic so they might escape overland unmolested (yes, this sounds ridiculous to us now, but they had been separated from the fleet by a gale and had no way of knowing that the armada's invasion of England had not been successful). Findloss had no long-range weapons to defend itself, and the villagers were completely at the Spaniards' mercy, but a second volley was never fired. Before the cannon could be reloaded, the ship suddenly capsized and sank beneath the waves, pulled down by some invisible vortex.

Again, there are wild stories about this. No one is entirely certain what happened that day, but every tale agrees that after the ship capsized there was a massive explosion that threw parts of the shattered dreadnought on shore, and the galleon sank without a single survivor into the completely calm sea. From time to time one may still find bits of twisted, tarnished silver plates and Spanish coins along the beach. Most people leave them there, unwilling to tempt fate by touching the belongings of doomed men. This demonstrates how deep the belief in spirits is in this poverty-stricken village.

The sunken galleon, haunted by the ghosts of dead sailors guarding a lost treasure, is more local color to write about. No treasure has ever been reclaimed from the wreck, but I have a cannon ball beside the door of the cottage. I assume it is the one that chipped the western cornerstone of the building and knocked a fist-sized piece of stone free.

"Hello, Herman," I said to my cat, as he rushed for my ankles and began making a noise that I imagine to be purring. Herman came with the cottage, and I have no idea what his real name is. He is large and black and looks ferocious, but is actually quite the gentleman. He is also a fisherman and sometimes brings me small fish and seaweed that he has hunted up in the tide pools. I have yet to think of a way to cook starfish or seahorse, but I appreciate the generous gesture even when I return his gifts to the sea. Occasionally he brings me tufts of fur as well. This pleases me less.

The fish are not the only animals that have returned to thrive in Findloss. The many hares that seem content to live on bent grass and furze are large and sleek. (Likewise, the foxes that hunt the hares are glossy with health and of an unusual size; a cat would be an easy meal for them. They too have forgotten to fear men and are quite bold about approaching if humans remain still.) Though I have tired of a menu of fish, not being as ichthyophagous as Findloss natives, I haven't yet suggested to any of the locals that they break out their snares and hunt the conies. I doubt they would do it even if asked; there seems to be an almost superstitious dread about the land animals that live here, including the seals that sometimes sun themselves on shore. I haven't the stomach for the bloody task either. I never even got the knack of wringing chicken necks, so certainly I could not garrote a rabbit. Instead I had to be content with the occasional egg and bit of cheese to vary my diet.

I went first to use the privy. The cottage has a few modern conveniences, meaning that an appropriate area was built against the back of the cottage so one needn't go out into the night or storm to answer the call of nature. In addition, there is also a hand pump in the kitchen to draw water so one needn't go to the old well outside, whose windlass is in disrepair. Cooking is done on a small cast-iron stove, and bathing and laundry are done in a brass washtub—also in the kitchen, so that the water may be heated on the stove. There is strong local belief that bathing in cold water builds character and keeps the Devil away. Unfortunately, it also makes for chilblains, so people go for long periods without bathing. This does not suit me. I was raised with the idea that cleanliness is next to godliness; and, frankly, a scrubbed body was about as close to holy as I was going to get, given my current anger with God. I was grateful for what I had— truly—but it was only after I moved here that I realized how much I enjoyed indoor plumbing and having a real bathtub.

Heating is done in the fireplace, which is situated

in the middle of the cottage, allowing all four rooms to touch it and theoretically share warmth. The chimney is large, quite adequate to accommodate a man or a small bull. Perhaps that is why it has been fitted with iron bars. Certainly the bars do nothing to keep out the birds that find their way inside whenever it rains, and I could not imagine any other creature that would attempt to gain entrance in this manner.

The hearth is strange, a sort of mosaic made of shells that might once have been pretty but is now badly damaged, perhaps deliberately defaced. Only enough remains to suggest that the theme was aquatic, perhaps a tribute to that local sea monster that gobbled up virgins and buried the village.

It was early yet, but I lit one of the lamps. Storms come in fast and can bring about a near-twilight state in a matter of moments. I've no love for the smell of burning paraffin, but it is better than shark oil, which many of the locals use in their lamps.

The cold had not yet crept over the sill and down the chimney, but I decided to light the fire as well and put the soup kettle on to warm. Herman did not object. Being a cat, he was fond of warm places. When possible I burn driftwood, but recently—in spite of the storms—it had become hard to come by. This meant using coal or peat.

The fisherman's words once again put me in mind of some of the wilder tales of Fergus Culbin, and I found myself again feeling reluctantly curious about the man I'd never met or even heard of until after his death. I had found no personal artifacts in the cottage beyond clothing that was old but of good quality, and the solicitor assured me that nothing had been removed from the premises. I was sure that something had to exist, some correspondence or a diary. But where?

There weren't that many places where one could conceal a journal or letters. The first that came to mind was the ridiculous desk, an overwrought Louis the Some-teenth that was tucked away in the bedroom, perhaps a family relic from more prosperous times. Duncan once said that his family had gotten evicted from practically every country in Europe, for always being on the wrong side of the endless religious wars. I had been promising myself for weeks that I would take the time to examine it for secret compartments. There were bound to be a few, and the moment was appropriate.

The walls and ceiling about me were thick and strong, but a glance out the window showed the wind was blowing the rain nearly horizontally, and handfuls of water and sand were occasionally thrown at the narrow panes. The sound was rather like someone scratching at the scarred glass, and I did my best to ignore it while I searched the desk.

In the end it was Herman who found the hidden compartment for me. I should have perceived that one of the drawers wasn't as deep as the other, but I didn't notice the stubby compartment until Herman got in the drawer and began shoving one side of the back wall. Immediately the pane pivoted outward, and I found what I was looking for: a small book, leather bound and worn. A quick glance showed me that the pages were handwritten.

"Thank you, Herman!" I said, and offered a scratch

under the chin that he accepted gratefully. "Let's go have a seat by the fire and see what this has to say."

Herman meowed plaintively when I stopped petting him, reminding me that it was a good night for a nip of whisky in my tea and perhaps time to share a small bite to eat. They call whisky *the water of life* here in Scotland, and having withstood a couple of their weeklong storms I understand why. Without some help for the nerves, the weather would be unendurable. As it was, there still were suicides every winter. At home we called it cabin fever. Here they said a man had gone sea-daft.

After getting some food, I sat down and began to read.

Moving onward with eyes shut . . . I was met by a blast of wind which seemed to work altogether beyond the common operations of nature . . . I caught it by the handful as I passed. I felt as if a dozen thongs were lashing me around the body . . . I felt a pressure of weight on my body, which had the effect of dragging me down and retarding progress, as if the power of gravitation had increased tenfold. For a moment I stood like one petrified—perspiration starting from every pore—I put my hand in my pocket in search of handkerchief and found the pocket crammed with sand. Every pocket about me was filled with sand, my clothes completely saturated with it, my shoes like to burst, my ears, eyes, nostrils and mouth were like partakers.
—Lachlan Shaw in *The History of the Province of Moray*

Chapter Two

I squinted in the faint light, my eyes tired but my mind too fascinated to stop reading.

Blue men of the Minch, Sruth nam fear Gorma: powerful sea spirits of the Outer Hebrides thought to be Fallen Angels or souls of Moorish slaves forced into sailing Viking longships. They calm treacherous waters when residing in underground caves. Can sometimes be defeated in battle by rhyming contests, or by singing unknown songs. Might be selkies, roane, fin folk or merrows. Note: Shedding their blood will cause epic storms. *Able to transform at will by shedding their skins or by use of a red feather cap. Might they be Nickers or Nokke??? Possible link to kelpies (water demons) and needing to devour human flesh every day they remain on land. Review history of Clan MacCodrum . . .*

Clan MacCodrum? I lowered the journal for a moment and rubbed my eyes, unable to believe that my maternal grandmother's family name was mentioned. I knew very little about Morag MacCodrum or any of her Scottish kin. My memories of my grandparents were dim. My father's view was hostile, and my soft-spoken mother rarely mentioned them and only with great nervousness on the rare occasions she did. I always suspected that there was some scandal or mystery associated with them because Father was not universally xenophobic. Indeed he showed no dislike of any of our neighbors, though many came from Europe.

Thunder crashed right outside the window, bringing me back to my present surroundings. The rain had grown ferocious while I read, and the wind all but screamed. As the saying goes, it was a night "fit for neither man nor beast," so nothing could have surprised me more than to have my late reading—if the slow deciphering of the symbols of the book I examined by firelight could be called that—interrupted by a pounding on the cottage door. The blows were heavy and spaced evenly, like the tolling of a funeral bell, and I couldn't help shivering as the echo died away. This was the sound of doom calling, and it demanded I answer.

Herman jumped up and hissed. His hair stood on end and he would have looked comical, but as the cat was habitually calm, even in bad weather, this display alarmed more than amused me. A dozen ridiculous thoughts ran through my head as I sat frozen—among them that the Devil had come to call on Fergus Culbin—but at last good sense prevailed and I seized on the most likely explanation to flit through my mind: A fishing boat from another village had perhaps been driven ashore and the fishermen, not knowing the path to the village, had headed for the nearest shelter. They had seen the light in my window, and it had guided them to the cottage, which was the closest building.

I put Fergus Culbin's journal aside slowly and laid another book atop it. Then I took up the lamp with a hand only vaguely troubled by tremors and forced my reluctant feet to move.

I had a welcoming if insincere smile pasted in place when I pulled back the heavy bar and opened the ancient door, but it faded very quickly as I surveyed the creature on my doorstep. He was male—oh, definitely male—and quite the most beautiful being I had ever seen. But there was also something about him that seemed sinister and made me feel very weak and insignificant as I stood before him. Perhaps it was the fierce black eyes or the alabaster skin, or the long hair that fell in a sleek cascade to below his shoulders. Or perhaps, most alarming of all, it was how not a drop of rain seemed to cling to him—not to his hair, not to his skin, not to the old-fashioned sark and kilt he wore most sloppily. A drop of blood ran down the side of his face, and he had an odd fur coat slung over his back.

"*Co tha seo?*" The voice was deep, the eyes compelling, and I thought of the entry about water demons I had just read. "*Nach eil thu 'gam aithneachadh?*"

He was speaking Gaelic. My grandmother had sometimes spoken the language, and my husband had used it with his few friends, so I recognized some of the stranger's words. The man was asking who I was and if I recognized him.

The voice was a bit like a rusty razor that was perhaps not often used but capable of cutting deeply if needed. Against my will I answered. "*Is mise* . . . Megan. And I don't know you." I gasped the last bit, and it sounded something like laughter—hysterics, though, not girlish giggles meant to attract a man.

The stranger inhaled deeply. His eyes widened and his pupils expanded, blotting out the dark irises and then even the whites. All the stories about Fergus being in league with the Devil came rushing back at me, and I did something I had never done before: I put a hand over my heart and fainted.

As the world went black, I remember seeing arms reach for me, and I felt a small measure of relief. Not because someone was there to break my fall and catch the lamp before it started a fire, but because I momentarily had my legends confused, and my last thought was that this man couldn't be the Devil, because he had passed over my doorway without an invitation. It was only later that I recalled this idea and realized that I was confusing vampires with devils. The Devil may come and go as he pleases. And anyway, if gossip were to be believed, the Devil had already been invited into the cottage by its former owner. He didn't need my permission to enter. This was a definite down side to living in a cottage old enough to recall the Dark Ages.

When I awoke sometime later, it was to an empty cottage and the first light of dawn toying with the sky outside the uncurtained window. I might have assumed that I had been caught up in a nightmare, but it was obvious that someone had been in the cottage. I knew that I had not hallucinated the event, because peat had been added to the fire and there were a pot of tea and a mug on the table at the left arm of the settee where I was lying with a blanket from my bed draped over me. Of my strange visitor there was no sign.

Herman was sitting on the hearth looking unruffled, and I envied him his peace of mind. I was still thoroughly alarmed by the trespass. Especially when I looked to the front door and found it closed but unbarred.

A quick search revealed that Fergus's journal was gone. So my mysterious visitor was a thief—but per-

haps a kind one, since he had bothered to make up
the fire and drape me with a blanket. He also felt
enough at home to make a pot of tea before depart-
ing. Not that anything would induce me to drink it. I
could think of no reason why this stranger would
wish to poison me, but in my uneasy state I was not
prepared to take chances. I felt suddenly very young and
inexperienced.

The loss of the journal annoyed me, and I seized on
this emotion since I liked it better than fear and be-
wilderment. The book was nonsense, all of it. Flesh-
eating water demons and fallen angels? What rot! I
hadn't read such nonsense since my days of childhood
fairy tales. But the book did belong to me, and might
have been a nice addition to the local tales of sea monsters that I had been collecting. If the stranger came
calling again—and I sincerely hoped he didn't—I
promised myself that I would demand the journal's return.

Houses will build themselves,
And tombstones re-write names on a dead man's grave.
—Andrew Young, *"Culbin Sands"*

Chapter Three

Fear is paranoia's chief handmaiden, and therefore sometimes an evil influence on even the most rational mind. I had calmed considerably by the time I made porridge and brushed out my hair. It takes patience and time to add the oats little by little to boiling salted water. I don't care for lumpy porridge, and it is my experience that alarm can only be sustained for a short period of time in the absence of any new threats, especially when doing something so prosaic as whisking oatmeal on the stove with a cat looking on. Still, I was a long way from being completely at ease in my thoughts as I prepared my meal.

I didn't need to light the kitchen fire since the embers were still glowing, a further confirmation that my visitor had felt free to make himself at home. However, by the time I had stirred the oatmeal into something nearly edible, my thoughts had turned from tales of devils to stories of night visitors of the amorous variety. Legend had it that the area was once populated with *sleagh maith,* the local Gaelic term for fairies, notorious for seducing humans. The thought of my alarmed reaction brought the first smile of the day: If my guest wasn't of the Satanic persuasion and had indeed come looking for a bit of carnality, then I must have seriously alarmed or offended him by fainting. There was no way that my reaction could be mistaken for any kind of coquetry. My faerie would not come calling again.

Feeling much calmer after this brief flight of silliness, I nonetheless decided to walk into the village to see if there were any reports of boats washing up on shore, or anything else that might reasonably explain why a strange man would be abroad on such a terrible night. I thought that perhaps I would even meet my guest again, since it seemed likely he would have sought out help for mending his boat as soon as the storm abated.

The day was sunny but the wind brisk, so I bundled up well before leaving the cottage. I thought of taking the iron key that turned the rather stiff lock on the door, but decided against it. No one in the village locked their doors in the daytime. In spite of my nervousness at the invasion the previous night, I decided to observe the custom. After all, sandstorms blew up without warning and a neighbor in some dire straits might require shelter in the cottage. I wasn't on the best of terms with the other villagers, but I certainly would not begrudge protection to anyone in need. I also left a shutter and window ajar so that Herman could come and go as he wished. I had made the mistake of shutting him in once and found an ample expression of his displeasure waiting for me right inside the door when I returned.

But in the village, instead of reassurance for my paranoia, I found the uneasy populace gathered in the street around a visitor I learned was from Keil. A quick look assured me that this elderly and heavily bewhiskered man of the cloth was not my uninvited guest.

"Who is this? What has happened?" I asked softly of Mistress MacLaren, one of the few women in town and a gossip. She and her husband ran the general store and post office where the more-or-less weekly ferry made deliveries of goods and mail. She was what the locals call a *carlin of ugly mein*, just what children imagined when they thought of a wicked witch. I tried to wear my bitterness at life's disappointments lightly and not inflict my unhappiness on the world, but not so Mistress MacLaren, and her perpetual anger had warped her expression into something unpleasant.

"'Tis Reverend MacNeil," she whispered back excitedly. I could smell whisky on her breath. This was not uncommon. "The De'il was seen abroad last night and Callum was sent tae fetch him o'er. He'll hae some idea of what tae dae aboot this."

"The Devil?" I repeated, the reassurance in which I had wrapped myself falling away like silk in a violent wind, not because I was afraid of the Devil—not in the cold light of day—but because such strongly articulated ideas are more dangerous than casual notions kept to oneself, and actual belief—especially of the religious kind and especially in a crowd—is most dangerous of all. History has shown us that belief can make otherwise reasonable men do things that are vindictive or even insane. There had been a lynching in our town when I was a child, and I feared I was about to again see something of that nature. "But . . . what can he do? If it was truly the Devil?"

"Listen," Mistress MacLaren instructed, and I reluctantly did.

The minister had a fine voice, one that would have done splendidly upon the stage but I suppose suited him as well in the pulpit. His choice of material was rather grim, though, and I found myself feeling oddly offended, both that he thought his audience gullible enough to believe that his brand of religious witchcraft would do anything practical against intruders and the contradictory though equally strong belief that if my night visitor had been of the supernatural persuasion, that he would be immediately driven off by this man without even an inquiry into his purpose for visiting. It seemed unneighborly to me and even a bit shocking, given that by tradition the visitor seeking shelter in Scotland is sacrosanct.

"Brethren, be sober! Be vigilant! Because yer adversary, the De'il, goeth aboot as a roaring lion, seeking wham he may devour." The minister looked heavenward as he continued. "O unquiet spirit, who at thy release from the contagion of flesh chooseth tae remain earthbound, hear the words of exhortation and admonish now addressed tae thee!"

The Roman exorcism rang strange when delivered with a Scottish accent, but it was still terrifying, and looking at the mesmerized faces around me, I suddenly felt a bit ill and wary of my neighbors in a way I never had been before. There is something horribly inflexible about religious passions in a mob that frightens outsiders. It wasn't that I desired to have unwanted visitors about, perhaps getting up to mischief and stealing books, but surely strangers in the night weren't as damaging as, say, termites, or as vicious as the midges who came out at sunset; and trying to cast a person out into the spiritual void for making a late-night call seemed drastic. Even if he were a book thief.

Not that I believed in the nonsense the reverend was speaking. His were just silly words that couldn't really hurt anyone. But still. Mobs, having no infirmity of purpose when aroused by fear and a seductive voice, are known to inflict more than spiritual ill will or exorcism on strangers. In many ways, the mindset of this village was still quite medieval.

"I exorcise thee by the element of salt, by the Almighty God who, by the hand of Elijah, the prophet, mingled thee wi' the earth, that the barrenness of the land might be healed. Receive this salt from which the spirit of evil has been cast out, for the eternal rest of thee and of all the faithful, that there may be vanished frae this place every kind of hallucination, wickedness, craft and de'ilish deceit." Reverend MacNeil lifted up a candle and a piece of bread. "I carry here the symbol of Christ, the light of the warld and the food of the angels."

Unable to stand any more, I backed away. I wanted answers about the night visitor, but this wasn't the moment to ask questions of the frightened crowd, which was clearly ready to embrace any kind of superstitious gobbledygook and perhaps do something violent. I did not want them invading my home looking for devils if their fear turned in my direction. I had not forgotten that not so many years ago Scotland was in the habit of burning witches, werewolves and other creatures of that ilk.

I meandered among the dunes, heading for the shore at a slow trudge, where I could hear waves pounding away with more than usual vigor against the shallow sea caves that were filled except at low tide. At ebb tide there is a thin bar of sand and rock that allows one to cross the headlands and remain dry-shod almost all the way to Kiel. One must use caution, though, because the mats of sea wrack on the shore can hide pools that will turn and even break ankles. I was not used to such highs and lows of tidal waters, and the water can turn quickly. At high tide a small boat may pass safely over the bar, assuming the water is not so violent with storm that it dashes the craft upon the rugged cliffs; then it is deep enough to drown a tall man.

The jetty stood at the south end of the cove in whose arms Findloss sheltered. It was an old structure in the shape of an E, its long spine thrust out straight from the island. On the shorter arms, the largest boats were moored. Smaller boats were often pulled up onto patches of sand between the gullies cut into the cliff face; these few scattered beaches were safe from most high tides. It is said that a cave lies below the bottom leg of the pier, which was partly quarried stone and part the cliff face itself, whose lowest shelf had been smoothed into a sort of table and then expanded with the need for more pier. This cave is accessible only at the lowest of spring tides. I have never seen it, but would like to because it is supposedly inhabited by several species of colorful anemones that can be seen nowhere else in Scotland. People who described it to me had made it sound like a fairyland.

I was feeling more annoyed than forlorn at that point, but was aware of a growing melancholy trying to possess my mind as rapidly as sand filled my shoes. There is no shortage of sand on the plateaus where the village sits, and with the wind in the west there were enough dunes for the Sahara desert. This low mood threatening me was in part due to the returning clouds that promised more rain, but also the recurring suspicion that I had made a terrible mistake by coming to live among these strange people, and that a winter in Scotland might be more than I could stand.

Anxious to distract myself from this avenue of pointless thought, I let my brain return to the mystery of my visitor and how he had gotten to my cottage. At one time there had been a sort of road to Findloss. I gathered that it had not been a real road or even a path as most people back home thought of it; the trail had been a sort of zigzag switchback affair, a series of a dozen traverses some sixty feet apiece and rather steep, which climbed the far side of the hills that ringed the village. The natives had shunned it, both because it was built by the British—for the purpose of more efficient tax collection and also chasing down Jacobite rebels—but also because the gravel had hurt the unshod ponies' hooves as well as the bare feet of the villagers. (Yes, I lived in a place where shoes were once—and not so long ago—considered an effete and foreign invention, a modern convenience that eroded the moral fiber of the inhabitants.)

In any event, the road is gone now, the hills having reclaimed the space with marron grass, and the village is again what I once heard described by my solicitor as "inaccessible from without and not to be left from within." So, my stranger was most likely to have come from the sea rather than by road, and probably not from the north since the currents were tricky, and if you sailed incautiously into the marshlands or stony shoals during dark, you were likely to end up adding to the collection of derelict boats whose broken ribs were bleaching in the rare sun at low tide. But if he had come from the south, where was his boat now? It must not have been badly damaged if he had taken off again as soon as the storm abated. Of course, if he were still about somewhere, perhaps trying to mend his vessel, then it was my duty to warn him of what was being said in the village.

I topped a sandbank and looked out at the empty patch of shore between two spits of rock and then back up at Fergus's cottage hunkering in the dunes well up from the ancient shoreline, whose edges were fringed with sea grass that had somehow survived a half century buried in sand. I put up a hand to shade my eyes from the sun that was still on the incline and bright enough to burn the eyes when it peered around the clouds. None of the cottage windows were visible, just the roof. Though the stranger was taller than I, how on earth had he found me in the dark if he came from the shore?

I turned back to the ocean, still searching for the

stranger or his boat, and as I watched the more peaceful water and listened to some distant seal's plaint, an entirely comforting thought occurred to me. My visitor had probably been a friend of Fergus. A normal, human friend. He probably hadn't heard that Fergus was dead—or perhaps had heard and assumed the cottage would be empty and that he would be able to pass the night there, when the storm came on suddenly and he was caught away from home. Doubtless he had visited many times and knew the tides and where it was safe to stow a boat. And he had even used the kitchen before, because he was human, subject to the cold, not a devil or a sea monster who had no need for tea. And he had come at night because of the stupid villagers who were so hostile to strangers. Look at how they still treated me! Findloss was necessarily hermetic given its geography, and while not inbred in any physical sense, it was unusually xenophobic and superstitious. Perhaps because the people who had chosen to inhabit this haunted place had no claim— legal, historical or moral—to the abodes they had appropriated, they always feared being removed if anyone in authority ever found them. Though, who would desire this land I couldn't guess. No one else wanted to live here with the sand and curses.

Poor man. My presence must have shocked him every bit as much as his had startled me, hence the sharp questions in Gaelic. It was still the preferred language of the nearby villages.

That didn't explain why he'd taken the book, however. Unless it had been his to begin with? I had assumed the journal had belonged to Fergus Culbin, but maybe not. Perhaps this man had simply retrieved his own property. That might even have been the purpose of his visit.

And the lack of water on his clothes and hair? A trick of the light, I decided. The lamp had been turned low and flickering even inside the chimney because of the wind. My eyes, abetted by panic brought on by the vivid entries in the journal, had deceived me. And anyway, he might have just removed his coat, which perhaps had a hood that kept his hair dry. And as for that tiny bit of blood on his head, perhaps he had tripped in the dark and hurt himself.

Feeling much better—and completely scornful of the villagers and their silly exorcism—I started back for the cottage, determined to finally make a start of organizing the local tall tales into some kind of manuscript. I wanted to get down the words of the exorcism while they were fresh in my mind. If I had to live in a cursed village full of superstitious peasants, then I thought that I might as well profit from it. I would write a book.

Roar ye torrents down the steep,
Roll ye mists on Morven.
—"The Maiden of Morven"

Chapter Four

Back at the cottage—which was happily empty of all life save Herman—I made a fresh pot of tea and stirred up the ash on the hearth so that I could build another fire. The villagers would sneer at my weakness, but I was from a warmer clime and didn't like the cold. This task took me a while because, unlike my unwanted guest, I hadn't the knack of building a peat fire and had to use some coal to get the blaze started.

I brought a cup with me and set it on the hearth, where I could sip as I battled with the stubborn, smoking fire. The smell of tea would hardly terrorize any uncanny visitors, but it subdued the worst of my nervousness with its familiar calming scent. As was bound to happen when wrestling two-handed with a job that needed at least three or maybe four, I upset the cup, which was unsteady on the uneven shell surface and spilled tea over the mosaic. The browned water spread quickly into the grout and in only a moment I found myself staring into a familiar face. It was the stranger.

Of course, it wasn't really the stranger, just a being with long black hair and dark eyes who seemed to be floating on ocean waves, surrounded by tentacled and finned monsters. I knew that I should blot up the mess immediately, lest the stain be permanent, but I found myself unable to touch it or even look away. Fear can make wild thoughts cohere in odd and unreasonable patterns. My new, or I should say returning, suppositions were frightening, and quite ruined my tenuous sense of comfort, yet I found myself unable to dismiss them completely, no matter how irrational they sounded.

"This is insane," I said to the cat, who was also staring intently at the mosaic. But I had to know, one way or the other, who the night visitor was; I would have no peace until then. I needed more information, and my only real hope of getting it was if Fergus had left some other journals or letters behind: Surely if this stranger had been a friend, Fergus would make some mention of him. And if he wasn't a friend . . . ? Well, he would probably mention that too.

My Aunt Sophie—acquired through marriage and thought of without affection—was originally from Texas. She always said to my mother that I had a lot of quit in me. The stupid woman didn't know me very well. What I had had were a lot of good manners drilled into me, and that kept me from contradicting her even when what she said was idiotic, self-serving or vicious, which was most of the time. I also did not

waste energy fighting hopeless battles such as changing someone's long-held prejudices. Though Mother
never said a word against her sister-in-law, I believe
she considered Sophie a blight on her brother's happiness and once said to my father that Thomas would
regret spending his "sinister years" with his chosen
helpmate. I had a different B-word for her.

It was probably just as well that Mother never got
to know my own husband. She would not have liked
him either.

In point of fact, I can do "stubborn and secretive"
with the best of them; it is just that I smile while I go
about it. It was this stubbornness that had gotten me
on a boat to Scotland, though the faraway world across
the ocean was terra incognita to me then. And the fact
that I had ended up in a place far stranger than I had
ever imagined—and perhaps more unpleasant than I
actually deserved—didn't change facts one bit. This
was my home and I wasn't leaving now that I had
clawed out a small space of contentment. This meant
I needed to know how to make myself safe here.

Mother had been a firm believer in the idea that
some people were just not meant to be happy. She never
said why, and I didn't think to ask until it was too
late. Given my recent history I was almost willing to
believe that I was one of these fated people, but if God
were merciful, and if she and I were both wrong, then
knowledge might save me and give me the opportu-
nity to be free of my devils. Particularly the tall, dark
and handsome one.

Lamp in hand, I checked the desk again and actually found another hidden compartment. This one held

a small leather bag of coins. Gold coins. *Spanish* coins. I put them back hastily, in that moment no longer completely confident that the relics were not haunted by the ghosts of drowned sailors, and unwilling to tempt fate by handling them.

A frustrating hour later, I was certain the desk held no more secrets, but, not yet discouraged from the task of discovery, I started on the cottage's other pieces of furniture. There weren't many, but I was thorough and it took some time. I was storm-stayed anyway, since the rain had returned, so I made a full-frontal assault on all of the cottage's secret places and its dust; I have always felt that dust is inimical to one's health, a household equivalent of the coal dust that gives miners black lung. The activity took me through to dinnertime, and I stopped for some bread and jam and to light the lamp as it began to get dark and the rain grew stronger.

Feeling less enthused but still determined, I added more peat to the fire and then began to examine the wainscoting and baseboards—a strange addition to a stone cottage whose exterior walls would not readily accept nails, I then realized. I found one section that was loose and managed to pry it from the wall. The thin piece of paneling had had its back inscribed with runes written in reddish brown . . . ink? Again, disturbed and more than a little baffled, I pushed the board back into place and went on with my search. The cottage was soon rid— at least from my hips downward—of dust and the cobwebs that bred with such speed, but of hidden documents I found no sign. There had to be more books. More letters. There were people who possessed only one book, but that was usually a family Bible. If a man were interested enough to be collecting stories of deadly faeries, then he was bound to collect other materials.

The privy was the sole location left to search. It isn't a warm place. Built on an old design, a slice of stream runs through it, under the wooden seat, carrying waste away to what I liked to imagine was a leach field. The water is sometimes pungent with the smell of hawthorn, though how this could be I do not know, since no hawthorn blooms nearby. In a poplar trunk at the back of the small addition where ancient and brittle linens were kept, I found beneath the yellowed fabric a set of shackles made of what my brain insisted was cold iron. There was also a kind of carpet beater, which I was willing to bet was made of yew.

I recalled from Fergus's journal that both yew and cold iron were considered effective weapons against the *sleagh maith* and other faeries. What was odder still, my late husband had also had a set of these shackles and a yew switch, which he'd kept in his private desk. Duncan had once sneeringly intimated that they were for sexual purposes. I had believed him then, since his tastes were so depraved. Now I was not so certain, and the idea that my husband might have been keeping still other secrets from me was saddening as well as disturbing.

I caught a glimpse of myself in the small mirror I had hung on the wall; vanity should be hidden away, and this was as "away" as it could get. The eyes that looked back at me were filled up with anxiety and perhaps a bit more whisky than they should be. I would

have to watch that. I didn't want to be too at home
with either of those things.

"Herman, I wish you had hands instead of paws,
because I could use another pair," I said to the cat,
who had followed me through the cottage, watching
intently as I pushed the furniture about. "Better yet, I
wish you could just tell me where to find out more
about our strange visitor. Did you know him?"

The cat looked from me to the front door. The gesture was so deliberate that I found myself expecting to
see someone in the doorway.

My mother always warned me to be careful what I
wished for, because often the heart's desires are overheard by the mind . . . and sometimes by someone or
something else. The brisk but light knock on the door
brought both dread and relief. I piled the stale linens
on top of the shackles and beater; then, closing the lid
of the trunk, I shoved it to the back wall of the privy
and dusted my hands as best I could on a scrap of
towel. But the effort was wasted. Nothing was going to disguise the fact that I had been cleaning. I just
had to hope that whoever was visiting would not find
my seeming mania for housework at such a late hour
to be too odd.

Preternatural: differing from what is natural.
Irregular: in a manner different from the
common order of nature.
Supernatural: being above the cause, order or
power of nature.

Chapter Five

"Good morrow, mistress," the ill-dressed but familiar stranger said pleasantly enough. This time he spoke in the heavily accented Scots you hear near the Borders.

There is a mistaken impression among some Americans and especially Englishmen that use of Scots connotes a lack of, if not refinement, then of education. This isn't necessarily true. Proper English was passed along north of the border along with the new tax system hundreds of years ago. The use of Scots dialect in the modern era is a matter of comfort, and to a great degree, defiance. More complete defiance for a Celt is to use Gaelic, which was certainly true in my grandparents' case. Scots, after all, is a form of old English, and Gaelic was the native language of the Gaels thousands of years before the Sassenach usurpers wandered over the border and smashed their culture.

"I am glad tae see ye have suffered no ill effects from my last visit," he went on. "I have returned as hastily as I may tae see tae yer . . . state of health."

I wasn't sure what he classified as an ill effect, but was willing to bet the list didn't include a perturbed mind. The naked intensity of the stranger's gaze as he examined me was startling, and I realized how much I counted on unfamiliar persons to disguise their feelings in the proper way and avert their eyes after a second or two of inspection. Surprise kept me silent and I hoped undemonstrative of my mild alarm, which manifested itself in a quickening of my pulse, which I could feel in my neck and behind my eyes.

"Ye may call me . . . Lachlan. I have always liked that name." The man I might call Lachlan went suddenly to one knee and inhaled deeply. His dark hair fell forward, hiding his face, and I was glad of the veil between my body and his gaze. "So, they've sown the nearby sands with salt. It may keep out their devil, but it has no effect on my kind. Or the other. Silly humans, sae slow to learn. Sae swift at forgetting. Was not the burial of this village lesson enough?"

The visitor's voice was soft, and I wasn't certain if I was supposed to hear. Demosthenes might have expressed himself more eloquently, and without the thick accent, but these words were plenty direct and frightening, delivered though they were in a pleasant burr. Leaving aside the implication that there had indeed been something supernatural about the sandstorm that buried Findloss—a large matter to set casually aside, at least for me—the people of this village were so hostile against this stranger that they had performed an exorcism against him, apparently in my own yard, and he showed not the slightest concern at their antagonism. This meant he was either very foolish or so very dangerous that he didn't need to care. Or perhaps both. Certainly he wasn't human. I could only wonder that I had ever thought him so.

"Now you, Mistress Silence, are another matter entirely." He rose, and when I failed to say anything, brushed past me into the cottage.

Though he offered me no violence, I was still ill at ease and wondered wildly if threatening him with a lamp or knife would do any good. Then I recalled Fergus's note saying to shed fey blood was to summon brutal tempests, so actions manslaughterous must be put on hold unless I was directly threatened. I was beginning to feel completely overwhelmed and helpless when I remembered the shackles in the trunk inside the privy. Perhaps there *was* something that could contain this creature if he got careless and let me leave the room unattended.

I glanced at my uninvited guest with some disfavor as he took up a place near the fire. I saw that he was studying the damp mosaic on the hearth. His fingers, which he drummed on the mantel, were exceptionally long and narrow, but in no way effete.

"So, not all of them had forgotten me," he said softly. "I believe this was done in the year before the inundation."

Little attention is paid to the regular calendar in Findloss; everything is calculated in years before and after the town's burial and subsequent resurrection, so the manner of his marking time didn't faze me. Lachlan's faith and certainty that he was something not human was different, and it was stronger than my assumption that he must be a normal person because monsters and faeries don't exist. My insufficient confidence in what I had previously known as reality kept me from arguing either with him or myself. And under the surface alarm, I was very curious. It took an effort to loosen my frozen tongue but I forced myself to speak.

"I'm sorry if I've been a bit impolite. It is just that my previous life was bereft of . . . preternatural beings. I am afraid that for a while I could not even admit your existence, and I found your inhuman presence on a particularly late and stormy night to be frankly menacing. My wits were temporarily addled by what I thought was a hallucination."

Those dark eyes turned my way. "And now?"

I spread my filthy hands and then took a seat on the edge of a stiff-backed chair. I hid my soiled palms in my skirt, strangely annoyed at my lack of presentability. "I am attempting to keep an open mind. Perhaps you are not menacing. After all, what do I know of your customs? Perhaps by your standards you are being charming!" I made myself smile as I said this, and it seemed to strike him temporarily dumb: Perhaps few people were inclined to be friendly to his kind. "You did after all make tea for me. That is usually accounted a friendly gesture." Unless it is poisoned, of course.

"And the people of this village?" he asked at last. "How do you find them?"

"Menacing," I answered. "Xenophobic, ignorant and superstitious—though I shall have to rethink the 'ignorant and superstitious' part now that I know you are real. And obviously they are ill-informed as to the nature of their unwanted guest, since their exorcism did not work."

"Nay, yer correct. The villagers are ignorant and superstitious. And one of them is allied with a very dangerous being. That is why I am here and . . . charming ye with tea and such." He did not smile but the head tilted slightly. The action reminded me of something an animal might do.

"What sort of dangerous being?" I asked, though this wasn't anything I actually wanted to hear about. I didn't comment on his claim to charm, either. "I assume you are not speaking of yourself."

Lachlan considered the question a moment before answering. "A rogue finman. A wizard, ye'd call him. A nasty, evil beastie wha can nevertheless pass for human when he chooses. I would be very careful aboot opening my door tae strangers in future. The finmen possess an absolutely devouring hatred of your kind."

My kind? Did he mean humans? Or did he refer to the Culbins? Or to the MacCodrums. I should not forget that my grandparents' clan had been mentioned in the missing journal.

"I see," I said. I didn't, but this didn't seem the moment to encourage a lecture about supernatural beings that hadn't actually visited me yet. I took a small steadying breath and pressed on to the matter that was more urgent. "And you are . . . ?"

"My job is to discover who has been daft enough tae call this monster back tae the village."

"I gathered that—but what *are* you?" I asked again.

"In what context?"

I hadn't expected any show of humor, and I found a real smile tugging at my lips.

"In the context of your visiting me late at night, scaring me half to death and stealing the book I was reading."

"Could ye read it?" he asked, avoiding the first half of my question.

"Parts of it, after a fashion. I have some Gaelic from my late husband and grandparents." I leaned forward in my seat, hoping the gesture was inviting of confidences and not threatening or impolite. "So, are you a blue man perhaps?"

"Nay."

"A fallen angel?"

"Certainly not!" The idea seemed to amuse him.

"A selkie?" I suggested, undeterred. I was willing to name the whole list, at least up to the water demon. If one of those were sitting in my parlor I preferred not to know it; that would be one straw too many for the poor camel in my brain that was in danger of running mad from the load of suppositions I was piling up. I was already feeling a bit mad, but only a bit. Some are born into a state of unreasonableness—poor mad souls—and some achieve unreason with the diligent application of alcohol or other stimulants. Some have unreason thrust upon them by outside sources, such as nonhuman visitors in the night. I am of the latter variety.

In spite of the most unreasonable—indeed unthinkable—circumstances in which I found my-self, a degree of reasonableness seemed to be gradually returning. And insane as it sounds, the amalgamation of my old logic with a new belief in the impossible had brought about a kind of calm acceptance of my situation, an end to my mental discomfort. There were the rules for my old life, and rules for the new. In one place, there were only human monsters. Here they apparently came in many shapes and species. I was adapting. Perhaps in time I could see a unicorn and think it normal.

"I am a hunter. That is all you need to know. For now." He said this flatly and I did not doubt him. As with my other neighbors, a little humor went a long way with him and he was done jesting.

"Did you know Fergus Culbin well?" I asked.

"I knew of him. The Culbins lived here for a lang while. By human standards."

From his tone, I adjudged that Lachlan hadn't liked my in-law. That made it universal. No one had liked Fergus, apparently not even his nephew or the village monster who should have been sympathetic to a fellow evildoer.

"Since it seems that we will probably be at this for a while, would you care for some tea?" I asked, deciding to disengage from a fruitless line of questioning, at least for the time being. I looked about for Herman but the cat had wisely gone missing.

"Thank ye, but nay. I dae not find your tea tae my liking."

"Some whisky then?" Alcohol helps one say things to and of persons that one would normally shroud in silence. In fact, it can lead one to contentions that had previously never entered one's head. Duncan had drunk almost all the time, and it had often freed his tongue. I had learned to do so too, in self-defense, and rather fancied myself to have a larger than normal capacity for strong spirits.

"Again, thank ye, but nay. Your company is intoxicating enough."

I did not attempt to either believe or disbelieve this gallant claim, but there was a tiny amount of exasperation in my voice when I asked, "Then, if it is not for tea or whisky, would it be too much to ask why you are here?"

"Not at all. As I said, I am hunting." Lachlan's head tilted. "And you have aroused my curiosity."

"However do you mean?" I asked, ever more reluctantly. "I assure you that I am unacquainted with any finmen or wizards, or in any way knowledgeable about hunting anything. I never met Fergus Culbin, who died before I ever heard his name. In short, I cannot see any way that I may be of service to you."

"When I knew that someone frae Findloss had summoned the finman and offered him refuge whilst he worked his evil ways, my first suspect was the duplicitous mage, Fergus Culbin. I was quite surprised tae find him dead and you here in his place. I didn't ken afore last night that there were any of yer clan left."

"Clan?"

"The MacCodrums. You are hereditary enemies of the Culbins, did ye know? For a brief moment, I wondered if ye'd killed him yerself."

I blinked a few times. Over the years I have been accused of many things, but never murder. My first reaction was to be insulted. My second (and completely reprehensible) thought was that it was a bit flattering that he thought I was capable of such ruthless action. Of late I had been something of a doormat upon which my husband wiped his feet.

"I'm afraid I am indeed the last—at least of my immediate family. And my husband and I were certainly . . . adversarial. But I assure you that I killed neither my husband nor Fergus Culbin." I took a small breath. "How did you discover that Fergus was dead? Did someone in the village tell you?"

"Nay, I could smell it. He died violently, killed by the finman. Ye didn't ken this?"

"No, the solicitor somehow failed to mention that detail. In fact, I believe he said that Fergus died in a boating accident." My voice was even, but I was beginning to be angry, and planned on asking Mr. Waverly a few pointed questions the next time I wrote to him. The former owner being murdered in my cottage seemed something that he should have mentioned.

Lachlan snorted. "The sea is unforgiving of ineptitude and carelessness, and many drown, but Fergus Culbin wasnae careless. He was killed here and his body dragged down tae the water." The stranger paused. "I believe the finman may have imprisoned his soul before killing him."

"Imprisoned his soul?" I tried out the phrase, not liking the way it sat on the tongue and immediately wishing that I could take it back. Not that silence would stay Lachlan's answer. I sensed that I was fated to hear this dénouement and to test the extent of my new beliefs, whether ready to encompass the story or not.

"That is what finmen dae to their victims. They need souls tae work their dark magic. I cannae tell fer certain since I didna see the corpse, but it seems likely. This finman is voracious."

"You can tell if a corpse has had its soul stolen? I mean, doesn't the spirit leave on its own once the person is dead?"

"Aye. But ritual theft leaves distinct marks on the nose where the teeth grip it."

The hair on my arms lifted and I shuddered. This was the pièce de rèsistance, and yet my mind was too resistant to this particular piece of information to allow itself to dwell on it for any length of time. I asked, "Would you mind stirring up the fire? I am suddenly chilled."

"Certainly. Would you like me tae make you some tea?" Lachlan replied.

"No, but I will take a glass of whisky." I gestured at a small sideboard where a decanter and two glasses sat. The second glass had been bought in an early misplaced optimism that I would have friendly neighbors with whom to share hearth and refreshment. "And then you can explain why this creature killed Fergus and why he would hate me when we have never met."

"Certainly." Lachlan walked to the sideboard and picked up the decanter. "Have you ever heard of the *Cailleach-a-Phluc*?"

No, I hadn't. And I didn't want to, since even the words sounded evil. In the usual course of events, I am not an unregulated neurotic who is ruled solely by instinct and emotion, but these proceedings were hardly usual and I thought a degree of trepidation and even fear was in order. And yet, I could not omit any knowledge that might improve my safety. Caution was required but I could not afford ignorance, however taxing the truth on my sanity.

Putting a glass in my hand, Lachlan turned to the fire. I didn't gulp the contents, but I wasn't sipping daintily either. Lachlan continued speaking.

"The *Cailleach-a-Phluc* was a black witch of unsurpassed evilness wha often visited this village. It was the finmen's theft of her wicked magic that turned them tae creatures of ravenous hunger and depravity. Made strong and bold by this stolen magic, the chief wizard of the finmen worked an evil spell that he sent against my people who lived aen the caves that stretch beneath the village and up the coast a day's journey." Lachlan's voice was cold. "Findloss had been warned about what would happen if they didnae expel the finman from among them, but they were greedy and anxious to keep their nets full of enchanted fish. And so they let the finman remain. Our wizard and I managed tae turn back the terrible storm of sand that the finman had sent tae Avocamor, also called *Tir-fo-Thuinn*—Land under the Waves—and instead this village was buried . . . and the finman along with it.

"We thought that was the end. The others of the tainted tribe were hunted down and banished or killed. But we were wrong tae relax our guard. The most evil of the finmen didnae die, and eventually he was able tae unbury the village and escape. I believe he survived all those years off the souls of those trapped in the church. They were his personal larder while he schemed and eventually discovered the means tae escape his own curse."

"And now someone has called this monster back?" My voice was barely a whisper. "But why? That seems like madness."

"Aye. And I am at a loss tae know wham it may be. Only twa humans survived the inundation and would have known of the creature. And Fergus Culbin is now dead—at the hands of the finman. Unless they had a falling-out after the summons, I cannae imagine why the finman waud kill him."

"And the other survivor?"

"Died without issue a decade ago."

I thought about this. "You know, you are making an assumption that may not be true."

A dark brow lifted. "Aye?"

"We know that only two survivors ended up in Keil, but that doesn't mean that someone else might not have escaped to somewhere else if they fled overland. If they never mentioned the storm or the finman, no one would have thought anything about a traveler passing through Glen Ard or elsewhere." Lachlan nodded slowly, and I went on without considering. "I think the trick may be to have a look at the church records and see exactly who was in the village at the time of the storm and then see if any of their offspring have come back. Assuming the offspring are witless enough to use the family name."

Lachlan shook his head. "I have ceased tae marvel at how witless some people can be. I shall look on this when I am finished wi' other inquiries."

I doubted his investigation involved any methods

with which I was familiar, but sadly, I had to agree about the general state of human witlessness. Was I not even now being careless with my trust? How could I know if anything Lachlan said was true? For that matter, how did I know that he was even real and not a figment of a disturbed imagination?

I pulled my chair closer to the hearth, getting as near as I could without setting my shoes on fire. It was a wasted effort. I simply could not get close enough to drive off the new chill in my bones.

*The wind comes rushing down through the openings
between the hills, carrying with it immense torrents of
sand with a force and violence almost overpowering.
Clouds of dust are raised from the tops of the mounds
and are whirled about in the wildest confusion, and
fall with the force of hail. Nothing can be seen but
sand above, sand below and sand everywhere. You dare
not open your eyes but must grope your way about
as if blindfolded.*

—John Martin of Elgin, describing the village
of Culbin during a 17th-century sandstorm

Chapter Six

Lachlan's late visit—and promised return by the next
full moon—left me disturbed and with my brain
seething. I didn't know if I was more frightened or
amazed or exhausted by the constant low-grade panic
and lingering disbelief engendered by what I had
heard; all three emotions took turns being in ascen-
dance and I found myself pacing the cottage instead
of preparing for bed.

As I walked through the rooms, I discovered that

there was something bothering me about the second bedroom, some deformity of space that tugged at my eyes every time I entered. I was using it for storage of unneeded household items, and it was therefore far from tidy, but every time I walked into the room, it felt smaller to me than the time before. This should not have been the case, because the cot in that room was actually smaller than the bed I slept in and the space should have felt more spacious instead of less.

Eventually, to satisfy my nagging brain, I paced off the two rooms and discovered that the smaller-seeming room *was* smaller. By two large paces. Once the anomaly was identified, it took little effort to discover the loose stone in the back fireplace chimney that hid the latch that released the false wall. The reason for the paneling in the cottage was then clear; secrets and not warmth or ornamentation had been the cause of its installation. Someone, perhaps several someones, had wanted to conceal something from their neighbors.

The air that puffed into the bedroom from the dark hole was not unpleasant, though a bit stale. It reminded me of the lending library back home, and I felt a degree of lessening in my trepidation as musty air and nothing else rushed out at me. Fetching the lamp, I ducked into the secret cupboard and let my eyes adjust to the greater dark. Herman followed reluctantly, sneezing from time to time.

There were dust and cobwebs in abundance, telling me the narrow room had not been cleaned for some while. If the cottage had been grander and more on the beaten path of Europe's traditional religious turmoil—or on any path at all—I would have suspected the hidden room was a priest hole. But of holy relics there were no signs. Nor were there any secret staircases leading to hidden passages used by so many smugglers in Robert Louis Stevenson's stories. This sudden idea of smugglers was fostered by the discovery of a heavy keg of brandy in the far corner of the closet, which was mostly full. How old it was, I could not say, but it smelled potent when uncorked and the oak of the cask was quite dark, suggesting that some liquor had seeped through.

Though I saw no place in the walls, floor or ceiling where another secret door might be, I did take the time to tap the panels and pound the floorboards. I had not forgotten Lachlan's insistence that Fergus Culbin had been murdered in the cottage by a rogue finman who must have found some way inside. The lack of secret passages was therefore doubly reassuring. Since the chimney was barred and all the windows too small to admit a human, the only place the creature could enter the cottage was the front door, and I had a heavy bar and sturdy lock to take care of that.

What the tiny room lacked in religious icons, it made up for in books and folios. Most were written in Latin and Greek—the second, a language for which I had little facility—but one handwritten journal was done in some form of Gaelic, which Fergus (I assumed) had glossed extensively in English, and another was penned in an older form of border English. These I put aside, though I hadn't any reason to assume that I would be able to translate the villainous handwriting that was faded, had some water damage and was blithely unconcerned about conforming to any of the grammatical rules with which I was familiar.

That was all of the room's contents, except for the one chair—taken from the dining room, I assumed, since it matched the others, though it brought the total to thirteen, an unlucky and odd number of seats—and a small table with a dusty lamp, a pot of dried ink and a broken pen. Taking the two books with me, I closed the panel back up and decided to wash and then retire to bed. I also retrieved the yew carpet beater and iron shackles from the linen basket and put them beneath my pillow. Perhaps my faith was misplaced, but I felt better having them near at hand.

I feared that my mind would keep me awake, but fear is exhausting. After reading for a short while, I put the disquieting books aside and fell into a deep sleep that was disturbed only once, when Herman jumped on the bed and insisted on wiggling his way under the covers. I patted him once in sympathy: The journal had revealed something nasty that I hadn't previously suspected of Fergus. Duncan's uncle had been attempting to find the lost Spanish gold through divination. His notes suggested that had he not been killed by the finman, Herman would have been headed for a sacrificial death and mummification at the next dark of the moon.

I am not an early riser, if I can avoid it. It is not that I am slothful or unnaturally indolent, but I see no need to be up before the sun when it is cold and I will need to make a fire just to be comfortable. Neither coal nor peat was cheap in Findloss, so I felt justified remaining in my bed until normal inclination told me to rise and rub the laziness from my eyes. But even for me, that morning was making an exceptionally late start. The sun was high in the narrow bit of scarred glass that I had forgotten to shutter before retiring to sleep.

Looking at the situation optimistically, I decided I could skip lumpy breakfast porridge and just have an early lunch.

I had previously resisted the temptation to pay a visit to the local *Sithean Mor*, a supposed abandoned faerie mound mentioned by the locals and in one of Fergus's handwritten books, believed by the natives to be a tomb for a race of giants, though Fergus did not mention this in his notes. The mound is reachable on foot if one is undeterred by hard climbing and the possibility of broken bones and drowning. None of those things appealed to me in the least, but that morning I found myself sufficiently curious and willing to consider the existence of what had previously seemed impossible that I tied up a lunch and a small sketchpad and pencils in a large scarf, which I hung down my shoulder like a peddler's sack, and started off on my adventure.

First I stopped in at the post office, ostensibly to check for mail but really to mention where I was going. The post office is also our only shop. It is not a very impressive store, and Mistress MacLaren who runs it does not spend her time trying to lure customers into buying her multifarious wares with attractive displays or signs—mostly because she has no competition to lure customers from, and also because the wares are not all that diverse or alluring. What is it about a shop counter that turns a mere table into an insurmountable obstacle one would never dream of crossing? And why does the person behind it seem more in charge than the one offering custom? I have often wondered if Mistress MacLaren had a stool concealed back there that she stood on whenever she heard the door, because she seemed much taller on one side of the counter than on the other.

Mistress MacLaren was not a licensed grocer (or even a postmistress), which probably explained the lack of variety in her goods and why we sometimes ended up with wooden seeds in supposed raspberry jam. (I had never encountered counterfeit jam before and found the experience at once amusing and annoying). But, to be fair, I doubt she would have made enough money in commerce to pay the license fees the government required, so we were grateful for whatever she carried. My main purchases were oats and eggs. Though as thrifty as any native, I had found it hard to do without certain things and so had asked my solicitor before I arrived to arrange for a shipment of a few luxuries, among them potatoes, dried apples for baking, fine milled flour, some sugar and a small amount of cinnamon. I don't think Mistress MacLaren ever forgave me for buying these things from an outsider.

To the villagers, I am slightly tainted by sinful worldliness because of where I was born. This also makes me foreign—as in, not a Scot—a fact for which I am to be pitied. If they were not themselves also transplants from several other villages, I should likely be completely ostracized, but none of us here can say we actually belong to Findloss. And frankly, I have the best claim, having been left one of the original residences by my late husband's uncle. Perhaps they would have trusted me more if I had explained that my mother's family was of the MacCodrum clan. Or perhaps not. There were a lot of blood feuds here, and the people have long memories and some rusty claymores in their cupboards.

Mistress MacLaren clearly wanted to ask me why I was taking such a strenuous hike, and I considered being teasing and refusing to answer her curiosity. But it seemed best not to alienate one of the few people who would talk to me, however reluctantly, so I volunteered that I had heard there were still some sea-blooming orchids out that way and I was going to sketch them. This satisfied her as to my intentions and also allowed her the chance to later gossip to the others about my foolishness and eccentricities. I tried not to begrudge her this entertainment, since she would be the one, I hoped, to send a rescue party to find me if I did not return by nightfall.

Outside of Findloss the cliffs rose almost immediately, hence the village's preference for sea rather than land travel. There is a narrow strip of sand that one may traverse around the cliff arms for the few hours that the tide is out, but it is stony and wrack strewn. The terraced crags loomed large on either side of the pier, which had been built on the only bit of smoothish beach in the tiny harbor. The town was erected on the second low terrace of the mountain, except for my own cottage, which sits on its own out-thrusting hillock on what I am told is an igneous extrusion. There were stairs to the beach and a path of sorts that led to the cliff tops by a series of switchbacks, but one could also scramble both up and down the giant sheets of limestone that had pulled away from the cliff and fallen like dominoes. The cliffs would probably not seem formidable to anyone who had lived in the Alps, but to me they seemed quite impregnable and scary, being inhabited only by screaming birds whose shrill cries seemed mean and aggressive.

An hour on, I stopped at a small stream that spilled out of the white cliff walls and had a drink. The water was clear but tasted peaty, so I did not drink deeply as I squatted among the small rushes in the miniature quagmire of moss and bog myrtle, which was blazing the shade of candle flame as it huddled in the tiny and cold oasis in the sand. Along the way were curved beaches where the cliffs had been carved out into a chaotic series of arches and caves. Most were shallow, but a few seemed deep. I was not tempted to explore them. I had heard too many stories of people being trapped in caves when the tide came in and drowning for their curiosity. This seemed a terrible fate to me: life choking out of you in total darkness, your body perhaps swept away at the turning of the tide. Also, I heard, or imagined I heard, a low-voiced crying. This belonged to a seal, one of the supposed emissaries from the court of King Lochlann that frequented our shores on sunny days. The seals are lovely from a distance, but knowing what I did in that moment—and not knowing a great deal more—I thought it best to stay away from a creature that might not be exactly what it appeared.

I continued a while more and then stopped at a

grassy meadow, called a *machair*, where I found my-self a flat rock in the sun to sit on. There I had my simple lunch of bread and jam, and one rather tired apple that nevertheless tasted delicious because of my hunger. If I had had any worries about being observed in my travels, they would have been allayed. I had seen only one boat, and it was far out at sea. Other than the noisy birds and a few curious hares, I had no companions in my narrow meadow. Feeling generous, I tossed my apple core to the nearest of the doe-eyed bunnies and a small crust of bread to the sharp-eyed curlew that had stood patiently at the base of the rock, watching as I ate. My offers accepted, I rose slowly, had a stretch and then resumed my travels.

The entire way I kept an eye on the tide. At the first sign of it turning, I was giving up and turning back for home. Fortunately, the sea continued to ebb, and I was lured onward by the rare sunshine and the increasingly smooth sand bar. I decided that if the next day were as nice, I would make a trip to the cockle beds and dig up my own dinner. Herman always enjoyed digging in the sand and I was ready for a change in diet.

As I walked, I discovered that my brain was soon back to pondering the same two questions that had bothered me since Lachlan's visit. Why, if my husband had in fact known that his family and mine were par-ticipating in some kind of family feud, had he mar-ried me? It is said that in Scotland it is a tradition for enemies to put rings on each other's fingers and dirks in each other's hearts, but he had come to America to make a fresh start and knew well that this wasn't our custom. It made his behavior confusing and mysterious.

Perhaps even sinister. Was he something more than he appeared? Certainly he had been keeping secrets.

And now, more urgently, I wondered who and what Lachlan was—and could I trust him? After all, my current relieved supposition that my husband may have had some compelling outside reason for disliking me came from this stranger. How did I know that he was telling the truth? My instinct was to believe him, but my instincts had been wrong before. Attraction affected judgment and I had to admit that at some level, and against all wisdom, I was attracted to Lachlan, whomever and whatever he was.

Ponder as I did, no answers came to me and my bafflement remained, somewhat spoiling my walk. Duncan's name had stupidly been invoked, and like a zombie he rose from where I had buried him and hurried across the sea. The mind is determined to relive certain events, and I recalled with some pain standing in the judge's chambers with my heart, if not in my hand, then at least as open as hope in the face of parental disapproval could make it. I smiled happily while we said our vows in front of a clerk who stood as witness to our marriage, and for a while I remained emotionally undefended and expecting we would have a happy marriage, because Duncan, though a lot older and sometimes impatient in manner, was kind and affectionate in an offhand way. He was even a helpmate when my parents died and I was left feeling guilty for my unhealed breach with them. Had it all been an act? Was there *never* any affection in his heart?

One day, Duncan had received a letter from Scotland. What it said I never knew, because he burned it, but he locked himself in the parlor he used as a study and when he emerged hours later, he was drunk and rude. From that day forward, I don't think he was ever entirely sober again. He never touched me after that day either. His words and manner grew increasingly cruel and repulsive as he strove to drive me away. I offered sympathy, but my pity only infuriated him.

He did touch whores. Many of them. And he turned to a new love: cocaine. Duncan's sudden passing had left me with a bittersweet incense of tragic memory that smoldered in my thoughts for weeks after his death. I thought I had doused the last spark, but apparently some embers lingered.

Had Fergus Culbin been the author of the letter that caused the change in my husband? It seemed that I might never know the answer. One thing was certain, though. My failed marriage had cast a long dark shadow over my life, deepened by the loss of my parents before we made up our quarrel, and I was tired of being lost in memory's evil twilight. Duncan was dead and buried, and I needed to find my way out of his shade. I had to become my own woman again and put this blight from my soul once and for all.

On this thought, I rounded a headland and came face to cliff face with the *Sithean Mor*. The sight immediately shook me from my unhappy reverie and caused my nerves to shrill with awed alarm and unhealthy fascination. The mound was not the green of grass or moss that I had expected, but rather a salmon pink stone shaded through with the colors of a strong sunset. It stood some two stories high and had no windows or doors—a fact for which I felt oddly grateful. Had there been an opening, self-respect would have demanded that I step inside and look around, and this was not something I wanted to do.

The islands had never held me in thrall any more than the supposedly enchanted lowlands or highlands, but I could sense that this was an uncanny spot. Lonely, a place of spiritual desuetude and perhaps something worse. It was what the natives called "feart." Still, at some level it called to me, a familiar voice whispering in the closed-up basement of my brain. I had never been here before, but this place knew me.

Megan MacCodrum, come near.

Terror is a strange beast. It can be repulsive, an urgent warning from that inner voice of sanity to stay away from something. But it can also be oddly enthralling, even addicting, and the foolish urge to rush out into the dark when one hears a noise, or to look beneath the hood of the cloaked stranger to see perhaps a monster can be very strong. At its worst, this mixture of fear and fascination can become a parasite in the blood that takes up residence in the heart and stays with you forever, always urging dangerous confrontation when common sense says to flee. This was the way my mood trended. Angered at what I had willingly endured at Duncan's hands, I was ready to lash out wildly, to prove that I would not be subdued by anything or anyone again.

The whispering voice encouraged me: *Come closer and we shall make you strong!*

Then, unbidden, a paragraph from Fergus's book came to mind:

> *The savior of Man, enraged with the spilling of Christian blood on this, the most Holy of Days, allowed the phantom candle to appear at the stone as a sign of disgrace, and it burned throughout the night with unnatural brightness. All who beheld it were dead within a fortnight, a judgment upon them for their impiety.*

The words, feeling suddenly quite real and crying out louder than the foreign whispers in my head, caused me to shudder and I was suddenly more than ready to leave that haunted place to the whispering ghosts who owned it. Surprised from my trance, I belatedly noticed that there lingered in the air, so unnaturally still for being hard upon the shore, a trace of something foul and threatening. I did not think the troubling residue was from the mound itself but from something nearby, and it made me recall Lachlan's contention that he could smell Fergus's murder. This seemed something similar.

Then I saw a most disturbing thing. As though conjured by my thoughts, a glow, rather like a small sunrise, began at the north side of the mound. Cautiously I skirted the *Sithean Mor*, keeping well back from the stone walls and praying that no door or window had opened while I wasn't looking.

The light was not from the mound itself, but rather from something outside which quickly grew from a few inches to something taller than a man, though in a man's general shape. The phenomenon has many names, both in Scotland and in the United States—will-o-wisps, Saint Elmo's Fire, hobby lanterns, spook lights, ball lightning and, most disturbing, corpse candles. Learned men in ivory towers would have us believe that they are caused by swamp gas escaping from the ground, but of what use is this theory when the seven-foot-tall shaft of painful, glowing light was appearing on a rocky beach where there was neither swamp nor gas?

Some think they are evil spirits turned away by both God and the Devil and doomed to roam the earth forever. Others believe they are the guardians of buried treasure. I could not help but recall that locally, these effulgent lights supposedly appear in places where the dead have been—or will soon be. And not just any dead—only those who die in violence.

Nerves shattered, I fled.

Come as the wind comes, when
Forests are rended;
Come as the waves come, when
Navies are stranded.
—Sir Walter Scott,
"Gathering Song of Donald Dhu"

Chapter Seven

I ran blindly, my feet guided by panic that did not in the moment seem so unreasonable, and it was some minutes before I realized I was stumbling through surf that had overrun the narrow beach. It took a moment to understand that this meant the tide had turned . . . and that I might not be able to return the way I had come.

Shocked back into my senses by a larger and more tangible fear of being trapped by the ocean, I slowed my galloping feet and heart and looked about to see how far the sea had progressed inland. My heart was dismayed by the view. How long had I been at the faerie mound? It had not seemed more than a few minutes, but I saw that the sun had actually swayed far into the west and was preparing to set. On the horizon, another storm was gathering.

I squinted into the harsh light and perceived that thirty feet of my beach was gone, already under a foot of water. The sea's breathless murmurs had become hissed threats from which the birds fled in disorder, all species winging together in panicked flight, which only added to my alarm. I was certain that the fishermen I had seen earlier had already paid heed to the warning and had brought their boat to shore without detouring to sell their catch at the fish market in Glen Ruadh. There would be no help there.

Could I make it along the shore, if I tied up my skirts and ran? As though to discourage me from any courageous but foolhardy thoughts, a wave washed over my knees, hitting hard enough to unbalance me, and biting my legs with icy teeth and making an effort to ensnare them with seaweed; cold wind, sharp as the flensing knives used by the fishermen, cut over my face and gouged tears from my eyes, which ran down my cheeks and then fell into the surf. Gasping with shock at the physical assault, I looked back toward the mound. The corpse candle was still burning brightly, taller and wider than ever. It might even be visible from the village. More unnerved by this sight than by the turning tide that seemed to be herding me back toward the cliffs, I shuffled carefully in a circle, looking for some option other than the flaming devil or the deep blue sea.

There was one. I had not noticed the fissure in the cliff face as I journeyed up the beach, but with the sun now casting long fingers of fiery light into its recesses,

I could see it clearly. It was some sort of upward slop-
ing though narrow tunnel, and most happily for me, I
could see from the bent marron grass that a breeze
was blowing down it. That meant it opened somewhere to the air. Not hesitating, since the waves beating at me had reached my thighs and were threatening
to drag me by the skirts right out to sea, I reluctantly
waded for the opening.

Once inside, the air grew quite sultry, as though
heated by some geyser. Quite oddly I began to feel
sleepy, and to have gluttonous fantasies about eating
toast with jam as I sat by the fire at the cottage and had
a doze. So real was this vision that I almost stopped
then and there to sit in the rough shells that had gathered in one of the depressions in the tunnel floor. Only
the cries of the terrified birds and the hissing tide kept
me moving.

Megan MacCodrum—come back!

The eerie voice had me moving again. The sunlight
faded with every step, but I had no trouble seeing,
because of a strange phosphorescence that covered the
walls. I did not touch the luminance, for it smelled of
ammonia and sulfur though it was rather pretty and
conveniently bright. The floor of the cave rose gradually, promising eventual safety, but I had to walk
quickly to outpace the water that rushed in behind me.
It was difficult because my limbs were growing wooden
and graceless.

Though feeling increasingly sleepy, I began to notice
that there was an odd kind of sterility to the tunnel
now that it had passed inland. No crustaceans or bar-
nacles had taken up residence here, perhaps because

of the strange green slime, or perhaps because of the unpleasantly warm temperature that made my skin bead with sweat, which I knew would feel disagreeably chilly when I finally reached open air again. Or maybe it was because the water at high tide ran too fast through the tunnel to permit anything to lodge there. Urged to greater effort by this thought, I moved faster, fighting sleepiness and cursing the wet skirts that hampered and chafed my clumsy legs.

Fast as I trotted, the water was closing in faster—and the dark with it. And I found the gullies, both large and small, which increasingly laced the tunnel floor and walls, to be treacherously corniced with crumbling stone that gave easily, foot traps hidden by rotting sea wrack and loose scree and strangely shaped shells that waited just to turn my ankles. Haste was foolish, but dallying was not an option, and the inevitable finally occurred when I stumbled into a hidden hole, twisting my left ankle. The pain was sharp enough to make me feel sick. I leaned against the slimy rock wall, using blasphemous language as I reached for my pained joint and suddenly feared that even if Mistress MacLaren allowed herself to be inconvenienced enough to notice I was missing and send out a search party, help would come too late. Looking upward, I could see that the tunnel's walls were wet all the way to the ceiling at this point. If I did not find another way out, I would drown in this narrow tunnel.

I looked back the way I had come and was not encouraged. I could see no sign of daylight, only white water that thrashed about as if there were creatures in it. My ankle would have to hold my weight, or I would have to crawl. Hissing every bad word I knew, I forced myself to hobble around the sharp bend in the tunnel—

I ran straight into Lachlan. I couldn't help noticing that he was shirtless and his kilt had been hastily donned. The bottoms of the uneven pleats were damp and smutted with sand.

"*C'aite am bheil thu dol?*" *Where are you going?* he demanded, catching me by the shoulders. I had the impression that he was not entirely happy to see me, and startled enough by my presence to use Gaelic rather than Scots.

"Out of here," I answered, feeling immediate relief at not being alone in that terrible place, even if my companion was also rather frightening.

"Aye. That would be best. The white horses are running hard," he said, looking past me; and when I turned I could see the cold green water was topped with white foam, which suggested great turbulence. "A storm is coming on. An unnatural one. Follow me noo—and make haste. We havenae much time tae spare." He let go of me and started off.

The water roared behind me, sounding angry that I might escape after all. I made haste as best I could but fell behind almost immediately, and Lachlan looked back with annoyance and perhaps a bit of concern. He had a general damn-your-eyes attitude that afternoon, which left me confounded. I couldn't imagine why my presence was bothering him. Surely he didn't live in these caves or think that I was spying on him . . . ?

"My ankle is sprained," I snarled defensively. "I can't go any faster."

Frowning, he doubled back. Lachlan leaned in uncomfortably close, and before I could ask what he was doing, he pulled back his lips in a snarl of his own and scraped his rather long and sharp teeth along my earlobe and jaw.

"Ow!" But before the echo of my cry died away, he had followed up with a long lick along the injured skin, which also lapped up the last of my tears. "What are you . . . ?" I trailed off. I had been given ether once when I'd had my tonsils removed, and the anesthetic had produced something similar to what I was feeling.

"'Tis the quickest way." Lachlan's long-fingered hands held me up while I fought for equilibrium. My sudden and unexplainable dizziness left me feeling helpless and grateful for his careless support. I noticed more than a touch of sin in those dark eyes that studied me, but whether it was the beginnings of lust or sins more deadly, I couldn't say.

I became aware of his scent, something sort of spicy, and I was suddenly glad that Lachlan didn't smoke. Duncan had, and I hadn't liked it. I agree with James VI that tobacco is a weed fit for nothing but diabolical fumigation, and Lachlan smelled too nice to have his odor hidden.

"Is that better?" he asked, as I rediscovered my knees and shook the cobwebs from my head.

"Y-yes." And it was. I felt no pain in my ankle or where he had bitten me. My limbs were again warm and flexible.

"Let us go on then. The tide willna wait," he warned, releasing me more slowly.

"I know."

"Can ye think of nae reason why Fergus Culbin might have called the finman?" The question was abrupt, and he turned away right after.

"Maybe. I found some more books and it seems that he was hunting for Spanish gold from that sunken galleon." I hadn't meant to say anything about this, but in my dreamy state I felt compelled to answer Lachlan truthfully. Lying was not even considered.

"Was he in earnest aboot it?"

"Earnest enough to be making plans to kill the cat. He was going to try some divination ritual that needed a blood sacrifice."

"Unpleasant, but that wouldnae necessarily involve a finman. Unless he thought to compel him tae swim tae the depths and bring up the treasure . . ."

This sounded reasonable.

"You've had no luck discovering who has called the finman back or why?" I asked.

"I havena. Not yet. But be ye sure that I shall. I cannae fail. Tae much rides on this resolution."

"Rend your clothes and gird yourself with sackcloth," I muttered, thinking of King David and his battle with Goliath.

"He's one of the Old Testament killers, is he not, this David, King of the Jews?"

I opened my mouth to protest the description, but then reconsidered. To a non-Christian, the Old Testament's violent heroes and prophets could seem quite crazy and their actions questionable enough to merit such a label. "More of a cad really. And in his own way, brave—in a sneaky sort of manner."

"I recall him noo. 'She saw King David leaping and

dancing before the Lord and she despised him in her heart.' He is a strange man to admire. As a woman, he doesnae offend thee?"

"Who said I admire him?" I was very surprised that Lachlan would recall anything from the Bible, and flattered that he would ask me this question. Absolutely no one in my old life would have posed such a query. "And, yes, I find men who have relations with many women to be objectionable—particularly if they are married. I simply don't dwell on it because he's been dead for thousands of years and it would be silly to carry a grudge for that long." Duncan was another matter. I was entitled to hate him forever if I so chose.

"Ah." Lachlan stopped abruptly and looked upward. There was a narrow chimney overhead, smooth as glass and slightly wider than my would-be rescuer's generous shoulders. My heart was somewhat gladdened when I saw the red light of sunset glowing above.

" 'Tis a blowhole. A bit tight but serviceable."

"We're going up there?" I said doubtfully. I wanted out of that tunnel, but this seemed impossible to scale without rope.

"What for nae? I came down it safe enough when I heard ye running. I canna see why it shouldna take us back up again." I realized that the heavier Scottish accent had reappeared and he sounded amused.

I looked down and could see clear tracks in the sandy silt at the bottom of the chimney that had fallen in from above. He had obviously passed this way, though why he should be near the caves at all was a mystery.

"Up with ye noo. The *gair na mara* is unhappy and tracking us hard," he said, stooping down so that I could climb onto his back. I was embarrassed and somewhat reluctant to do this, but Lachlan was correct. The water gurgling behind us in an ever-growing voice of anger kept me from shilly-shallying.

What he did then I cannot explain, but somehow he managed to spring upward, grip those glassy walls with fingers and toes, and pull us both up that stone chimney. His muscles flexed and rippled under my clinging limbs and in less than a minute we clambered out onto a flat rock surrounded by the beautiful feather grass nature sometimes sows on her stony shores. The fronds shook like a snoring gnome's hoary beard. The wind was sharp with the smell of coming rain, and as I had feared, I was very cold. Especially when the clouds covered the setting sun and further depleted the sky's dying light. I felt rather as if something had reached inside me, grabbed at my lungs with icy fingers and ripped my voice away.

I slipped around to the sheltered side of a largish rock, trying to hide from the wind, and startled a covey of fall-muted grouse seeking shelter in the grass and a lone winter-coated ptarmigan that froze in terror at our approach. I knew how he felt. Lachlan sometimes affected me that way.

"Thank you," I said, when I found breath the cold had momentarily stolen.

"*Cha ghabh mi luach,*" he murmured. *I'll take no reward*. I was made nervous by his sudden affability and found myself turning away so I wouldn't have to confront that intent gaze and the strange half smile on his lips. Or that mostly naked chest. How was it that he did not feel the cold? I was already half numb.

"*Nam bithinn-sa thusa, bhithinn as a so am mairech.*" *If I were you I'd be out of this tomorrow.* My Gaelic was not fluent but I had no trouble understanding him.

"Unfortunately, leaving isn't an option. The ferry won't come for several more days, and it may not be able to moor even then if the weather does not moderate."

Also, I had nowhere to go.

Clouds thickened as I watched, forming hellishly fast. They carried the eye down to the horizon and the heaving sea, which was being driven inward by the wind. And I was suddenly certain that I had seen this once before.

"Yer knowing this place then." The voice was languid, hypnotic. He moved closer.

Looking about confusedly as I mastered my uneven breath, I could see my cottage in the distance, and beyond it the steeple of the kirk painted orange by the last of the setting sun on the horizon that hadn't been swallowed by the clouds. The rest of the town was invisible and mute, embraced in the hollow of the shifting dunes that hissed and whispered slyly. Talk about the foolhardiness of building a house on shifting sands! Both buildings were dark and deserted, and I was struck with the unwanted knowledge that we were in a place whose time was past—not far past perhaps, but still belonging to an age and people who were gone, amputated from the rest of the world by the Storm that had buried it years ago. We were trespassers in a dead place and Findloss's inhabitants were living on borrowed time. This filled me with a vague sort of atavistic fear and also resignation. I should have been more alarmed, but terror of other things had exhausted me and mild concern was all I could muster as the deadly cold crept into my bones.

"Come on. Yer shivering. We shall speak of this later," Lachlan said, laying a hand on my arm and pulling me to my feet. I didn't explain that it was the chill in my soul more than the one on my flesh that made me tremble. Though I was embarrassed, I turned my freezing cheeks against the heated flesh of his chest and allowed myself a moment to warm both skin and spirit.

Lachlan did not repulse me, and after a moment even stroked a hand over my fallen and now wild hair. "What a strange lass, ye are, and it's mad I maun be. Yer tears have driven me here. I'd nae thought of this ever happening again." I could not swear that he said this aloud, yet I heard him.

Behind us, the *gair na mara*—that mocking laughter of the sea reported by fishermen—bellowed loudly and then spat cold green water out of the chimney we had just climbed. I knew that, had Lachlan not found me, I would be dead, my lungs filled with green water and my body battered against the walls of the sea cave until it took me back out to the depths. The thought had me shuddering in spite of the immense comfort I found in his arms.

"Donnae think on it. I *was* there," he said, and turned me toward the cottage. "Ye called tae me in time."

Had I called to him? Surely not aloud, though he had been in my thoughts when I cried with despair.

However he had known of my predicament, I was grateful that he had come.

Leave untended the herd,
The flock without shelter;
Leave the corpse uninterr'd,
The bride at the altar.
—Sir Walter Scott,
"Gathering Song of Donald Dhu"

Chapter Eight

With food in my stomach and a glass of whisky in hand—I wanted brandy but wasn't willing to drink anything in Fergus's hidden room, since who knew what he had been doing with it—I was feeling much less undone. And a bath, once the water had finished heating, would conclude the repairs to the inner woman. The outer woman would have bruises for a few days.

Knowing it wouldn't calm me but feeling compelled nonetheless, I picked up one of Fergus's books and began reading where he had translated the text in the margins:

And she was delivered of a boy childe. Pushing the gamp [midwife] aside, the tall and ferocious man who had paced at the bedside, his gown of blackest velvet which looked more like the fur of some beast, snatched up the infant and retired to the fire he had blazing in preparation. He threw the babe into the flames and crushed it with his bootheel until its body disappeared into the coals. When the gamp attempted to rescue the child, he choked the life from her. He said to the babe's mother that he would have no selkie bastards in his house.

Nauseated, I put the book aside. Knowledge came at too high a price. I wasn't ready to seek out any more answers.

"It wasnae Fergus's ancestor wham did this. If ye care," Lachlan said softly from over my shoulder. I hadn't heard him reenter the cottage, but his presence didn't surprise me. "It was the finman. And his 'gown of velvet' was a selkie skin—the wee murdered bairn's father. The woman's name was Heather Macbeth. She took her own life a few days later. This happened right afore the village was buried."

I shook my head, unable to comprehend such evil.

"The Culbins were nae sae innocent themselves, though. Fergus Culbin's father should hae been put tae the horn and hanged—and likely wadha been had the family been less feart in the village."

I thought for an uncharitable moment about how much simpler my life would be if someone had wiped out the Culbins before Duncan had been born.

"I don't know why, but I've been thinking of my husband today," I answered, speaking the words aloud before I had time to consider the wisdom of inaugurating another unpleasant and extremely personal subject. Some minds are backward-looking; mine is not usually so, and I had to consider why it was harkening consistently to the past when I prefer to face forward. Perhaps some part of me knew that answers to my current problem waited there.

"Aye?"

"I'm wondering—still—why he married me. The longer I consider the matter, the more I see that it was all very deliberate. He wooed me without love. With affection, perhaps, in the beginning, but not out of romantic attachment."

"For protection mayhap," Lachlan said.

"From what?" I hoped I didn't look as stunned and stupid as I felt. Protection?

"Frae his family. Yer a MacCodrum, after all. They would have avoided ye. Or perhaps he feared the finman and hoped you would repel him as well. Yours is a race of olden renown, hunters and killers every one."

I still felt stunned and stupid. My family was renowned? For being killers? Me? My mother? My granny? That might explain my father's dislike of his in-laws, though.

"But why? And how? For heaven's sakes, we had an ocean between us and Scotland. How could there have been any danger to Duncan from his family or the finman?" My questions were mostly voiced in a tone of denial rather than inquiry, but I knew Lachlan would answer.

"Normally an ocean wad be enough. But this situation is far frae normal. The finman is after something and he wants it verra badly. Perhaps badly enough tae chase down your husband aen the other side of the warld."

I thought of that letter from Scotland. Could Fergus have broken the news of the finman's return? Had that sent Duncan into a depression or an orgy of fear, especially when he came to believe that I couldn't do anything to help him after all? My ankle twinged and I realized that I was beginning to feel more myself again, both physically and mentally. I wasn't sure it was an improvement. I don't like being out of control, but for a time it had been nice to feel comfortably numb in both body and mind.

"Not that I would dream of complaining," I said to Lachlan's back as he poked at the fire. "But what exactly did you do to me in that cave? I've felt drugged and alienated from mind ever since."

He paused to search for a word, I am sure, rather than to find a careful explanation for me. When he chose to answer my questions, he usually answered straightly. Finally he turned. He spoke in formal English, facing me. His switch in diction was odd, almost as though he were offering a quotation, and underlined that he was being especially serious.

"I anesthetized you. My saliva has certain properties, among them, the ability to block pain."

Lachlan had a habit of saying things that no other person could or would. On another evening, this reply would have upset me. That night I was still too drugged, or too exhausted, to protest.

"Yes, indeed you did—and thank you. I couldn't have walked so quickly without aid. I'm just grateful that the paranoia and mental deterioration that went alongside were short-lived. I can't say I enjoy being estranged from my . . . will, or seeing all those bizarre and frightening things."

"Paranoia?" he asked interestedly, putting up the poker. "Did ye sense something in the cave?"

"Maybe that isn't the best descriptor of my state. If I were more . . ." It was my turn to search for a word. "If I were of a fey turn, I would call what I felt out there the second sight."

"Would ye now? And how so? Ye saw a vision?"

"No, but . . . Findloss is going to be buried again. Soon. Isn't it? That's why that corpse candle was so large. Something is going to happen."

Lachlan's eyes widened. "Now, that is a verra interesting question, lass. And that ye saw the candle is most odd." But more than that about the subject he would not say. I was beginning to know him.

"The bite and salt I gave ye opens the doors of perception," he pointed out.

"Opens them? For a moment I thought they'd come unhinged and I'd never be able to shut them again. Is there any way I can control what I see?"

He shook his head. "Nay. Ye see wha and wham ye see. That is the way of it."

"Wonderful." I sighed. "Is Gaelic your native language? You seem to use it when you are surprised." Or annoyed.

He blinked. "Nay. 'Twas the first human language I learned and the one I've used the longest. It reminds me of happier but dead days when my wife still lived. She was human just as you are, a spaewife—a healer."

I made an involuntary sound. "You were married?"

"It was long ago. There are twa worlds and I live in both as need be, but belong to neither anymore. I think my time is passing. Especially here. I shall not long be able to come and go among yer kind. The more industry ye have, the more dangerous ye become. The more ye poison the warld for my kind." He smiled a bit, but not with humor. "Yer inkling hard, lass. What troubles ye? Surely nowt my marriage."

I was troubled but would rather die than admit it. My eyes grew tired of looking at Lachlan, who was handsome but so very strange, now that my mind was clearing out its mental cobwebs and able to perceive his uncanny and inhuman stillness. Instead I looked at the dining room table squatting to the left of him and felt a stab of sharp disfavor. The entire room was being subordinated to the unattractive relic I loathed. It was suddenly important that I move it.

"Lachlan, are you very, *very* strong?" I asked.

"Aye." He didn't hesitate to answer, but I sensed no bragging in his reply. I knew he was watching me carefully but couldn't think why he would be so intent. "Why dae ye ask this?"

"Might we move this table? Over there against the wall?" I would have shoved it out the door and over a cliff, but realized it wouldn't fit through the opening. Which meant that the cottage had been constructed around it, hundreds of years ago. This thought, though only at the very back of my mind and not fully examined, made me shiver. Who builds a house around a piece of furniture? Only someone who is convinced the furniture is very important.

"Perhaps. Ye wish tae examine the floor beneath?"

The thought hadn't occurred to me, but once voiced I found that I did indeed wish to examine the floor. Though curiosity was mixed with a large helping of trepidation. If this was indeed some sort of altar, might there be something buried below? It suddenly seemed certain that there was, but I was not completely certain I wished to see whatever it hid.

"Unless you think this unwise," I replied. "It has been here a long time. Perhaps we should leave it." And let sleeping dogs—or demons—lie.

"Nay, I am now most curious tae see what may be hidden aen the floor."

"Wait!" I begged, and Lachlan raised a brow. "Your bite and its properties. Would one of them be . . . presentiment?"

"Aye, in some it can bring future- as well as past-seeing."

"And that is why you are still here? Because I'm see-ing?" I was getting distracted, but I wanted an answer to this.

He nodded. "I wouldnae leave ye until ye are returned tae your own senses. Others could possibly take ad-vantage of ye, perhaps influence or terrorize ye wi' vi-sions. Also, I wish to hear about your other . . . paranoid notions. They may be verra useful."

"Let's move the damn table," I said, feeling an-noyed and knowing it wasn't fair. Lachlan had saved my life by biting me and numbing my pain; that there were consequences to how he did it was not really his fault. And I could hardly blame him for wanting to know what I was seeing, if there were any hope of finding the finman. I didn't like that he was here solely for this reason, though, being female enough to wish pursuit for my own lovely self and not because I was merely useful.

The table moved unwillingly at first, but move it eventually did. I made no effort to assist Lachlan, instead keeping my distance and enjoying the play of muscles as they bunched in his back. I had thought to offer one of Fergus's shirts for his use, but he seemed undisturbed by his seminudity. Everyone else I had met in Scotland was reserved in thought and manner, prudish even. Lachlan, while remaining mysterious and stubbornly silent on some subjects, was quite uninhibited, at least in matters of dress—or undress, as the case more often was. It was a breath of fresh air in an otherwise stultifying situation, and a long-buried part of me welcomed it.

As I had half expected, we found a trap door beneath one of the massive legs, a plug about eight inches by eight. I would have broken a nail prying the panel up, but Lachlan's hand seemed to grow claws that curved into the floor's joint, and he had the hidden space open in a trice.

"Well, now." I leaned in closer and saw that in his hand was a small crystal casket about the size of a petite jewelry box. Inside was something the shade of liver, but which I knew was a heart. It was surrounded by something that looked like thin milk.

"Is it human?" I whispered.

"Nay."

I was relieved, but then seeing Lachlan's stillness I realized that I was being insensitive. After what I had read about in that horrible book, I knew it might be something far worse.

"Is it selkie?" I asked, even more softly. I couldn't bring myself to ask if it belonged to a child.

"Nay." His eyes met mine and I couldn't for the world guess what he was thinking. "I do believe it belongs tae the finman."

I swallowed the sudden lump that appeared in my throat.

"It's the finman's heart?" I asked. He nodded once and waited until I said, "I guess we know what he's looking for." I swallowed again. "And I don't suppose he'll ever leave the village without it."

"Nay, he willnae. And I should verra much like to know how it came tae be hidden in this floor. It would have taken a verra strong man tae have moved this table. Fergus Culbin's father was a strong man, but old, so I doubt he could have moved this table aen his own. And certainly Fergus couldnae, his left arm being withered." This was news to me, and I felt myself frown. Lachlan's head tilted as he studied me. "Could your husband hae moved it? Perhaps if he had rubbed wax on the floor? Or if he had aid frae Fergus?"

Duncan had been strong, especially when drunk, as I had good cause to know, but I had no knowledge of whether or not he had ever been to this cottage. It was possible, though, and my gut said it was likely. I started to nod and then gasped and jumped backward and fell into a chair. The heart had twitched.

"It moved!"

Lachlan smiled grimly and put the casket on the

table. I watched carefully and saw the organ twitch again.

"Aye. The finman wouldnae have much use for a deid heart." He looked at me, considering. "You'd be best pleased if I took this with me," he suggested.

"Absolutely. Right now." I recalled my manners. "Please."

"And yet I am uncertain that it is wise. The heart has remained well hidden thus far. Perhaps it would be best to leave it in place while I consult with . . . others. I've nae clear notion as yet how tae put this thing tae rest."

"Lachlan, no! I don't want it here. It's an abomination. I don't care who stole it—I want it gone."

But the casket was returned to its crypt and the table shoved back, though I flung myself on top in an effort to stop him.

"Sometimes you make it very hard to like you," I snapped, sliding to the floor and pulling my skirt back into place.

Instead of laughing at me, as I expected him to do, Lachlan looked rather sad. "Aye. It is one of the hazards of being wha I am."

"Just tell me this. What does the finman look like? Could he truly be mistaken for a human? Could I run into him and not know it? Could he knock on my door and trick me into letting him in?"

"Frae a distance mayhap he could fool ye. Close by, ye waud ken the difference. The finman can mask his character to a degree, but yer kind will always ken his true nature."

My kind. The MacCodrums, hunters and killers

every one. Familial rather than individual destiny. It was still strange for me to think of myself in any way that did not relate to my own behavior and failings. I was a MacCodrum just as I was a redhead, and had no say in either thing and did not see why it should dictate the parameters of my life. The thought that it could made me peevish.

Lachlan continued: "He smells a bit of rotting things and his flesh is always cauld and white. And look tae his eyes—briefly. They are black and cannae blink." He paused. "I shall make thee a charm and bring it aen the morrow. Hang it aen the door when ye leave the cottage and it will keep him oot. And bar the door when ye are within. He can magic locks, but not a bar made of yew like this one."

"I have this too." I reached for my blouse and pulled out the necklace Duncan had given me; I had put it on when I changed clothes. Lachlan's eyes widened. "It was from my husband." Then, because my mind seemed intent on thinking of all the worst things: "Won't putting up a charm on the door tell the finman that I know he is here?"

"Aye, but 'tis the lesser of evils. Any road, I believe he already kens aboot ye. Why else send the tide after ye today? He wants ye for some purpose—one ye'd best avoid."

The finman had sent the tide after me? He could do that? I had thought myself merely unlucky. And had it been his voice I heard calling to me? I had thought it came from the faerie mound, but was I mistaken?

"You must work harder on saying comforting things," I said absently. "People will like you better for it."

"I daena want ye comforted. I want ye alive," he said harshly, and strode toward the door. "Bar this ahind me. 'Tis the *theacht mean oidche*. The auld protective spell aen the door isnae powerful enough tae stand if the finman comes."

I knew these words and shivered. My grandmother had spoken uneasily of the coming of midnight, but only on Auld Year's Night and once at Beltane.

Angrily I followed Lachlan so that I could put up the bar, but after the door shut behind him I found myself strangely frightened and unwilling to do what I needed to do if it meant going closer to the outside. Under the lingering influence of Lachlan's bite I could see Fergus's spell. Spiked shadows, perhaps real and perhaps only in my mind, cast by some unseen thing brought on by the seeing, enframed the doorway. I was reluctant to disturb them as they stretched and swayed in their effort to guard the door. But by then storm and true night had encompassed the house and I surely didn't want anyone or anything lingering out there to enter the cottage. I would have to reach through these shadows despite my distaste.

"Bar the door!" Lachlan snarled again from outside. He hit the panel once. The blow shook the door and scattered the shadows.

"Go away!" I snarled back, lifting the bar into place as quickly as I was able. It was heavy and ugly, but I took comfort in that. Perhaps it would be more efficacious.

But pluck the old isle from its roots deep planted
Where tides cry coronach *round the Hebrides. . . .*
—"Cumba Mac-ille-Chalium Rarsaidh"
("The Lament of Ian Garbh")

Chapter Nine

Lachlan was gone—without the damned heart but
with more angry words from me, though he couldn't
hear them, being long vanished—and I finally had
my bath and then went to bed to sulk and read. The
wind and rain held a carnival outside, complete with
bright lights and what I swear was the distant sound
of a calliope that rang out from the *Bearlach nam
Cu*—the pass of the hound. Though sensible people
would say it was just the screaming of frightened seabirds or seals, I did not believe this, and it was with
some difficulty that I finally put out the lamp and
drifted to sleep.

That night I dreamed, which was not uncommon,
but it was a sleeping vision like no other. No dream or
nightmare has ever felt as real to me, and I came
awake with the alarmed conviction that I had experienced some kind of unnatural prescience brought on

by Lachlan's bite. It was through him that I *saw* into another frightening world. In my dream I stood before the faerie mound, facing the corpse candle that still burned there. The sun was setting and my shadow was very long, stretching almost to the dunes. Though I was enthralled by the corpse candle burning in the air, a slight movement at the horizon lured my eyes downward and I saw a little being, a poppet with the face of a catfish, made of aged leather and twigs and stained the color of peat bogs. He was rolling up my shadow, coiling it carefully onto a sort of spindle. As I watched, he finished with my shoulders and then started on my torso. I felt a sudden chill in my heart as his clawed hand touched my shadow's breastbone.

Another movement caught my eye. I looked down at my feet and there was a second of these creatures, armed with a pair of shears, which it was using to cut away my shadow at my bare toes so the first poppet could carry it away. This one I could see quite clearly. It had whiskers growing from its cheeks, chin and forehead. It was small, no more than two feet tall, and I might have thought it cute if not for it being busy chopping away at my shadow.

I screamed once in protest and kicked out with the foot farther from the shears, but my limb barely moved and my shadow not at all. The sensation was similar to the one that had overcome me in the cave, though pronounced to an extreme degree. The creature hissed back but did not shy away until Herman landed on it with claws outstretched. Then it gave an angry shriek and fell back, dropping its shears. The blood that ran from its wound was white, not red, and this stuck to the ground in mucuslike clots that steamed unattractively. This was the same milky substance that surrounded the finman's still beating heart.

Herman turned on me then, howling and swiping at my leg, perhaps attempting to break the spell that held me in place, though maybe only maddened with fear and lashing out at whoever was nearby. At the last moment, he leapt for my eyes. This worked. I came awake in bed with the cat on my chest, crying loudly into my face.

"Good kitty," I croaked, pushing him aside, and then I reached under the covers for my stinging leg. The warm wetness told me I was bleeding. Then my hand encountered something that chilled me all the way to my soul.

I pulled out the cold metal thing and laid it on the covers. My hands shook as I fumbled for the lamp I kept at the side of the bed. It took a moment for me to light it and then to turn the flame up high, and when I turned back to the bed—with the utmost reluctance, I might add—the shears were gone. But they had been there, of that I was certain, because they had left a bloody print outlined clearly on the white coverlet.

I thought then of the story in the village about how Fergus Culbin often went about without his shadow. Were these nightmare creatures somehow tied to him, perhaps some kind of familiars?

"Lachlan," I whispered, reaching out in a kind of prayer. "If you can hear me, please come back."

Morning found me on my bike heading to the village, though it was cold and the damp mist that sometimes turns into the light rain the locals call *smirr* seemed disinclined to surrender its hold on the shore. My body hurt, especially my leg, where I was scratched in four places, but I forced myself to keep moving. I was frayed at the edges of my nerves, unraveled by nightmares and worry, but as the saying goes: Sometimes the only way out is through. Hiding at home would not help me.

My attention was divided the whole way between the slick, uneven ground and the dim light of a paraffin bicycle lamp glowing eerily in the waves of fog that rolled by irregularly. I had trouble imagining a wicked wizard riding a bicycle with a generous-sized basket about town, but the bike had been in Fergus's storeroom, so I assume that he used it, withered arm and all.

It had not escaped my notice that I was without a charm to ward my door when I left and it was possible for the finman to enter in my absence, should he be able to force the lock, but so far he had preferred skulking about at night and I stubbornly clung to the belief that he had already searched my cottage and found nothing. He must have done so—if not on the night he killed Fergus, then sometime in the weeks that followed, while the cottage was tenantless. There was no reason for him to come back.

I would, of course, be very careful on my return, regardless of this reasonable rationalization.

Though I admit it only reluctantly, I must confess that I thought some of Lachlan as well on my ride, what he was and that he had been married. To a human woman. And unlike my own union, his had apparently been loving and happy. That made the end tragic. And he had not married again, which caused me to be curious in the way of my sex: Was he so emotionally scarred by his loss that he could not love again? Or was it that he thought no woman could ever be as perfect as his first wife had been?

At least, he hadn't said anything about marrying again. Maybe he had. Many times. Maybe he was married even now.

That thought was annoying, so I pushed it away in favor of other things.

If all roads lead to Rome—at least, the properly paved ones—then this would explain the lack of them in Findloss. The Gaels, especially those returned from the Great War, seem to have no desire to travel again outside their own lands. They have a lot of poetry and mysticism in their romantic souls, so what would be the appeal of a world built on logic and in the accruement of our greatest material desires? So many of us, at least for a time when we are young and less wise, spend our souls and limited will on the pursuit of shiny material things, but that seems not to be the way of the Gaels. These people always had very little and knew how to make do with the bits and pieces their villages provided. Pleasures were rare and entertainment limited, but it seemed to make their happy moments all the more appreciated. Here I did not feel my poverty as I had at home.

Sometimes I miss the superficial world of my childhood and its conveniences, but never entirely. Lachlan was not alone in feeling alienated; mechanization and modernization frightened me. It seems in many ways that machines will control us and not the other way around. Certainly clocks and schedules run most modern lives. These call us to work and to worship, to rise in the morning and retire to bed. They dominated the Great War. In Findloss it was different. This is not to suggest that Scotland has been laggardly in keeping up with the world, but the last war of their making happened nearly a century ago and was an internal affair. The people of the village—all but one of them, if Lachlan were correct—seemed content to fish and drink and once in a while make some music or tell old tales. They did not look outside themselves or their village for amusement or happiness. Nor did I. I had a cat and my books, though I brought very few to the cottage: the family Bible, a battered copy of *The Tenant of Wildfell Hall*, and a Murray's Diary, which was a sort of railroad map and timetable for the trains in Scotland. It included information on ferry services to the ports and islands, which was how I ended up with a tuppence copy. (This was also where I had learned that dogs may travel on the railroad. The fare is tuppence, unless they are working dogs. Herding canines are considered the same as a tool bag or a doctor's kit, and are allowed to ride free so long as they remain tucked beneath the master's seat. No mention was made of cats or livestock.)

I wasn't at all sure where I would go when I was forced to leave Findloss, and that I would soon have to leave I now believed with all my heart and soul. Lachlan's bite-caused sight had left me, but the conviction that the village was in danger had not. And Findloss had an unenviable record for deadly storms, even before the final one that had buried it completely.

Eventually I reached the post office, and was relieved to see a light inside. But I had barely entered the store when Mistress MacLaren leaned over the counter and hissed: "Lights were seen in the kirk last night. They say it was the Devil abroad again. And did ye hear the storm? It's an ill wind, ye see, wha blaws naebody guid."

"How can anyone be sure it is the Devil?" I objected, dispensing with the usual wishes for a good morning. "Might it not have been someone walking about who . . . decided to go in and pray?"

"Would *ye* be sae daft?" she demanded with a touch of indignation.

"I don't wander at night," I hedged.

Mistress MacLaren snorted. "Neither does anyone else in the village."

She had a point, which would make things convenient for the finman. Or for Lachlan. It could have been Lachlan, after all. Hadn't I suggested he look for records in the church? He hadn't said anything about being there last night, and what with all the other distractions—like nearly drowning and finding an undead heart in my floor—I had forgotten to ask what he had discovered and what future plans he had made.

"And, someone has been visiting cottages, searching them for something. The villagers are salting their doorways and ye'd best be doing the same."

It was on the tip of my tongue to tell the woman that salt wouldn't keep the village's visitor out, but I kept my peace. So far, no one had been harmed. As long as the finman was just searching, I felt no need to admit to any involvement or knowledge whatsoever. This was perhaps cowardly, but I would not have put it past the frightened villagers to kill the messenger. In this case that meant me, as well as Lachlan.

"Was anyone seen leaving the kirk?" I asked.

"Nay, and we watched 'til dawn," she admitted, making me glad that my cottage was beyond eyeshot of her own. I wasn't afraid of gossip in the normal way of things, but would just as soon not have people know that I had a male visitor coming and going at all hours of the night.

"Does the kirk have a basement—a crypt perhaps?" I asked.

"Aye," she said slowly, horror beginning to fill her eyes as she considered. "There was a crypt, and also they say it was part of a sea cave used by vile creatures until they bricked it off."

I chose to misunderstand. "That's probably it then! Smugglers are using the kirk again. They likely knocked down the wall and are coming and going from the caves on the shore."

"Smugglers?" This arrested her panic and I could see her turning the new idea over in her head as she examined it on all sides. The notion lacked some of the drama of the Devil or sea monsters making an appearance, but it was a lot less frightening.

Unfortunately, I didn't believe my own suggestion. Not unless the finman was smuggling something. Evil, if not the Devil himself, was definitely abroad at night and I feared that I knew what it was looking for.

But then so was Lachlan about in the night, and also in sea caves as he hunted his prey. I'd thought he intended to go immediately to "consult with others" about what we had found, but perhaps he had made a stop at the kirk on the way. Or perhaps he hadn't. Until I knew which it was messing about in the church, I would have to be crazy to visit the kirk, though the urge to rush out and confront my fear was strong. My mind had somehow not accepted the idea that this time the monsters were real and not just phantoms of the imagination. At least in the daylight, I wanted to strike at them before they crept up behind me in dreams.

"I've read about the smugglers in Cornwall," I said, fingering a bolt of cloth. It was poplin, but in a nice shade of blue. I had a few frivolous frocks, but they were old. I had not dressed in gay inconsequence since my marriage. "They actually had everyone convinced that there was some demon driving a coach with a team of headless horses. It was quite clever of them. They went on their way unmolested for many years . . ."

"Ye're not going tae the kirk, are ye?" Mistress Mac-Laren demanded, sensing my curiosity.

"Not today," I agreed, letting go of the fabric. "It's too foggy. And I would as soon give the smugglers time to shift their wares before I explore. I've no desire to meet one face-to-face."

"Aye?" She sounded incredulous.

"I don't care about smuggling, per se. Most of the taxes on imports are iniquitous, and who can blame a man if he has to do a little extra to help his family?" I shrugged and finally saw a faint smile of approval touch the postmistress's thin lips. Smuggling was an enterprise that fishermen had engaged in for centuries. Most people saw it as a way for poor families to supplement their income and to put one over on the English. There was also the added allure of limited danger hereabouts: The long arm of the Sassenach law rarely extended to Findloss; its nearest limb of any type was an elderly man with a wooden leg in Glen Ruadh.

I bought some honey and dried plums for the scones I decided to bake; the honey from the local hives is a bit strange to me, being made from the pollen of sea grasses rather than the blossoms of fruit trees or flowers, but I have come to enjoy it on my porridge and bread. I waited while Mistress MacLaren fetched the requested items and then departed from her relentlessly grim company. I did not ask about the faded photograph of a young man in uniform that she kept on the counter, though I had seen it before and wondered. Because of the Great War, Findloss is also haunted by the ghosts of the Lost Generation, the boys who had gone off and not come home. A full third of many highland regiments had been killed and many more maimed while fighting honorably in a war that many considered dishonorable.

I knew from past conversations that Mistress MacLaren had lost a son, a brother and two nephews all at Vimy Ridge on Easter Monday in 1917. Poor woman. When fate decides to bludgeon you, all you can do is duck and run and pray the cudgel is short enough that you can escape. Sometimes you get away; sometimes you don't. Knowing how my own losses had affected me, I bit my tongue when she was especially sullen or nosy. We all grieve differently, and she offered no true incivility.

The death-cold cloak of storm and mist had parted by the time I left the shop, and when I looked seaward I could see the weekly mail steamer coming our way. When I say "weekly," I mean that according to Murray's Diary it endeavored to come every seven days. It was often delayed by bad weather, as I'd pointed out to Lachlan.

The distant whistle shrilled again as I tucked my small parcel into the bicycle's basket, and I noticed a small boat setting off from the chafed jetty where the larger fishing boats were usually moored. Securing a mooring between the two vessels would be tricky because the sea remained rough, but I had no doubt that the harassed men would manage in spite of the turbulence. Angry seas were nothing new to these fishermen, and they did this every week—or ten or twelve days, or whenever tide and fog permitted.

The whistle sounded again, shriller than birds, which called to mind the sound of the calliope I thought I had heard the night before. Had it perhaps been a ship at sea and not the storm winds singing through the pass that had frightened me? The throbbing in my leg said no. Something unnatural had been abroad last night. Something evil, and it had come close.

I shrugged deeper into my cape and realized with surprise how much I had come to appreciate the usual quiet of Findloss and how much I resented losing it, now that it was threatened. I was beginning to feel knit into the fabric of this country, albeit on the very edges. Perhaps it was the blood of my ancestors at last awakening in my veins. Maybe it was just finally being free to make my way in the world.

Wind blew back my hair with a salty breath that was unique to this village. I marveled again that though raised in a city, most days I did not miss the bustle of the exciting annoyance of my earlier and more materialistic life in the United States. Industrial progress no longer seemed as much like progress to me. I did not like the noise and agitation that came with the convenience of my old life enough to wish its return. Like Lachlan claimed of himself, I lived in two worlds and probably couldn't stay in either. What would become of us? Where do people go when home isn't home anymore?

I looked seaward, but the ocean offered no answer. The tiny bit of aureate light that slid between clouds brought no real warmth, and the sun's routine creepings toward the western horizon—growing shorter every day—seemed suddenly sinister. Did Sol, like the tide, conspire with the finman? Evil surely went about in the day, but it was most active in the dark. There seemed an increasing number of dark hours where wickedness could hold sway.

The storm shall not wake thee,
nor shark overtake thee,
Asleep in the arms of the slow-swinging sea.
—Rudyard Kipling, "Seal Lullaby"

Chapter Ten

I prepared a pot of tea and baked some scones, and enjoyed them; though, since I am not British enough for tea to be a panacea, the ritual calmed me only slightly, even with a dram of whisky added to the pot. Some of the local whisky is appalling, unsafe unless you are a ruminant with more than one stomach to spare for digesting toxic things. I paid extra for something drinkable, but used it sparingly. I simply couldn't afford to be an alcoholic.

A part of me was watching the sun creep westward, waiting impatiently for Lachlan and his promised charm of protection, though this wasn't reasonable; he had never come to visit the cottage except in full darkness.

The sleet that attacked at sunset was sudden and fierce, and I lost heart that Lachlan would come, but appear he did, just before the midnight hour. On his shoulder was a fresh wound that I knew could only be caused by the bite of a shark. Or maybe a finman.

I did not immediately ask questions, just went to fetch linens and some hot water for cleaning the wound. Once again he'd been out in the cold without a shirt or overcoat, but this state of semiundress seemed almost normal now. Certainly it was no hardship for me to look upon him.

"Take off that plaid before you freeze," I said, handing him a large sheet of toweling and turning my back politely until I heard the sodden wool hit the hearth.

"I am modestly draped," Lachlan said, and I thought I heard some amusement in his voice. This surprised me, given the depth of the bite and how much pain he had to be feeling.

"I understand from my most recent reading that drinking from a selkie's footprint can cause a person to shape-shift." I said it lightly as I set about washing the jagged tear that was healing even as I dabbed at it. That was fortunate, because I am fainthearted and don't do well with the sight of any blood other than my own. Setting stitches would have been out of the question.

Lachlan didn't laugh at the superstition as I had hoped, and his next words indirectly confirmed my belief that he was a seal man. "Nay. But it might just be possible that a bit of . . . anesthetic might linger there. And if the drinker were someone who had previously been exposed, they might be affected in the mind." His face was very close to mine and I could feel his breath on my cheek. As ever, his body was warm. He also smelled heavily of clove, and I realized that it was his blood I was scenting. A part of me wanted to taste that, and the thought made me a bit dizzy. I had to put out a hand to steady myself but opted for a lower arm instead of the chest.

"I shall be careful what footprint I slurp from," I joked, then changed the subject. "Mistress MacLaren tells me that the Devil was seen in the kirk last night. I don't suppose that it was you checking on church records as we discussed."

I felt the weight of his eyes as they settled on my own. "Nay."

"Then I suppose we had best have a look at it to-morrow and speak to a few people. Perhaps someone else in the village saw something useful."

I guessed that this suggestion probably wouldn't be met with enthusiasm, and I was right.

"I will gae out and ask questions when I deem it prudent. Ye'll stay here and not gossip wi' the villagers wham may be dangerous tae ye. Wi' this hanging aen the door," he added, leaning over and pulling something from under his sodden plaid. He laid the small wreath of sea wrack and a metal spike on the table.

I was tempted to ask what else he had had under his kilt but refrained. I also decided against arguing with him about the kirk. I was beginning to believe that Lachlan was from the kick-over-the-wasp-nest-and-see-what-crawls-out school of investigation. No fan of Conan Doyle's detective was he; subtle examination and clever interrogation were clearly not his forte. But why should they be? After all, he was a hunter on the trail of deadly prey and intended to kill, not question it. Yet I had a feeling that something subtler might work better, at least as far as questioning the superstitious villagers, and I was very curious about the church now and wanted to see it before Lachlan pulled it down stone by stone, or whatever else he had in mind.

Lachlan wouldn't like hearing this intention, though, so I decided that it would be better to seek forgiveness than permission. "Did the finman attack you tonight?" I asked, keeping my gaze on his wound, for fear he might read the intentional disregard of his advice in my gaze.

"His minions, aye. There were twa sharks waiting near the shore. They were big nasty brutes. I had a bit of a battle killing them." I looked at the size of the bite. Its diameter was twice the length my hand. Then I tried to image how large the shark that had bitten him was. My mind faltered when it came to imagining how Lachlan might have killed two sharks of this size. What sort of seal man was he?

"And they weren't just . . . passing sharks?" I asked.

"Nae. Hae ye ne'er noticed the talk among the villagers? There are nae sharks in these waters. My people have made these seas safe for the sea pups and their mithers that come tae the beach fer birthing."

I had heard something like this before. "Someone must be getting desperate then."

"Aye. I've inkled and spoken wi' others frae nearby clans, and 'tis believed by the merrows that the finman may have tae find his heart by the winter solstice or perish."

"What will happen on your way . . . back? Will there be other sharks waiting to attack you?"

" 'Tis the maxim of the wise man tae never return by the same road he came—providing there is anither road free tae him. This I shall remember, since I hate tae slay the beasts of the sea wham are but innocents enslaved." He changed the subject. "Have ye read anything else of interest in Fergus's cursed books?"

"I have been reading some about pookas."

Lachlan snorted. "Be glad I am nowt a pooka."

"Why?" I asked, genuinely curious and glad that Lachlan seemed in a mood to talk. This was not his normal state, and I felt that I'd best take advantage of any loquaciousness.

"Because in general they're rather nasty and hae an indefatigable sense of humor. Their relentless cheer and pranks are exhausting and can lead them intae trouble. It nearly also leads tae humans being deid."

"I'll remember that," I said. "I was also reading about brownies and wondering how I could go about getting one, since there is no such thing as a house-keeper in this village and I would love someone to spin some yarn for me. I'm actually a pretty capable knitter." No one would admit it to an outsider, but I had noticed that the few women who still spun their own yarn took down their spinning wheels at night so that no supernatural being might use them. Until I met Lachlan I had told myself this was just more local nonsense. Now I was less sure.

"That's just silly superstition," Lachlan said with a sniff.

"Is it now?" And then I laughed. The sound was weak and tentative, but quite real. "How am I to know what is real and what is not? You are all fable to me."

"Sweet reason, woman. Magical housekeepers?"

All I could do was shake my head and reach for some strips of linen to tie over the makeshift bandage, which was hardly necessary now. "I rarely see you during the day. Is it because the sun hurts you?" I asked, since he remained in what seemed for him a fairly garrulous mood.

"Nay. There are twilight people and Night Side people, but very few fey gae about aen the day anymore. There's too much ill will and cold iron aboot. I had an uncle wha used tae visit a lady friend in daylight, though he was warned tae stay away, but he tempted fate once tae often. I think he was more than a bit mad frae the contamination in this warld and none tae gifted with sense tae begin with. It happens sometimes when we are tae lang alone. He was hunted down and his skin taken."

"Every family has its black sheep—or seal," I added with a small grim smile, making note that in spite of the harsh tale my mood had lifted. In fact, I felt a bit intoxicated and suspected it was the prolonged contact with Lachlan. "Ours was Uncle Milo—though he was not a blood uncle, so the title is only a courtesy. He was an elixir salesman and dishonest enough to have you counting your fingers after you shook his hand. As the saying goes, he would steal candy from a baby—or in this case, a niece—and then resell it as soon as he found another buyer. That was usually my cousin, Torquil. I think he may have been a bit mad too. Certainly he had no grasp of what was acceptable behavior in our home." He had, for instance, once tried to reach under my dress. I had poured my milk on him and threatened to tell my father. Now, as an adult, I sometimes wondered if Milo had not perhaps been doing things to Torquil. If he had, it warped my cousin into a sadistic and dishonest man.

"And where are this Milo and Torquil now?" Lachlan's voice was gentle, but I was not deceived. Somehow he had guessed that there was more to my story and was angered on my behalf, even though in that moment I felt no rage myself.

"On the road to fame and fortune, or so my aunt says. I haven't seen them in years and likely never will again." I had finished wrapping Lachlan's shoulder. The temptation to drop a kiss on his wound almost overcame me, but I managed to step back without doing anything foolish. My breath was a bit rapid, but I could always blame that on the sight of the injury if Lachlan said anything. "There! That's tidy now. And I didn't faint on you—so there."

"I thank ye. I can tell that ye are near swoonin'." He flexed his arm and rotated his shoulder.

"Well, it is expected from a gentlewoman when confronted with blood," I pointed out, wondering what my parents would have thought of Lachlan and my reluctant physical attraction to him. They would probably be shocked by my romantic transgression. Or perhaps not. They might have considered him a step up from Duncan. Certainly I did, though I also knew he was far more dangerous.

"Yer smiling. Now, why? The sight of my blood amuses thee?"

"I was just thinking how much my parents would have disapproved of my friendship with you."

"And this makes ye smile, lass?"

I shrugged. "I have always had an odd sense of humor. Perhaps I am not entirely sane either. At least, not around you. Somehow you affect me even when I am not drugged. I just wonder sometimes if it's deliberate. Do you like me off guard? Can you make me so by some other means than a bite?"

" 'Tis better than making ye struck dumb, aye?"

Struck dumb. That reminded me of my dream, and all playfulness fell away in a rush. "Lachlan, have you ever heard of a . . . a kind of pixie or familiar who would try to cut off someone's shadow?"

"Aye. Ye've seen one?" He wasn't smiling anymore, either.

"Yes. In a dream. Last night. When I woke up . . . well, come and see." I led him into the bedroom, for once unconcerned about having a strange man near my bed. I pointed at the bloody print of the shears. "It's my blood, not theirs. That thing bled white glop."

"This is all?"

"No. I think Herman saw them too. He attacked them and then scratched me to wake me up."

"Herman?"

"The cat."

There was silence for a long moment. "What cat?"

"Fergus's cat. I call him Herman."

"Megan . . ." For once he seemed disturbed. "Fergus had a cat called Og. But it likely perished when he did, killed the same night. He was a big black beastie."

"Yes. But . . ." I was blank. "Then it must be a

neighbor's cat. I mean, it's a real cat. And black cats are quite common."

"Yer certain it is a cat? Where is it noo?"

"I . . . I don't know. But Herman is real, Lachlan. He—he relieved himself on the floor one day when I locked him in by mistake. A . . . a *ghost* wouldn't do that."

"Nay, not a ghost. There is a task I maun dae tonight, but I shall be back tomorrow eve," he said abruptly. "Meantimes, worry nowt about the apparitions in yer dreams. They'll nowt return noo that the salt has worn away. Fergus's creatures cannae reach ye unless yer . . . influenced. And ye'll stay away frae the kirk, aye? And keep yer *cat* close if he'll dae it. He'll ken in which quarter the wind blows."

"Go to the kirk? At night? Do you think me stupid?" I asked evasively, forcing myself to meet his eyes. That seemed the innocent thing to do.

"Nay. But by yer aen admission ye maun be a bit mad."

I opened my mouth to argue my state of complete reason, but he laid his index finger against my lower lip and narrowed his eyes. Instead of answering I made my gaze limpid, and not knowing me well, Lachlan was fooled. I did not let myself believe that he was actually distracted by my charms, though the longer he touched me, his expression grew closer to bemusement and further from chiding.

Before he left, Lachlan took up the spike he'd brought and with one blow, drove it into the outside of the door. "Don't forget to hang the charm when ye gae out," he reminded me. "The finman has become bold, and I'll not hae you risk yerself needlessly."

"I will hang the charm," I promised with all sincerity. "Thank you for it."

Lachlan nodded and then closed the door softly behind him. It was only when he was gone that I realized he had left his sodden plaid behind along with the borrowed linen. Apparently wherever he was going, it didn't require clothing.

I did not go immediately to the kirk upon rising the next morn, though this was not because of Lachlan's admonition or any change of heart. The sun was out, so I made some porridge and fed the cat, who had mysteriously reappeared, and then hung my charm on the door. I took a stroll down to the emerging beach where I could get an unimpeded look at the village and surrounding cliffs—and the various tunnels and caves carved into the terraced cliffs by the ocean or man's hands. There were a lot of them. Too many to explore in a day or even a week, supposing one was capable and brave. I hoped Lachlan had some means of limiting the search.

The water shushed and gurgled as it withdrew from the land. Until recently the sea's murmurings had been an excellent barometer of things to come. (*Voice in the north, sailors gae forth!* A voice from the south was another matter, or so the fishermen said.) But now the tides and storms were unpredictable, the weather able to turn without warning. The waters remained rich with fish so men ventured out, but they all knew that the danger had grown.

To calm the turbulent sea, some of the fishermen

resorted to old superstitions and towed behind their boats a mealy pudding made with the fat of seabirds found dead on the beach, usually nestlings whose first flights from the cliff face had ended disastrously. Where this less-than-charming custom originated I do not know, but according to Fergus's books it is often used in the Hebrides. One had to wonder when the danger would grow so great that they would move away from Findloss.

Tawny bladder wrack had washed up on the flattened boulders around me where it blackened in the sun. The odor was not unpleasant, but every now and again a swelling bladder would burst, making a sound not unlike a pistol being discharged. The tide had mostly stilled. It was nearing slack water, tempting to wade out in, but I didn't trust it for a minute; this area was notorious for its undertow and I had not forgotten what had happened on the day I had gone to see the faerie mound. Unnatural forces were at work all around—why did no one else see it?

Bright fingers of water wriggled among the crevices before surrendering to the pull of the tide and retreating ever farther down the shore. Of course some pools remained here and there, and on another day I would have stopped to investigate the creatures that braved the sea's retreat to remain in these rocky puddles. That day, I had other things on my mind—like defying Lachlan and doing some exploring on my own.

In the distance were the remains of a few lazy beds, raised plantings called *feannegan* in the Gaelic. These had ridges of soil, fertilized with seaweed, and between the rows lay furrows for drainage so planted root crops did not rot and so the farmer need not stoop so far to plant and harvest. It gave such land a mesmerizing rippling effect as wind passed over the wild grass that had claimed the old farmsteads. The villagers still grew some oats, turnips, potatoes and some stunted carrots in their cottage gardens; this land would never be farmed again.

The southern end of the cliffs was steep and deeply pocked and had become a sort of gullery in the last decade. No one walks in its shadow for fear of bombardment and the birds have grown fearless and fat. Their sound, while pleasant from a distance, is overwhelming up close, particularly if the gulls are alarmed by a predator. It did not seem a likely place for the finman to hide. My readings seemed to point to definite behaviors and divisions in the supernatural world: Creatures of the air did not mix with those of the sea.

The north end of the cliff was another matter. Nothing lived there except perhaps bats and a few tenacious plants that didn't mind the bitter salt winds assaulting them daily. One needed to be nimble and careful to move about without mishap if one hiked there, especially when the tide was on the turn. It was difficult to judge the depth of the pools. Above the waterline and below, things were treacherous. There are many stretches of coast in the world where more ships have come to grief than the rocky shoals of Findloss, but none where the sinkings are more inexplicable. But then, this entire village and its haunted environs were impossible to explain to the rational twentieth-century mind that does not allow for things like sea monsters and faeries. I don't like to think of how many souls have drowned and disappeared in these unforgiving waters, never to be seen again until the day when the trumpet is blown and the sea renders up her dead for good and for all. Not that I much want to see them. Ugh.

I watched for a quarter of an hour as the birds rushed in and out of their stone houses, but nothing moved in any of the larger caves or tunnels; to all appearances I was alone on the finger of exposed beach that led up to the uninhabited cliff face. Which meant it was time to go to the kirk. Just to look around. Not in the crypts, of course. Not unless I was absolutely *certain* that I was alone.

Reason pleaded with me to reconsider my intention, but I did not. Fear stabbed my heart and belly, but I did not turn away. I couldn't. Later I would understand that it was a compulsion coming from outside myself, but at the time I simply believed I was asserting my rights as a free person to investigate what I chose. At last reason threw up its hands and said, "Do as you like! I take no further responsibility for your safety or sanity."

Reason's voice sounded a lot like Lachlan. Would that I had listened.

Plead my cause, O LORD, with them that strive with me: fight against them that fight against me . . . Draw out also the spear, and stop the way against them that persecute me: say unto my soul, I am thy salvation. Let them be confounded and put to shame that seek after my soul: let them be turned back and brought to confusion that devise my hurt . . . Let their way be dark and slippery: and let the angel of the LORD persecute them. For without cause have they hid for me their net in a pit, which without cause they have digged for my soul. Let destruction come upon him at unawares; and let his net that he hath hid catch himself: into that very destruction let him fall.'
—Psalms 35:1-10

Chapter Eleven

I met one person on the way to the kirk. Niall Magee was a "collateral"—a bastard, for those who prefer plain speaking—of an English lord who had come hunting in the North some twenty years ago and found a maiden he liked better than the local hart and grouse. Niall had, according to Mistress MacLaren,

the fair coloring and height of his father's Nordic ancestors. He was also, because of the wages of sin, a
seven-month child and a bit simple.

I liked him because he was always cheerful, if pain-
fully shy except with Herman. If I had had the cat
with me, he might have spoken to us, but since I was
alone I got no more for my greeting than a quick duck
of a capped head and a mumbled salutation as Niall
fled down the path toward the cottage he shared with
his mother and grandparents. So much for my plan of
questioning any passing villagers.

I paused at the churchyard fence that ringed the
cemetery, hand resting on the iron gate for a moment
before entering. Prior to that day I had not paid particular attention to the graves, but that morning I
stopped to read the stones that had been brought
there as remembrances through the ages. The century
was young yet, but had already been devastating to
both Europe and America. It turned out that Fergus
was not the only person buried in the churchyard;
Mistress MacLarens's soldier sons were there too.
There were also graves for unknowns, strange fishermen whose bodies had washed ashore and never been
claimed. It bothered me that anyone rested in this
unhallowed ground, but I couldn't really blame the
villagers for using the churchyard for its intended purpose. After all, what was one to do with unclaimed
and unidentifiable bodies?

I could see my blackened chimney stack from the
churchyard and felt heartened by the small curl of
smoke coming from it. Herman and a fire would be

waiting for me when I returned home. I missed the smell of wood fires, the narcotic of my childhood. The scent of hickory can still conjure up feelings of safety and a desire for sleep. But any fire would do fine in a pinch and I was glad I had left one burning.

The cottage, before the Culbins, did not have an especially evil reputation—at least not one remembered by the villagers or the people I had spoken with in Keil or Glen Ruadh. But I could not entirely forget that there was that disturbing mosaic on the hearth, the heart-sized crypt in the floor under a table that looked a great deal like an altar, the secret room filled with horrible books—and perhaps most telling of all, a witch's roost on the chimney. This flat stone projecting outward about one quarter of the way up the stack had been built deliberately so that witches would have a place to rest on their travels to and from coven meetings. It was hoped by the builders that the witches would be happy to rest there and not enter the cottage itself.

As I have already said, Findloss, and my cottage in particular, were not normal places. It was odd to think of this village as being my refuge from an even greater evil.

The kirk's massive wooden doors were ajar. This gave me a moment's pause, during which I listened most carefully for sounds of occupation. There were none, but I could not shake off the sudden dislike I had of entering the place. Unlike my cottage or the post office or any other place in the village I had visited, this building felt not just abandoned but tainted by evil, an arrogant erection by arrogant men and now tenanted by arrogant spirits. Reverend MacNeil's exorcism had done nothing to improve the atmosphere.

There were some obvious reasons for my abhorrence of the place. Architecturally it offended. Being from the United States, which is a new land, we don't have many of the reminders of our barbaric ancestors that Europeans do. For instance, my church at home had not possessed the type of rusty chains and shackles hanging from the wall of the kirk: *Jougs*, they were called, which I knew from my reading were used for a special form of medieval pillory that had made religious disagreement so much fun in the old country. Nor did our town square have an iron pole where witches were chained for burning. Instead we had rose gardens and a gazebo where bands played concerts on Sunday afternoons when the weather permitted. All religions mixed harmoniously at these events. Though, yes, once there had been a lynching in a shade tree at the edge of the park, I recalled unhappily.

The door swung halfway closed behind me without a sound, but with what I swear was an air of anticipation. As I walked slowly down the center aisle, there was still light enough to see by but shadows clung tenaciously between the patches of light let in by the sandblasted windows; and I felt pursued by the echoes of my own footsteps.

The kirk had a dusty pipe organ tucked away behind a wooden panel, which did not at first seem odd to me, but became stranger the longer I thought on it. Many churches have organs, but not the ones I'd seen in Scotland, particularly those of the United Free Church, which this had supposedly been. The kirks I had seen were plain and unadorned by "popish" statues and stained glass. Or organs. Most Ecclesiastical edifices had been purged of idols back in the sixteenth century, when they were purging Jews and witches and Catholics and other "undesirables." That meant they had gotten rid of gilded crosses and marble saints and especially pagan gargoyles. Stained-glass windows and ironwork were supposed to remain untouched, but those old-time religious mobs were apt to get excessive once they had a bonfire burning, and many things had disappeared.

A stray beam of light found its way through the maze of clouds and was resting on the organ. A part of me wanted to walk up to that keyboard and play "Drink to Me Only with Thine Eyes," the only song I could at the moment remember, but I knew the bellows would likely be broken and leaking. Also, a part of me was afraid of what secret message might be whispered from those pipes' rusty throats as the sound crept through the building's deeper shadows—and who their breathless whispers might attract.

I missed Lachlan keenly. Having him at my side would have made me more courageous. But had he been around, I would be stuck in my cottage, assigned to the task of keeping the hearth fires burning while he explored in my stead. At that moment, this did not seem an entirely bad thing, but still I went on.

There were a few gargoyles hiding here and there in the rafters—hermaphroditic creatures with fins from what I could see, and I again had to wonder why such carvings had not been destroyed during the Reformation. Had the villagers been too frightened of their sea monster to follow governmental and church decrees?

I searched halfheartedly. There was both relief and disappointment in the fact that there was nothing obviously incriminating in the church: no strange muddy footprints, no freshly drowned corpses hidden in the pews, no barrels of smuggled whisky or mono-grammed and bloodied handkerchiefs left by the vil-lain who had called the finman back to the village. If such a person existed. I had begun to doubt this the-ory. Couldn't the finman have returned on his own to seek his lost heart? Surely he did not need an invita-tion. And, for that matter, who had taken his heart? And how? Was it the selkies? This seemed unlikely. Lachlan had been as surprised as I when we found the crypt in my floor, and selkies would most likely have simply killed the finman, had they ever seen him in their power. The best candidate for this theft was Fer-gus Culbin or perhaps his father, but if that were the case, why had the finman waited so long to retrieve his heart? Surely he knew the person who had stolen it.

Thinking about this gave me a headache. There was too much that I didn't know. Speculating was fruit-less, and it was also making me more nervous with every passing minute. Tired, I turned back toward the door, but then I heard a noise: a sigh. Unable to ig-nore the sound, I turned back. Normally I would have called out, but prudence kept me silent.

I had no trouble finding the stair down to the crypt Mistress MacLaren had mentioned. There was no door, only a decorative iron rail at the top of a circular iron stair that descended into darkness. This I ventured onto with extreme caution, since the iron was badly corroded and I did not entirely trust it to hold my weight.

The daylight followed me for two turnings of the stair but then no more. I retreated on the shuddering staircase, unwilling to take any more risks. Had I not spotted the oil lamp sitting behind the pulpit—whose Bible, I couldn't help but notice, was opened to the thirty-fifth psalm—I would have left, but the lamp was sitting there, a clear challenge against cowardice. Again, fate could have turned me away by failing to provide a means of lighting the lamp, or by leaving the vessel empty of oil, but such was not the case; the lamp was full and there were dry matches beside it.

Sighing in frustration, I lit the lamp and returned to the twisting stair. Again I listened with all my might but heard nothing from below. Even the sound of the ocean was greatly muted by the thick stone walls, which wrapped me in a smothering embrace. I was alone.

Down, down I went, one slow step at a time, testing each tread before putting my full weight upon it. I counted as I went. There were thirty-nine steps that corkscrewed through what appeared to be a natural chimney in the rock. Everything smelled wet and slightly rotten.

The basement of the church was a surprise. The slanting floor was lined with shards of broken glass and porcelain that sparkled cruelly, and I hesitated a moment before stepping carefully into the fragments of pottery and glass. What was this vandalism and where had all the glass come from? Had the locals thought, on that stormy night when the sands came roaring ashore, to discourage the evil finman from coming among them by spreading glass on the floor, perhaps to cut his naked feet? Or was it to deter the unshod selkies who chased him? Or was this all more recent? Was this something to dissuade the Devil with his shoeless hooves, just in case exorcism didn't work? Why else destroy every pot and glass and bowl?

I shuffled carefully as I approached the crypts built into the wall. The niches were made of limestone, which had been dug out with a pick. No bodies rested in the empty crypts. Like all those who had perished in the storm, the crypt's dead had disappeared. There were twenty-six shelves and no markers, though I could see small holes where plaques had once been affixed.

Not unexpectedly, I found a tunnel leading from the crypt. It angled downward toward the sea. Men had finished the narrow passageway by smoothing the floor, but the walls and ceilings looked a great deal like the other natural tunnels I had seen, though this one was mercifully dry. There had once been some sort of stacked stone wall blocking off the tunnel, but it had collapsed outward. Not inward—not pushed in by smugglers coming up from a sea cave. Something in the crypt had pushed the wall down when it escaped seaward.

I had traveled perhaps a dozen steps into the tunnel when suddenly I could hear the sea begin to roar and gurgle. It seemed that I had again lost track of time and the tide had turned while I explored. Or was it the finman, somehow aware of my intrusion and sending the sea after me again?

The need to retrieve my courage and conduct after my panicked flight from the faerie mound kept me moving steadily if rapidly backward until I heard something scream with fury. The sound shook the very walls of the crypt. Then fear came upon me again, washing away whatever compulsion had lured me into the kirk. Being careful not to upset the lamp, I turned and fled back to the metal staircase and climbed it with much less caution than I had used in my descent. Survival before dignity. It is probably miraculous that I did not collapse the old spiral of rusted iron.

Still, enough was enough. I knew now that the kirk did indeed have tunnels that opened to the sea and could be used by the finman. Or by Lachlan. Or by anyone who did not want to visit the village in a conventional and honest manner. There was nothing else to see there, though, no parish records to investigate, not even graves where I might gather names. I wouldn't come again.

> *There are certayne sorcerers, who having annoynted their bodies with an ointment which they make by the instinct of the Devil, and putting on a certayne inchaunted girdle, does not only unto the view of others seem as animals, but to their own thinking have both the shape and nature of animals, so long as they wear the said girdle. And they do dispose themselves as very beasts, in worrying and killing, and most of humane creatures.*
> —Richard Verstegan, *Restitution of Decayed Intelligence*, 1628

Chapter Twelve

The sea was having convulsions as I left the church-yard, and I prayed it was localized to our bit of shore and that the village fishermen were beyond the water's angry reach—I suspected I had provoked it with my trespass, and any ill that befell them could be laid at my door. The village itself could be in danger. My brain chose that moment to recall that tidal waves were not unknown in Scotland and Ireland. In 1640 Aranmore had been struck by a giant wave, carrying off fifteen fishermen repairing nets on the stony shore, which was ironic, considering it was home to the graves of so many Irish saints and supposed to be blessed and looked over by God. We are not so fortunate in Find-loss.

The scene outside the kirk had turned bleak in other ways, and the grass and I alike were numb from the sudden assault of a livid wind, which I could not help but note now seemed to hurl itself angrily both night and day, clearly at the whim of some unseasonal agency. It did not escape my attention that rain came nightly now as well, and these sudden storms seemed invested with a deliberate and supernatural malevo-lence that reminded me of the rain that had fallen on the day we buried Duncan. Did everyone in the vil-lage sense this as well? Was that why no one was abroad? Normally I did not seek out my neighbors, but that day I wished for a familiar face, friendly or not. It was all too easy to imagine that I was the last living person in Findloss, which itself seemed not long for this world.

In that moment I feared for the village and for Lachlan, and especially for myself. Nothing had fol-lowed me out of the crypt, but I felt marked, observed and hated. A part of me wanted to try to placate the monster, return his heart and pray he afterward left us alone. However, I knew that Lachlan would not be deterred from the hunt, and what else could I do but stay and help him in the hopes that the village would be spared? Thinking practically, I had perhaps enough money for three weeks at some modest hotel in some city, but that would eat up my meager savings. I hadn't enough money for passage home, even if I could bring myself to face my family and former friends. Something would have to be done, though, if the others took panic and fled Findloss. I could not stay in the village if it were abandoned by everyone else. I hadn't the means. Or the courage.

Though my hearth called to me, the path to my cottage was a lonely and shadow-filled one and I was too nervous to take it at that moment. Instead I pulled my scarf tight and set out at a brisk pace for the village and the comparative warmth of Mistress Mac-Laren's company.

"*Cha d'thainig ne math raibh bh'l tuath ad goath fhuer 'san fhoghar,*" I heard as I entered the shop, shutting the door with some difficulty against the wind. This saying I knew: *There never came a good thing out of the North but a cold wind in autumn.*

The speaker was a stranger. This behemoth of a man wore workaday clothes, dark cord trousers belted at the knee, a patched shirt and an enormous belt that suggested he was accustomed to lifting heavy loads as part of a daily routine. His middle quarters bulged around the leather in a way that was almost comic, and I pitied the woman who might deal with his immense appetite; she was doubtless a slave to the stove. His only spot of color was a green muffler wrapped approximately where his neck should be, with the ends tucked into red braces.

As curious as everyone else in the shop, I waited and learned that the stranger's name was Miles Cooke, a cousin of the Magees, and he brought with him the news that Mill's Circus was coming to Keil.

I smiled politely when he looked my way, though inside I was repelled at his words. I have never liked the circus. Poor wild beasts, guilty of nothing, are made to serve life sentences in rolling prisons. They are forever exiled in a foreign, treeless land filled with gawking strangers and unkind wardens. Nor had I ever been one to take pleasure in staring at human freaks who were every bit as exiled from their families as those beasts who went about on four paws. And, I must admit, clowns had frightened me as a child. I had a distrust of anyone who hid behind a mask of paint.

This circus did offer one thing though that I thought might be of interest to Lachlan, and perhaps to the finman: The preserved body of a shark man, which one could see for six pennies. (It was surely an impressive relic, because this was a ruinous price for most children, who would be the main audience for such a thing.) It seemed that I would have a great deal to tell Lachlan when we met again. Perhaps this clue at the circus would distract him from his annoyance that I had gone to the kirk alone and perhaps further enraged the finman.

Night delivered its usual tempest. Warmed by the fire in my hearth and by a small glass of whisky and a book, I did my best to ignore it, though the wind seemed to take personal umbrage and battered my barred door with grit and detritus. Though I read until nearly twelve, the ticking of the clock on the mantel reminded me of the passage of time—and of Lachlan's failure to appear. Unable to sleep, I read on, feeding the fire recklessly.

My ears had grown attuned to the sound of Lachlan on my doorstep, so I did not at first feel alarm when I heard a louder scrape at the outside of the door. But when there came no knock, I hesitated to rise. Lachlan always announced himself with a deliberate blow; this night there came a light scratching that sounded something like a dog's claws, except from too high up on the doorframe. And if this were not enough to give me pause, Herman's arched back and silent snarl would have been a warning. The cat had hissed at Lachlan's knock, but he had never frozen in place, seeming caught between the two equally powerful emotions of terror and revulsion.

My logical side, the one still grappling to accept the abrupt supernatural intrusions into my life, suggested that it might be Lachlan, perhaps injured again and too weak to call out. But deep down I knew it wasn't Lachlan. Especially not when a faint but nauseating odor began to creep under the door. The Devil or worse was on the other side of that thick wood panel, listening and scrabbling as he tried to find a way in.

Herman remained silent and frozen. I too made no sound as I picked up Lachlan's charm and retreated to the bedroom, where I had taken to openly sleeping with the yew beater and the iron shackles; the shears-wielding beasties had not returned but I was taking no chances. They seemed pitiful weapons against a creature like the finman, but also all I had. A knife would not aid me. Hadn't someone already cut out this creature's heart?

It took all the will I possessed to enter the parlor again when the noise ceased, and when I did it was to find Herman and the terrible odor both gone. I ran through the cottage, making sure that no window was open, but I knew that I had closed them all long before the advent of the rain. Of the cat there was no sign; nor was there any sound or smell or other sensation to suggest I was anything but alone.

It was on my second, less frantic turn through the cottage that Lachlan's knock at last fell on the door. Certain as I was that this was he, I nevertheless called through the door before opening it.

"Lachlan—he was here!" The words were out before the door was completely open. Relief brought tears to my eyes and made my voice waver.

"Aye, I tracked him frae the kirk. He's gone intae the sea caves again." Lachlan set me away from the door and closed it carefully. I noticed that he was dressed, though the plaid he wore was more worn and faded than the last. "Sit down, lass. Yer whiter than sand. What did the creature dae?"

I allowed myself to be coaxed to the fire. "He just scratched. But the cat's gone. I can't find him. He puffed up like an adder when that thing came to the door . . . and then he disappeared. I know he must be hiding somewhere, but I can't find him. Could the finman have gotten him somehow?" My voice was quavering shamefully, but I truly feared for Herman.

"Donnae trouble yerself over the moggie. They're canny beasts. He'll return when it suits him. Now, drink this wee dram doon and tell me all that's happened. Something has provoked the beast and brought him here tae yer door."

So, this *was* my doing. Should I confess? It seemed wisest.

Usually I am not soothed by a *there-there* and a pat on the head, but Lachlan seemed so certain that Herman was fine that I allowed myself to relax and blink back my tears before they spilled over. Taking a deep breath, I began telling Lachlan first about my journey into the bowels of the kirk and the certainty that the finman had sensed me. Then, at the onset of Lachlan's frown, I related the news about the shark man at the circus in Keil and my feeling that the finman would go there to destroy it once he learned of its existence.

"I could tell ye that ye've an active imagination and tae not worry . . ."

This time, I rejected the soothing pat on the head and settled for a scowl. "But I don't—have an imagination, that is. I had my imagination removed with my appendix when I was twelve. Along with common sense, apparently." This was a lie, but I was damned if I would admit to being more than usually anxious. My near-hysterics over the cat had been emotional display enough. As close as I sometimes felt to Lachlan, he really was almost a stranger, and I didn't want to admit how much Herman meant to me.

"As a selkie, I donnae have an appendix."

This lighthearted answer was so out of character that I could only stare. At last I said, "You also lack the inclination to speak straightly with me. Lachlan, what are you thinking?"

Lachlan raised a brow. "If I am tae speak straightly, then it will be to tell ye that it was extremely foolish tae venture intae that crypt alone. Especially since I've already been there, tracking the finman's spoor. There is nae need to rush in blindly, lass. I hae matters well in hand."

"You might have shared this information before," I said in a tone of exaggerated aggrievement, hoping he would shoulder some of the blame. "And anyway, I believe in playing to my strengths. Impulsive action can take the enemy by surprise. I was there, the door was open . . ."

"I am sharing the information now," he said. "And yer impulsiveness maun be a surprise to yer friends as well as yer enemies. How dae they trust thee?"

I glared at him, not bothering to hide my annoyance at his suggestion. Usually I was very trustworthy— truthful, honorable, an upright citizen in every way. I asked instead, "Are we going to investigate this circus that has the shark-man mummy?"

"If I said that I waud investigate the circus, would ye be content tae stay out of it?"

"Probably not. Damn it, Lachlan! This involves me too. That cursed thing is in my home." I pointed at the floor beneath the table's ponderous leg. "Monsters are trying to cut off my shadow and that finman has tried to get me. Twice."

"Aye. Yer involved more closely than ye ken, and I've nae liking for it. If I could divorce ye frae these events I waud."

"What do you mean?" When he didn't answer I repeated the question. "Lachlan, what do you mean? How am I involved? Beyond the obvious." I paused. "What don't I know?"

"Ye've thought on wham it was wha stole the fin-man's heart?" Lachlan asked at last.

"Yes. Constantly. It was a magical kind of thing, right? Not just a physical assault? Could it have been Fergus's father? He would have been alive at the time of the inundation. Would his theft have caused the storm, or worsened it?"

"Aye, it could. But that wasnae what caused the storm, nor when the heart was taken. The theft was mair recent."

"No? Then when was it stolen?" I was beginning to get a bad feeling. "The year before last? It was Duncan, wasn't it? He took it."

Lachlan nodded. His posture was relaxed as he leaned against the mantel, but he watched me closely.

I spoke slowly as I thought it all through. "Duncan stole the heart and then . . . what? When the finman didn't die, he ran away to the States to escape retribution. Where he met me. And he thought, because of my family, I could protect him from the finman if the creature ever came."

Lachlan nodded again.

"But I couldn't. Because I didn't know anything about witches or finmen or MacCodrums. And eventually his family's hatred of mine began to surface. And he started to drink and . . . other things."

A third, smaller nod.

"But why? Why steal the heart? It seems such a crazy thing to do. Surely he knew that it would lead to bad things. And what could he gain by it?"

"Power mayhap. Tae aid Fergus in his diablerie in hopes of finding the lost treasure. I cannae say. But with Fergus's withered arm, Fergus couldnae hae done it alone. Nor could he hae hidden it in that crypt aneath the table. And I cannae believe he waud trust anyone nowt of his own blood."

"And so you're sure it was Duncan who did these things. There wasn't anyone else who might have done it?"

"Nay. Most likely he didnae ken that taking the heart wouldnae kill the finman. That must hae come as a nasty surprise."

"Have you always suspected that it was Duncan rather than Fergus who did this stupid thing?"

Lachlan didn't answer.

"Is that why you haven't trusted me? Because I'm his widow and I might have been involved?"

He blinked once, a slow and completely inhuman gesture during which I was able to see a second lid close over each eye. A part of me noted that this was probably how he was able to see in salt water.

He knelt by my chair so our eyes were level. "I trust thee now."

"Lachlan, couldn't we just destroy the heart?" I asked, leaning forward and putting a hand on his arm. As always, his flesh was hot to the touch.

"Possibly, wi the right spell. But the finman and his confederates need tae be flushed out of hiding, or the evil will simply gae underground and surface somewhere else," he answered, staring at my hand bemusedly and breathing deeply. "And be certain, should the heart be destroyed afore his ain death, that he shall bury this village again in vengeance, though it be his last living act. Every soul in it waud perish."

I felt cold and wrapped my arms about myself.

Lachlan's heat faded from my fingers as soon as contact was broken. "How can he live without a heart?"

"He cannae. He is using anither's organ. Perhaps Fergus Culbin's. But it cannae last long. He burns them out quickly and then needs anither. More people—yer kind and mine—shall die if he isnae destroyed along wi' his black heart."

I swallowed hard. "That's horrible. How many has he killed to steal their organs?"

"Countless. And aye, 'tis horrible. But everything aboot this monster is horrible. He waudnae have it any ither way. It is the nature of the beast. Dae nowt forget this."

A witch is a kind of hare,
And marks the weather
As a hare does.
—Ben Johnson, *The Sad Shepherd*

Chapter Thirteen

"*Bliadh an diugh, agus codagh am mairech,*" Lachlan murmured. I tried to decipher the phrase but failed. "Food today and war tomorrow," he translated, giving the small smile I was coming to know all too well.

We were sharing some chips, salty fried potato wedges, a new gastronomic experience for a suspicious Lachlan but apparently a satisfactory one. A small hostelry, The Alpine Inn, seemed to be serving customers, but we had chosen instead to patronize a street vendor. Lachlan had said obscurely that the inn had for too many years worn the sign of the peeled willow wand. I recalled that this had something to do with warning away witches or faeries or some such thing, and I was content to be led away to someplace with fewer bad memories.

This was the first time I had seen Lachlan in full daylight, and I have to admit that my eyes were pleased. I knew his hair was dark, but firelight did not show the deep chestnut and other autumnal hues lurking in those silken depths. His eyes beneath the brim of his tam were eerily black but utterly fascinating, and I had to make an effort not to stare as if besotted. We were attracting quite enough attention as it was.

We had gotten a ride to Keil in Old Man Mackenzie's fishing boat. The waters were calm that day, soothed by Lachlan though he would not admit to doing it, and we had reached Keil in under an hour. What Mackenzie had charged for the passage I do not know, but suspect that he enjoyed the benefit of a good day's fishing as well, since we needed him to collect us again around two o'clock and he would be more timely if his nets were full.

This did not stop him from being unnerved by his passengers, however, though he made an effort to hide his misgivings.

All this travel by boat was for my benefit, of course. Lachlan could have easily swum to Keil. Or gone without me. I was very glad that he had not. It suggested that perhaps he truly did trust me.

Keil was very different from Findloss. I noticed first that the docks in town were clean and attractive and bustling with activity. The natural skerries had been extended by a breakwater. Because the waters were so calm here, boats could rest safely at anchor rather than needing to be beached above the tide line as they were in our village, and they lent the sea a certain air of gaiety.

The men on the waterfront were mostly old and

there were also more women than I expected to see on the docks. I heard Norse, Gaelic and lowland Scots being spoken civilly, a thing not so common in days past. But times had changed and circumstances evolved, and the people had too. Many of the long, wearying clan conflicts of the highlands had been left unresolved, if probably not forgotten, when the last of the males went off to war, and there was no one left with sufficient spare energy to prosecute old battles. The few remaining old men and women were too grief-stricken or busy holding their families together to remain embittered. Perhaps it was better that way. Some conflicts never cease until the chain is broken by the death of an entire generation. Rather like those of finmen and selkies.

How to explain this most unusual day to you? It was autumn—normal autumn, with mild winds, brown grass and a scattering of twigs and cast-off leaves caught in the thistledown that had drifted at the side of the town's main street. Fishing boats went about their business in consistent but unhurried fashion. The docks were populated and busy, as I mentioned, though no one moved quickly there either, perhaps already responding to the onset of the fall torpor that was telling the world to prepare for sleep. Even the chiming of the church bells sounded drowsy and lacking in real ambition to call the sleepy faithful to worship. Winter did not yet reign here, not like in Findloss. We might have been visiting another country.

But what struck me most powerfully was how very sane the village felt. How normal. Unnatural evil had been growing in Findloss for months. I knew that, of course, but I hadn't realized how thick the miasma of doom had become while we fought what now seemed a losing rearguard action against a heartless invader from the sea.

The simplest animal, even the smallest of birds, makes reasonable preparation for the winter to survive the dead time. They dig safe dens and hibernate or, more wisely still, migrate away from the dangerous change. Unfortunately, I did not have that option, though I wished that I could be so self-indulgent. Probably no one else in the village had it, either. There was no villa in Italy, no chateau in the south of France. Instead I would stand with Lachlan and fight the cold killer who brought death upon us, as tempting as it was to stay in Keil and forget the horrors of home.

"What are ye inkling aen?" Lachlan asked.

"Winter."

"Ah."

In the past I had always associated the season with gentle rains and silent snow that muted passing voices and footsteps. It was the happy season of the Nativity and New Year revels. But not so in Findloss. There winter was turbulent and loud and threatening . . . if not that day. The weather that morning had been mild enough to justify wearing my one frivolous dress, which was a light blue linen about two years out of style, but still quite pretty.

"See ye those iron brackets on the wall?" Lachlan asked. There were a few old buildings near the docks, *bourachs* built of loose stacked stone and thatched carelessly on unhewn rafters of oak and birch trees grown in a wood that was now long gone. It had been burned down a century ago in an effort to discourage the brigands that lived there, no thought given to the animals and birds there as well.

"I see them, but please don't tell me anything horrid," I pleaded. "I should like to enjoy myself a while more."

He was amused. "In the days afore oil lamps, these held torches made frae the roots and trunks of fir trees dug up frae the peat bogs tae the south. The peat caused the resin aen them tae burn slow and bright, oftimes with a fire that was blue and green. I recall the smell fondly. My wife used them aen her home. Like sae many things, it is a custom that survives nae more."

"Oh," I said, not sure how I felt about his newest mention of his dead wife, whose existence I would prefer to forget completely. "That must have been a lot less smelly than paraffin."

Lachlan gave me a long look but said nothing, and I began to wonder if his wife had lived in that very village. If so, the visit might be troubling to him, and I felt a bit guilty for dragging him out on what might well prove to be a fool's errand.

We passed the kirk and a tidy kirkyard that looked quite old. I did not suggest visiting the graves, since his wife might be buried there and I thought it best to let sleeping ghosts lie.

Though I did not study the churchyard for long, Lachlan followed my gaze. "I've nae great liking for the joyless human religions, but I maun admit that there was one ceremony I enjoyed wi' all my heart." The words and sentiment were unexpected. "It was aen the year when Beltane Eve fell on a Sunday. Though they called the ritual a mass, the decoration o' the kirk was purely pagan. The aisle of the auld church was carpeted wi' a long rug woven entirely of herbage frae the garden, and showed every hue of green that is seen in the spring. The shredded crimson petals from the ancient rose bushes growing in the cemetery lent the air a rich perfume that grew stronger wi' every passing worshipper who crushed the blooms underfoot. It was one time when yer god seemed beautiful tae me."

There were no roses in the cemetery now, I noted sadly. No green either. "When was this?" I asked. "Long ago?"

"Aye. I cannae recall the exact date, but it was when the Catholics were new tae the land." He stopped and turned abruptly. "See yon stony table fast on the water? There was a castle there once, built aen top of a holy well. For sheer vulgarity and ostentation of furnishings it had nae rival in these parts. Nothing expensive and of bad taste was overlooked, and much of it was furnished wi' stolen goods. The builders were cruel as well, slaughtering every bird and beast they could lay hands and swords upon. Even our people were persecuted for a time." When I made a small noise he added, "The owners paid for their arrogance. The sea had its revenge. It started with the broad steps and pillars that supported the massive roof. The storms of winter—and soon of other seasons tae—threw spindrift and salt spume ontae the treads, and eventually the gale waters themselves came rushing up tae the castle door. It ate at the foundations. Then a pillar collapsed and then anither. They barred the door and retreated up the stair, but the tide was relentless and legend has it that the holy well water also rose up against the blasphemers. In less than a century the castle was gone, pulled back intae the sea, the sandstone pulverized and thrown up aen on the beach tae make a sandy bed for the very creatures they persecuted. Only the floor remains, a few pieces of marble that can be seen at low tide if the sand hasnae drifted o'er them."

Holy retribution? Or had the selkies and finmen had something to do with it? Maybe Findloss was not a unique case.

"You're not sorry it's gone."

"Nae. The humans hae all the land tae be lord o'er. They can afford tae leave the shore for the creatures wham dwell there." Sometimes when he said the word *human* there was unmistakable contempt in his voice.

"I agree," I said softly. We turned and continued strolling. The edge of town was scabbed with the tailings from old mines—tin or salt, most probably, though I suppose it might have been for anything.

Other than the piles of ancient discarded scree, furred now with grass stubs of autumn gold shorn down from their summer heights by the fluffy white sheep that dotted the landscape, the hollow was girdled by some dark scruffy pines whose strong and astringent scent mixed pleasingly with the salt air. The scene was quite pastoral, idyllic in a romantic way. There was even a stream to burble but it was placid, whispering quietly that day. There were hills beyond the small pines but no mountains majestic and no stony cliffs. No touch of the gothic or evil intruded here. It took no effort to enjoy the scenery.

The circus was set up at the edge of the village and not hard to find. Its tents, caravans and banners were not of subtle hue and the smell of the animals was also quite apparent when one was downwind. Chaos was being set into order with commendable rapidity by men who had obviously done this many times.

Memory is a fickle thing, and perhaps pricked by Lachlan's story of the arrogant castle builders I suddenly remembered a poem by Ralph Hodgson that had appeared in our newspaper about the time I matriculated from the Prescott Academy for young women. I had cut out and saved it until I married and disposed of many of my childhood mementos. I couldn't recall the first part, but I knew the end.

And he and they together
Knelt down in angry prayers
For tamed and shabby tigers,
And dancing dogs and bears,
And wretched, blind pit-ponies,
And little, hunted hares.

"What is wrong?" Lachlan asked softly, and I realized that I had stopped walking.

I thought about saying that it seemed a sin to step on the last patch of green grass that glowed vibrantly under the low-pitched sun, but that was as sentimental as my real thought, so instead I said: "I have always hated the circus. It's what they do to the animals—it seems so wrong to me. Even our worst criminals are not put in prison forever."

Lachlan nodded, either because he understood my

sentiment or because he shared it. Giving in to impulse, I recited the poem. Lachlan made no comment, but he took my hand in his and laced our fingers as if to offer courage, should any be necessary. I did feel much braver, but also a bit dizzy. His touch always affected me that way.

Everything was bright and cheery in a vulgar way, except for one caravan made with wood sides and a black canvas awning, painted around with strange and improbable animals from far-off lands and ancient lore. There was no need to ask which trailer held the oddities.

"They aren't open for custom yet," I murmured. "Should we try bribery?"

"Nay. There is naebody aboot just now. So ye'll wander over tae the men putting up the tent and do yer level best to be charming and vapid and perhaps a wee bit prone tae possibly sinning with strangers, and I shall let myself inside while they are distracted."

I giggled. I couldn't help it. I'd never attempted to act the part of a woman of low moral character; it is not my nature to stray so far from reality, and I had never been drawn to theatrics.

"I'll do it," I whispered when I had stopped laughing. "But be quick, please. I am not at all certain that I will be any good at this sort of thing, and I should hate to have to fall back on fainting. The dirt would ruin my dress."

"I should hope ye'd nae be experienced in such deception! Nae man needs that," Lachlan muttered, turning me toward the group of workmen gathered 'round a small stack of poles and giving me a small shove when my steps were too laggard for his tastes. Turning my head back, I stuck out my tongue, but Lachlan had already started toward the silent caravan.

Taking a deep breath and pasting on a smile, I began picking my way toward the workmen, who were arguing about something in French and what I thought was Italian. This cheered me considerably. We had a language barrier. It could take forever to make myself understood at this gathering of Babel.

Reaching up, I undid one of the pearl buttons on my dress and let the linen flutter at will. I was glad that I wasn't a society lady whose clothes buttoned down the back. My wrap fell to my elbows, where it did nothing to keep me warm, but where it would not impede anyone's view of my camisole and the tops of my breasts.

"Yoohoo—hello, y'all. Are any of you fine gentlemen from America?" I waggled my fingers at them in a manner I believed to be coy. Eight sets of blank eyes looked my way.

I smiled widely. The men smiled back, eyes no longer blank. The wind obligingly brought more of my décolletage into view and whisked my skirt a bit above the knee. Smiles widened.

This is going to be easy, I thought.

And glow-worms with lanterns,
Blue flowers for my breast;
And faeries to kiss me,
And lull me to rest.
—Alasdair Alpin MacGregor,
Miann An Fhogaraich (The Wanderer's Wish)

Chapter Fourteen

"Ye've said little of yer family. Dae the MacCodrums live yet in America?"

This might have been idle conversation to pass the ride back home, but since it was Lachlan asking, it seemed doubtful. He did not do small talk about family, particularly when I knew he was thinking hard about what he had discovered at the circus. The body in the freak show had not been a finman, but rather a merman—a different creature, I gathered—and the poor thing had had its heart cut out, probably by our least favorite wicked wizard, who was short one of his own.

Since prevarication was usually useless around Lachlan, and I had no wish to have any sort of liaison with a man who could not accept my personal quirks and habits for what they were, I decided to speak openly of my family and feelings and see what came of it. Especially since the sea guaranteed we would not be overheard by Mr. Mackenzie, who was at the other end of the boat, smoking contentedly on a large pipe and probably gloating over the haul of fish he'd sold in Keil.

"Some, I suppose, but none who are close to me. My parents are dead and I had no siblings. There is only my mother's brother. He did not care for my husband or for anything Scottish. No one did—like my husband, that is. Though, now that I think on it, no one talked much about Scotland and our family here either."

I cleared my throat, finding that once started, I actually wanted to talk about this but was uncertain where to begin. How did I express what had previously been inexpressible? How did I begin to tell the truth that no one had ever wanted to hear, least of all myself? One was supposed to love one's family and husband. All those rules I had learned at my parents' knee: rules for manners, rules of behavior, familial rules and societal rules. They meant nothing in this place and at this time. They had given me the skills I needed to survive in their world, but they hadn't helped me cope with Duncan and I doubted they would help me much with what I was facing. But maybe Lachlan could.

Lachlan waited patiently while I ruminated, and finally I said: "My home life was stifling. I felt that I was existing in an underused life designed for someone else, that I had been mistakenly placed in a family where I did not belong. I did not marry. Instead I worked—a very daring and scandalous thing to do. Then, at an age when I was considered past prayers, Duncan came into my life. And he was very different, exciting. Had I been a little wiser and not just older, I would have asked myself if different was necessarily better, but . . ." I shrugged. "So I married Duncan, who was as I said very different from the other men I knew, and who I hoped would let me make better use of my life. Unfortunately, after the first weeks, my marriage became a waking nightmare, a matter of endless performance anxiety and fear of being found flawed in new and previously unimagined ways. And I *was* found wanting. Every day, or so it seemed. And I could not turn to my family for help or advice because they had not approved the marriage and pride wouldn't let me admit I'd been wrong, even after Duncan became cruel."

I thought of the last time I had seen my grandmother. She had not aged well. Her face was as old and wrinkled as the sheets of an abandoned bed after a restless night's sleep. The bitter lines were entrenched, residents of old age and disappointment that would never be evicted. She had never been entirely at home in her life, and I once feared that this bitterness would be my fate as well.

"By the time my husband died and my aunt and uncle and various friends reluctantly reappeared in my life, I was too exhausted and soured to face them. And I found myself avoiding any chance of being presented with a list of emotional debts they thought I owed them for coming to me in my hour of need, especially since my hour of need had actually come while Duncan was alive. His death freed me, and I didn't need them. I was offended when they *forgave* me. And I did not forgive them."

Lachlan nodded. There was understanding and per- haps sympathy in his dark gaze, or so I chose to be- lieve.

"Because I feared that the emotional liability of these associations—mostly the guilt they could inspire—would keep me from acting in our own best interests, even when I needed to take drastic steps to survive, I ran away. Do you see why? I had failed to defend myself once and feared I would do so again. Duncan made me into a mousy coward, and I feared they would also be able to bully me."

"I believe that I ken yer meaning all tae well, though I believe that ye underestimate yerself," Lach- lan avowed.

"Yes? Perhaps. But you have come to know me now that I am more . . . healed. More certain of who I am. Then I was different. I was more afraid and bitter and hating. I speak now most specifically of hating my aunt and uncle. They infuriated me and always had. I did nothing that was actively hurtful to them in mar- rying a foreigner and non-Baptist, nothing that would cause pain and suffering and shame, except if some- one believed the whole universe revolved around their feelings and beliefs and wants, and indulged in the sort of self-destructive tantrums that bordered on hys- teria when they didn't get their way. I speak now more of my aunt—she of the voice that can damage brains and make ears bleed. My uncle was more the silently disapproving kind who thought whatever his wife suggested. Heaven knows that Duncan gave them ample to disapprove of. He actually seemed to delight in it—the whores and gambling and narcotics and drink, none of which he did anything to conceal." I sighed and then waved my hands, shooing the thoughts away. "I couldn't face any more recriminations. One more day of it and I should have murdered my aunt with her gardening shears and buried her body in the herb garden."

Lachlan actually smiled. "I've known people like yer aunt, people wham use emotion instead of wit tae forge a path in the world, and who see any disinclination tae participate in their wants, ha'ever stupid, as a personal attack. They cannae be reasoned with. Sometimes there is nowt tae do but leave afore ye dae bloody murder."

I was not certain he was speaking metaphorically, but I nodded anyway. "Exactly! My aunt seemed to have no conscience to play referee in a fight, and simply vomited her anger on whoever was nearest. Too often, that was me. So, I told myself that I was nearing the middle of my life and past the point of undertaking contortions of personality and habit to please family, or those who claimed to be friends but who actually offered a very conditional sort of approval and withdrew it when they were disappointed in my—or my husband's—actions. I chose emotional famine and freedom from family and their beliefs and ways of living. I chose Findloss . . . and poverty, and now danger. I still believe that I have made the right choice. Family and marriage are not for me. Mayhap that means I'm unnatural and unwomanly, but it is the truth. The only thing I am sorry for is that I did not have a child, but with Duncan as its father . . . well. I think fate was kind to deny me."

I cleared my throat. Enough was enough. I did not want to speak any more about Duncan or my kin. "And you, Lachlan? Have you any family?" Other than a dead wife.

"Aye. A cousin called Eonan. He is . . . young. High-spirited. He . . . travels a deal. Also two sons, Ardagh and Colm, though only Ardagh lived tae marry. Colm was born tae my human wife and did not survive tae adulthood. Also I've a grandson, called Cathair. And twa great-grandsons. They are Keir and Ruraidh." Lachlan looked out over the sea. The swells remained mild and the sky clear. The lingering smell of the offloaded fish was rather strong when the wind shifted to the south, but his words were too startling to waste time complaining. "Eonan is the only one I've seen in centuries."

I blinked, feeling the news as a blow to the head. "You have sons. And grandchildren."

"Aye." The smile was fleeting and wry. "And like yerself, my grandson married a . . . loveless being. She was bonnie but cruel."

"She was . . . human?"

"Nay. Better she had been. Human lasses can be . . ." Lachlan stopped, but I knew that he had been about to say that human women could be controlled. "We've been forced tae looking on land fer wives since the selkie women died. My first wife was the last of her kind. My grandson found a fae wife, caught by

accident in an entailing spell, and was thereafter unlucky in love. That has been the fate of sae many of
our men."

"That's . . . that's very sad. But, a family. How nice.
Will I ever meet them?" I asked brightly. I admit,
some of the manners I was taught as a child are still
useful. They provide the correct, polite question even
when one is in turmoil and has not yet formulated a
genuine reaction to unexpected news—like the ex-
tinction of a species you were unaware of, or a man
you had thought unattached actually having a large
family. Lachlan, a family man? I had thought of him
more as being hatched from the brain of a god like
Athena. Or was it Apollo? I can't recall.

He hesitated. "That maun be a wee bit hard tae arrange."

"Why? Do they live far away?"

His black eyes looked into mine. "They believe me
deid. Yer nowt alone in yer family toils. I also wearied
of the endless recriminations of my kin at my second
marriage, and thought it best tae leave my past behind."

I am no fan of pugilism, but I believe that in the
sport of boxing, this is what they call a one-two
punch. "Truly? They think you're dead?" Lachlan had
succeeded in knocking me off balance, and even manners could not find a proper social response to this,
especially when I was mad with curiosity and felt an
inappropriate desire to laugh. "But why? For heaven's
sake, how?" And why had I not thought of this? If I
were dead I would not have to send gifts at Christmas

or bother writing letters to friends I no longer cared about!

Lachlan sighed. "'Tis a long tale, but in the end it comes doon tae the fact that I was in nae fit condition tae lead my people after my wife—my human wife—died. Back then, taking a human wife was a bit of a shameful thing. My kin believed that the selkie women waud come back and they didnae make her welcome."

I shook my head but said nothing.

"Some selkies wha love human women choose a life on land. If they gie up their skins and stay ashore they donnae live vera long. My grandson believes that I died long ago." He looked away again. "Tae return waud be tae upset the order of things. My grandson is a guid king—he's welcome tae the task."

"A king?" This was a whisper. Shock upon shock had rendered me nearly mute.

"Aye, a king." Lachlan smiled a little. "Though 'tis not the grandiose thing that humans mean when they use this word. He is mair like a chief of a clan. There's nae crown of gold or jewels, nae robes of state. My home was a place called Avocamor. It is the first kingdom of the selkies, our last bastion aen this side of the warld. Our numbers are very few."

"Oh."

Lachlan had been a king? I digested this in silence. Did this change anything? Were his parenthood and elevated position in life, and his renunciation of it, reasons to retreat from this relationship? My impulses—stupid, greedy and impure impulses, which grew with every hour—said no. Perhaps a connection of a romantic nature would scar me in some way. But I'd been married to Duncan, the beast. How much more scarred could I get? Anyway, was his decision to run away from his old life that much different from my own? True, he had children, but they were grown and it sounded as though they had abandoned their father long before he left them.

And it was not as if I were planning to marry Lachlan. I had been sincere in what I told him. Marriage was not for me. And I could not even conceive what a marriage to a selkie would look like.

He was beautiful, though, and I desired him as I had nothing else in my life. I impulsively reached over and ran my fingertips down the palm of his hand. As always, I could feel my pulse leap at the contact of our flesh, which instantly warmed. I think he felt it, too, because I saw him catch his breath and his dark gaze fastened on me. His expressions were foreign much of the time, but desire is desire and I saw it writ plain on his face.

"I understand, you know. Running away isn't the worst thing one can do for one's children. Sometimes it's a kindness. As the saying goes—out of sight, out of mind. People grieve a bit and then move on." Or so I hoped. Everything else was too unpleasant to contemplate that afternoon.

"Nae, 'tisnae sae bad." Lachlan's face hardened, but he did not pull away. Instead he laced his fingers with mine. "But the finman is anither matter. His quarrel was made wi' me when I was king. My family will nae suffer for it. This creature maun die, and by my ain hand afore he harms anyone else."

I nodded. It was agreement but also a pledge. We would see the finman dead so we could move on with our lives—whether collectively or separately, I did not know, and in that moment did not care.

Omnes angeli, boni et mali,
ex virtute naturali habent potestatem
transmutandi corpora nostra.
*(All angels, good and bad, have the power of
transmutating our bodies).*
—Saint Thomas Aquinas

Chapter Fifteen

We made love when we returned to the cottage.

I know that this will be shocking and perhaps impossible for anyone else to imagine. How could I have sexual relations with a being who is not like me? Not my species? But humanity, as I define it, is not conferred merely by the blessings of speech and opposable thumbs. It is our capacity for reason and empathy that allows us to rise above the baser impulses of rage, greed, fear and envy. It is only when we triumph over these evils that we can lay just claim to being "human." In this way, Lachlan was one of the most human—and humane—people I have ever known. Lying down with him was natural.

And so it was that I slept with a king, one from a land more foreign than I had ever imagined.

Lachlan was not like Duncan, who was base and rough by comparison. My selkie's flesh was smooth, soft. The striking planes of his foreign-looking cheeks, his full lips that lingered enticingly, his long-fingered hands, all were as exquisite as the finest silk ever loomed for any Chinese emperor, for they possessed not the slightest hint of hair or stubble. Yet, with fur or without, he was infinitely touchable. My hands could not resist him and I did not try to stop their wandering.

His plaid was pushed away with great haste until he was naked and I could feel the beating of his heart beneath my cheek where it lay against his smooth chest. It was slow and deep, like the shushing of the ocean on a peaceful day just as the tide has turned. It caught me up, bespelled me more completely than anything ever before. I would have resented the surrender of will, the near mindlessness that happened with Lachlan, had I been alone in my bemusement, but I knew that Lachlan was likewise enthralled by the fiery enchantment building so quickly between us.

I did not cover myself or in any way try to hide my body when my clothes were shed. There was no need for modesty. I felt no shame and I was beautiful in Lachlan's dark eyes. Besides, it was too late to save my virtue. I was not an innocent bystander in this seduction.

"Are ye sure, Megan lass? There is nae going back once this act is done."

There was such terrible earnestness in this question that for a moment I hesitated. But then I caught a whiff of the scent that is uniquely Lachlan and somewhere

between my brain and my mouth the message translated from "Perhaps we should wait" to "Absolutely."

"I'm sure."

The sliver of waning moon that I knew rose behind
the storm clouds as we kissed started its journey across
the weeping heavens. A bit of storm wind—rising like
Lachlan's passion—crept under the windowsill, floating on stealthy wings. Its light caress danced over my
skin and through my hair. I opened my eyes wide and
noticed then that Lachlan's skin glowed as though lit
by the embers of a fire.

We lay on the bed, atop the woolen blanket with
which I had replaced the bloodied coverlet, and I wished
for rose petals and perfume and linens of silk instead.
It seemed an inadequate bower, too earth-bound and
common for someone like Lachlan, though he never
complained at our humble surroundings or at the
coarse fabric on his flesh.

His touch was deft and light, as though he handled
some delicate vessel made of fragile crystal. But I was
not glass; I was flesh and heated blood. The warmth of
my body grew immense and torturous even as my
muscles clenched in on themselves, folding tight like a
fist around the pommel of a sword that might run me
through. I believe that death or some other transformation was near, but I did not care. The warmth in
my belly quested outward toward my sweat-damp
skin, and inward as well, drawing muscles tight as it
traveled toward my womb. Streams of desire, yearn-
ing and even love flowed into one another, wove together and made my stimulated nerves dance wildly
when the combined emotions overflowed their normal

capacity to feel and sought new channels of sensation and understanding. Fire was conducted instantaneously from nerve to nerve, muscle to muscle and all along my skin as nameless emotion created new heights of consciousness—all in a part of my mind that had previously been locked away from me. Like Lachlan's skin, my own flesh came alive with an inner fire that made me glow, and it hungered for something it had never experienced but knew was possible on this particular night and with this particular man.

Perspiration glossed us both, and I was soon painted in the same warm glow that enshrouded Lachlan and made him luminous. For a time I was cautious, tasting only in moderation of his flesh and lips, but just a smallest kiss of the salt on his skin let the wild magic free. I was drugged and could feel myself yielding to his desires, anticipating them even. He could ask anything of me and I would not—could not—say no to any need. These were hours of freedom and forgetting.

There was no caution or second-guessing my decision to make love to Lachlan once we had kissed. Our coming together was correct, perhaps inevitable. He entered me, moved in me, and suddenly that clenched hand was flung open, releasing the sword and pitching me toward the clouded sky and past it toward the moon, hurtling me outward into a place so beautiful that it seemed imaginary, perhaps even forbidden to us mortals since we had been driven from the first paradise for defiantly tasting the Fruit of Knowledge. It was not death that came to me; it was life.

I came back to myself in time to see Lachlan arch

back above me, moved by the same ecstasy that existed next to both pain and deepest love. His eyes in the lamplight were bright, a black obsidian being consumed from within by some unknown but holy fire.

Was it degrading that I wanted him so very much? I somehow didn't think that he felt so. Again and again we joined, until he forced himself away and made me drink to slake an unrealized thirst. And I know that he desired me to the point of madness, too—something I valued above pearls because the world had so often seemed to find me undesirable and unworthy. He gave me the greatest of gifts that night—the certainty that I was beautiful, whole and perfect—and I was at peace for the first time in my entire life.

And in my sleep I hear the tide
Creeping beneath my window wide.
—Alasdair Alpin MacGregor

Chapter Sixteen

"I wasn't expecting a . . . supersexual being," I said sometime later, laying a hand against Lachlan's chest and again marveling at the feel of his skin. Dawn was beginning to light up the horizon, a pencil of red burning its way through the clouds.

"Yer likewise unexpected. I've made nae plans fer this event."

I could see the fact unnerved him a bit, though Lachlan's hands remained gentle and soothing as he stroked my breasts with a damp cloth. I said, "Sometimes things just happen." And for once that was a good thing.

"Aye. But they do nae happen tae me. At least, they havena happened fer a verra long while."

"Don't distress yourself. Nothing has fundamentally changed. I shan't be dragging you to the altar." The comment about changes felt as though it might be a lie, but I wanted to reassure him—and myself. I needed a while to assess what I felt. I did not regret our union, but I needed some reflection on the change it had brought over me. I had never thought to want a forever again, because I had not known how perfect one might be.

"Yer sae young tae have sae little faith. Gird yer soul wi' steel, but it willnae stop fate an she wants ye." Lachlan's voice was soft, almost as though he were speaking to himself. I was too tired to engage in the conversation, anyway, and decided to ignore it in favor of sleep.

"My head hurts. Like I drank too much whisky," I said, closing my eyes and letting myself be soothed by Lachlan's touch. "I must have gotten too much sun."

He nodded. "The clamber-skull is tae be expected. Fer we were greatly intoxicated wi' each other. That wasnae expected either. The madness hasnae come upon me in centuries of yer time, and I was careless and selfish." He took a breath and rose up on one elbow. "Megan, lass, I suspect that last night we conceived a bairn."

"What?" I smiled a little. I knew what *bairn* meant, but I was certain he couldn't intend the word that way.

"A bairn. A babe."

My eyes opened. I felt as if he had slapped me or thrown a carafe of water at my face. "No," I said flatly, sitting up and pulling the blankets tight across my breasts as I retreated to the edge of the bed. "We did not. I am . . . not able. Duncan and I couldn't . . . And anyway, you're a selkie. We can't have a child."

Lachlan's gaze was compassionate, but he did not

take back his words. "I assure ye that we can hae a child. Ye didnae conceive wi' your husband because yer body knew him for a mortal enemy. And ye have conceived wi me because yer body knows . . ." He stopped, his expression something very close to stunned.

"Knows what?" I demanded, my voice high and uneven. My peace was fleeing and I felt cold creeping in.

"Knows I am nae enemy of yers."

I opened my mouth to argue further, but he put a finger to my lips. Then he leaned over and laved behind my ear. I could feel the now-familiar dizziness that came whenever Lachlan drugged me.

"Why did you do that?"

"Sleep. We shall speak on it later. For now, best ye forget what I've told thee. We've a while yet afore it shall matter greatly and arrangement maun be made." Lachlan began humming in two-part harmony. It was lovely and alien.

As insane as it sounds, I did put the alarming subject out of mind. I didn't even scold him for drugging me without permission; I just slid back down on the pillow, listened to the lullaby and went promptly to sleep. When I awoke much later, it was to find Herman on my chest, peering at me intently. I looked about for Lachlan, but he was gone, and I vaguely recalled showing him out after dawn and barring the door behind him.

In spite of my claim to need time for reflection, I did very little of it that day. The joy of my illicit union I hugged to myself all morning, sharing my happiness only with the cat, who was staying quite close to me as I prepared porridge—without salt but with extra currants and honey because I had a strong craving for something sweet.

In spite of the porridge, the craving for sweets grew as the morning progressed, and I decided to walk to the shop and see if perhaps Mistress MacLaren had some kind of candy. When I opened the front door, however, it was to find the world beyond in the clutches of a gale. Unlike the previous storms, this one was strangely silent. The wind did not howl, though the rain was a torrent. I frowned, contemplating the twenty minutes of flood and sleet I'd have to endure if I went into the village. In addition to icy rain, the wind beyond the house was slinging sand with particular vehemence.

"What do you think, Herman?"

The cat stared at me for a long moment, no doubt wondering if he had heard me correctly, then turned his back. He is a great fisherman and loves the outdoors, but not obsessive about any fish breakfast that meant getting wet from whiskers to tail.

"I think you're right," I said, closing the door. Herman and I would share an egg for lunch. I also ate all my dried apples and the rest of the jam.

In an effort to distract myself from my growing craving, I began to read voraciously. Once upon a time I would have been burned at the stake for possessing the contents of Fergus Culbin's library, and a part of me had to wonder if I weren't endangering my soul with it. Certainly my reading did nothing for my peace of mind.

I found a poem in one of the books, "The Great Silkie of Sule Skerry." It made me shudder with horror, a reaction that seemed extreme when I thought about it later. The poem is sad, of course, but I told myself that it had nothing to do with me and Lachlan. Still, it stuck in my head and would not go away.

I heard a mither calm her bairn,
and as she rocked, and as she sang,
she dwelledt sae hard upon the verse
that the heart within her rang.

"O, cradle row, and cradle gae,
and sleep well, my bairn within;
I ken not wha thy father is,
nor yet the sea he dwells within."

It happened aen a certain day
When this mither fell asleep,
That in came her silkie lover
And set him down at her bare feet,

And up then spake a gray silkie
when he woke her frae her sleep,
"I'll tell ye noo where thy lover is:
he's sittin' close on thy bed feet."

"O, love, come tell to me thy name,
Tell me where does thy homeland be?"
"My home is great Sule Skerry,
And I earn my livin' aen the sea.

For I am a man upon the land;
but I am a silkie on the sea,
and when I'm far frae ev'ry strand,
my home is in Sule Skerry."

"Alas, this is a woeful fate!
This doom ye've laid aen me,
That a man should come out of the sea
And tae have a bairn wi' me!"

"Now foster well my wee young bairn,
For a twelve-month and a day,
and when that twelve-month's fairly gone,
I'll come and pay thy nurse's fee."

And soon the weary twelve-month gone,
he came tae pay the nurse's fee;
he had a coffer fu' o' Spanish gold,
and another fu' o' the silver money.

When he had taken of the silver and gold
And he had put it upon her knee,
He said "Gi'e tae me my little son,
And take thee up thy nurse's fee.

"But how shall I my young son ken
when thou ha' taken him frae me?"
"The one who wears the chains o' gold,
among a' the seals shall be he.

And now thou will marry a hunter good,
and a great hunter I'm sure he'll be;

and the first shot that e'er he takes
will kill both my young son and me.

And he shall come home wi' a gift,
chains of gold that he has won.
And ye shall ken by these chains
That he has killed yer lover and yer son."

Humans did kill selkies, as immortalized in this poem. Perhaps with cause, if the song was right. But there were other legends too, and those said humans also used selkies by hiding their skins and forcing them to use magic to call fish and calm the sea.

Then a stray thought: Where did Lachlan hide his skin when he visited me? I prayed it was somewhere safe from both finmen and humans.

The poem continued to run through my head as I ransacked the kitchen, looking for something sweet. One verse especially bothered me, and it chanted it-self over and over like a bully's taunt:

"And now thou will marry a hunter good,
and a great hunter I'm sure he'll be;
and the first shot that e'er he takes
will kill both my young son and me."

"My young son and me . . ." I said out loud.

It was only then that my last conversation with Lachlan came back to me. At first I assured myself it was only a dream, an unpleasant imagining of the type I'd had before, but the more the memory coalesced, the more certain I became that the conversation had been real. I had spent the morning tunneling along, as happy and as blind as any mole in the dark earth, but now I had popped out into the light and was forced to see what I had forgotten.

"Oh, my sainted aunt!" I said, sitting down hard on the kitchen stool. "Herman, could this be true? *Can* I be with child? And where has Lachlan gone?"

The cat looked at me sympathetically, but remained mute. I began to cry, unable to be happy, though I had been given my heart's desire.

May the tempest never rest,
Nor the seas with peace be blest
Since they tore thee from my breast.
—"The Maiden of Morven"

Chapter Seventeen

Many parts of that day remain a blur to me. I do recall going out after the rain and looking out at the clumps of dead grass that surrounded the cottage and feeling overwhelmingly sad. I wondered many strange things that morning I had not considered before. Watching the brown grass being flattened by the wind I wondered: Does it hurt, do you think—to grow old, wither and brown, then have the wind lay you low? The grass bursts from the ground each spring with joyous color; is it sorrowful at the end? Does it know that it is dying?

My thoughts grew more grim and fanciful as day turned to dark. The night wore on and Lachlan did not come. Feeling nervous, I paced the cottage and twice stopped to wind the mantel clock and my father's pocket watch; it seemed very important that I remain aware of the time. Finally, the cold compelled me to bed. My sleep was uneasy but there were no more tears.

The next morning, driven mad with the need for sweets and some companionship, I made the bike ride into the village in spite of the lingering rain and wind. It was there I heard that Bertie Stornmont, monger and sometimes rag-and-bone man possessed of no more than half his born wits, had chosen to end his rather unpleasant life the previous night by taking a long draught of some homemade kin of John Barleycorn and then following it up with another draught of lye. The latter had burned him badly about the mouth and, they said, the nose. But I recalled Lachlan's description of how the finman would suck out his victim's souls by latching his sharklike teeth onto the dying man's nose, and wondered.

I was horrified enough at the news to draw Mistress MacLaren's attention with a public display of gasping and swaying. She very kindly urged me to sit until I had regained my color, and I had no choice but to obey; my knees simply would not hold me up any longer. In that moment I wanted very badly to blurt out a warning to all those standing in the shop, but something held my tongue—probably fear of how these people would react. They were all to ready to believe in the Devil and his minions, and might turn their rage on Lachlan or me.

And where was Lachlan? Why had he been gone so long when he knew I must have questions? Did he know what had happened in the village? Was Bertie's death part of the reason for his absence? Surely there was some excellent cause for his nonappearance. He could never have simply impregnated me and then disappeared without a word. Could he?

I swallowed hard, twice. Heartache doesn't go down so easily when tears are welling up. Rejection and abandonment: These were my second skin, and I hated the familiar sight of them. I made myself a promise that I'd don that hair shirt only when all other possibilities were proven wrong; I didn't want to believe that once again I had been used, judged and found lacking. I had grown fearful as the day and night progressed—and with perfectly good reason, given our murderous enemy!—but it was time to decide if I trusted Lachlan and his judgment. Did I believe he was the kind of person who would abandon a pregnant lover, especially when the finman was still at large and looking for the heart buried under her floorboards?

Even as I asked the question, my gut rejected the possibility. Lachlan might have left his family once they were grown, but he would not abandon me—not when I was carrying his child and the finman was still running free. Perhaps neither of us was searching for a spouse and a life of togetherness, but we were not irresponsible and heartless. So, his absence had to mean something else.

Unfortunately, the list of something-elses was unpleasant. I found myself contemplating the idea that Lachlan could be in trouble. He could even be dead. That thought had me ducking my head and breathing slowly, again staving off a faint that made Mrs. Mac-Laren unbend so far as to pat my shoulder.

Lachlan was not dead! I ordered myself to quit being

morbid. I had quite enough troubles without borrowing from remote possibilities; he had disappeared before this without there being any sinister reason. What I needed to be thinking about was the finman and his actions in the village. The Minotaur of Greek mythology had obligingly stayed in his maze and out of human sight, but our monster was out of his lair. Herman and I would have to contend. There was no other choice.

Perhaps I could briefly put off taking action, but what would I do if Lachlan were delayed for many days and the finman returned while I was alone? Could I kill the creature on my own, a beast who'd had his heart removed but still managed to walk about and kill with impunity? I did not currently have the knowledge to do so. Gaining that knowledge seemed the first order of business, and having the beginning of a plan stiffened my spine and put strength back in my knees.

When I was able, I left the store with all the dried fruit and withered apples Mistress MacLaren had in stock. I stowed these in the basket of my bicycle, not sure how long they would hold back the cravings that roared in my belly. Perhaps I should have been more fearful of my standing in the human community, considering the circumstances. After all, a sudden pregnancy would be very hard to explain, and the judgment upon immoral women, even widows, could be very harsh indeed here. I might be shunned. Yet, this did not trouble me as much as it should have; at that moment, my mind was more consumed with the idea Lachlan could be in trouble (this in spite of my gut's fierce insistence that nothing had harmed him) or that there might be something wrong with the baby inside me—a child that could be little more than a thought in size but was already a reality to me in every other way.

Rather than returning to the cottage, which was feeling less a fortress of safety than a prison of unhappy thoughts, I went instead to the beach made visible with the tide at ebb, hoping to catch a glimpse of Lachlan. Instead I found a seal's carcass on the shore and had a moment of terror. But while it was not Lachlan, the poor beast had been attacked by sharks: I knew those bites now. Had the creature encountered the finman coming ashore to murder Bertie Stornmont?

Rising from the body, I noticed the low-tide beach was covered with silent seals huddled against the cliffs, as far from the water as topography would allow. Their eerie silence, so like Herman's on the night the finman first appeared, had the small hairs at the back of my neck rising in alarm. A frantic spin to look for danger revealed nothing, but I did not feel calm or safe. The water was too close.

I approached the seals slowly. Speaking in a voice only loud enough to rise above the wind, I said, "If any of you know Lachlan, please ask him to come back to me. I need him."

Part of me felt very silly doing this, but I did it anyway. Maybe they were just seals, but how else was I to get a message to a seal man?

The seals' heads all turned in my direction and exhaled in unison, their breath a mist that shut out the rest of the world. The earth and air shifted, and my orientation twisted and blurred as if through the lens of a spyglass focused upon something near, then something afar. Though previously inaudible, around my legs the marron grass whispered its dying secrets as it passed under the scythe of the besieging wind, not to rise again until spring. Or perhaps never. No matter what the calendar said, in an instant winter had overtaken fall, and the decades of darkness put off by its burial had caught up with the village in a matter of days. Like Dorian Gray's doomed portrait, age and decrepitude were racing in upon it. The evil beneath the village was seeping out, ensnaring everything it touched, and I could see this with my mind if not my actual eyes.

In this vision, as I watched, icy crystals of hoarfrost—what Grandmother had called *cranreuch*—bubbled out of the ground and decorated the terrified seals, sealing up their noses and mouths. It also grasped my feet and legs, raced up my body and then closed in over my head, nearly shutting out the morning light. I felt cold in a way I had never experienced, and knew it for a winter of the soul and not just the frosty season that chilled the flesh. Unable to stop a small sob of terror, I nonetheless used every bit of will within me and pushed the vision away. My frozen limbs were clumsy as I ran for my bicycle, but I forced myself to go on and not look back, just in case it wasn't all a waking dream but actually the end of the world.

Or have we eaten of the insane root
That takes the reason prisoner?
—William Shakespeare

Chapter Eighteen

Back at the cabin, my second night of uneasy dreams came and went, and it was with relief that I rose in the morning and saw that there was a break in the storms. Determined to take in some sun—and, yes, to stop behaving like a vaporish ninny who faints when she had better take action—I put on a cloak, a scarf, some old leather gloves and sensible boots, loaded my pockets with apples, and then set out for the beach to dig for cockles. During the night I'd had a sudden conviction that raw cockles drenched in honey would be delicious. Some species are poisonous, but I was convinced that I would be able to tell which kinds were safe. And I had to do something. The hunger was ravening, and the apples that I indelicately gobbled as I wrapped my scarf tightly about my neck and head barely appeased it.

Herman appeared to approve of this outing, so I assured myself that the finman couldn't be nearby.

The cat and I went to the shed together to fetch a spade and pail.

I soon discovered that there was a new acuity to my senses that was sometimes actually painful to experience. Sight, hearing, and especially my sense of smell were all now particularly intense. I was grateful that the air was fresh and crisp and the sun slightly veiled by clouds, because even the limited light made my eyes hurt.

My mind, like my stomach, seemed oddly empty. Fear and morbid rumination had been banished somehow, and I was existing solely in the moment. Occasional thoughts of the happenings in the outside world and its new uncertainties would enter my brain, but perhaps these cares felt lonely with no accompanying thought or ambitions beyond acquiring food, for they did not stay long to trouble me. My only companions were the raspy-voiced skuas that watched Herman and me closely as I worked and cheered my successes. Sometimes I would throw them small cockles, which they quickly learned how to open. Herman was polite and didn't chase the birds away, perhaps because I shared with him also.

Perhaps this harder life would be good for me. As I dug deep holes, I made note of the fact that I was getting stronger. Certainly I had no trouble digging through the wet sand to claim my prizes, though the task had always exhausted me before. Nor did I have any trouble finding the buried cockles; I *knew* where they were as surely as if I had a treasure map. It was as though my muscles and bones and all my senses were finally being put to proper use after a long sleep. For a long while, even the cold did not bother me, though the wind molested my hair and clothing.

A large shadow fell over shoulders as I worked, and I rose quickly to my feet, my spade held in what might have been a slightly threatening position. I looked about for Herman, but the cat was gone. He'd been helping me dig for cockles only a moment earlier, but as always, he was gone whenever someone else appeared. The skuas had fallen silent.

The man before me was quite tall and lean, and made me think of a racehorse. His clothes were old and his worn shirt barely hid his muscled chest and arms. I should have been alarmed at the proximity of this stranger but was not. He smelled good. He smelled a little like Lachlan, which was to say he was some mixture of spice and sin. I did not know if this pleased me or not.

"*Latha math*. I am Eonan. Lachlan's . . . cousin."

Certainly there was a general resemblance in the dark hair and eyes, though I sensed that this male was worlds younger and less serious than my missing lover.

"It is a verra great pleasure tae know thee," he continued.

"*Latha math*," I replied. "I'm Megan Culbin, Lachlan's . . . not cousin. And I am sure it will be a pleasure to know you too." I lowered the spade and stuffed it into the sand.

Eonan smiled—an expression devastating to any female heart, and I found my own breath stuttering as I took it in. "I've come tae look in on ye. Lachlan is gone tae Avocamor and may be a bittock longer than expected." When I looked blank, he explained, "He's gone tae see his family. They shall be . . . astonished at his return."

This news was a relief but was followed immediately by another uncomfortable thought. Lachlan was seeking rapprochement with his family? The ones who thought him dead?

"Good god. Why?" I asked baldly. "I mean, why now? Is something wrong?" More specifically, had I done something to cause this?

Eonan's smile widened. "Wrong? Nay. He's there because of yerself. And the bairn." The young man's smile faded at my silence. My own faded a bit too. This *did* have something to do with me. And our postcoital conversation hadn't been a hallucination; I was pregnant and Lachlan knew it as well.

"Lachlan doesnae want tae lose anither child. The bairn will be safest in Avocamor. If it is allowed . . . and it shall be."

"Good god," I said again, this time more weakly. I wasn't ready to admit to anyone that I was pregnant, let alone some strange relative of the father. I also did not know how to react to this news of Lachlan's making arrangements for me and my child that sounded like the rankest high-handedness. And what did Eonan mean about being *allowed?* Was this more of the prejudice Lachlan and Eonan had both mentioned, the bigotry that had kept Lachlan's clan from accepting his human wife? And if so, how was he so sure it would all turn out well?

I shook my head, willing myself to not get lost in the byways of speculation. "But why didn't he say something before he left? Did it not occur to him that I might worry when he disappeared?"

"Aye, it did, after he began to suspect that ye might recall what passed between ye both. He suggested first that I might want tae gae and break the happy news of his survival tae the clan meself, but I declined the honor. And that is why I am free tae be here and at yer service whilst he's away."

"And why would I not recall what had passed between us?" Later I would be embarrassed at this conversation, for it was far more likely that I would disrobe in front of stranger than discuss making love with someone I did not know. But for the moment I was too curious and annoyed to keep silent. Also, I had a strong suspicion that very little embarrassed Eonan.

"May I speak honestly, mistress?"

"Will it make me regret meeting you?" I asked in return. The question momentarily startled him out of his good humor, and I found myself amused. "I'm just teasing you. Please be honest. I'd prefer it."

Eonan smiled, comfortable again. "Weel . . . it happens that many lassies forget their encounters wi my kind. If we wish it." He did not seem repentant. In fact, the word *incorrigible* came to mind. I was very glad that I had not met him when I was young and persuadable.

"And you might wish this because . . . ?"

"If nae child comes of the union, then 'tis best a lassie doesnae carry any memories wi her," he said. " 'Tis a danger tae her and tae us."

This sounded unethical to me, but I didn't argue.

This was a discussion—one of several—I was saving for Lachlan. "But this forgetfulness doesn't work on me? This drug—"

"The *salt*," Eonan corrected. "Nae so well as Lachlan waud probably like."

The young man's voice was again slightly amused, but I found myself unable to remain annoyed. It was like feeling anger at dandelions for blowing seeds all over the garden: a pointless activity if ever there was one. Instead I said, "Well, you'd best come up to the cottage. Um . . . you don't happen to have any fruit or honey, though, do you? I've had the most awful craving for sweets, and I've eaten up nearly everything in the village."

"Nay . . ." Eonan bent down and picked up my nearly full pail and spade. We turned and started up the path, side by side but not touching, though the way was narrow. With every step we took from the sea, the wind grew stronger at our backs. I sensed that a storm wanted to push in but thought maybe Eonan was keeping it away. This did not seem strange. "But Lachlan shall be bringing something when he comes that will help wi' the cravings. They are strong?"

I sighed. "Unbelievable."

"That is marvelous news!" Eonan said.

"For whom?" I asked grumpily.

"For the bairn. A strong craving means a strong babe."

"Hmph." But I was relieved to hear this. My experience with pregnancy—even the human kind—was exactly zero, and I had been worrying that my body was not behaving normally. I had not forgotten

Lachlan saying that his other half-human child had died.

"It is a wee bit odd, yer remembering sae clearly and being sae calm in yer situation," Eonan mused. "Yer family perhaps knew of us frae before?" *Us*—the selkies. And by *before*, he meant when the MacCodrums lived in Scotland, I was sure. I wondered about this also, but had no answer.

"Granny MacCodrum might have. But she never said anything to me. My family was very . . . private about its dealings. This is all very unexpected."

"Ah—a MacCodrum! That waud explain yer resistance tae the salt."

I glanced at Eonan and laughed. "Maybe to you. I'm still baffled." But even as I said this, I felt my mind make the final separation from the old reality and accept the new one. I had a lover who wasn't human. I was pregnant, whether I wanted to be or not, and I was going to have Lachlan in my life at least for a time—again, whether I wanted him or not. And I thought I did.

I also might be headed for Avocamor, kingdom of the selkies. That, however, remained to be decided. I was not convinced that it would be the best thing for me, especially if Lachlan's people were upset by his return and inclined to dislike me and perhaps our child. However much I wished to leave Findloss and its dangers, I would not go to a place where I was hated and there was potential political turmoil.

"Eonan, I found a poem in an old book last night. It is called 'The Great Silkie of Sule Skerry.'"

"Aye. I ken this poem well." He didn't look happy.

"Why did the selkie take the baby from his mother?"

Eonan sighed. "The babe maun make the change tae sea life or die. There isnae hiding what he is, once the change happens, and history has proved that yer kind are none tae tolerant of us; our bairns were almost always murdered. And those wham were hidden still died when they stayed on land. A young selkie maun live in the sea a number of years afore he can safely shed his skin and walk on land again." He paused. "None of this waud happen if oor lovers could breed selkie females. But it is only males wham survive."

This wasn't news I wanted to hear, but I was relieved that it wasn't cruelty that made the selkies take their children from their human mothers. Given their apparent contempt for my kind, I had been inclined to wonder.

"But why human mothers at all?" I heard myself ask. "Lachlan said that he had a selkie wife once. And he had a grandson who married a faerie . . . ?" But I wasn't sure about this as I said it; a lot of my thinking was fuzzy, and I was having a hard time recalling past conversations. Had I imagined this?

"Aye, but she was the last. There've been nae female selkies born aen centuries of your time."

Lachlan had said this, I recalled now that I was reminded. It hardly seemed like the kind of thing I would forget. Unless I had been told to.

"Me own mither was of the fey," Eonan remarked.

"Really? Was she an elf?" I asked randomly.

"Nay. She was a pooka—a mischievous spirit wham could be a river horse when she willed it."

A pooka? Lachlan had said something about pookas. I concentrated hard, chasing down the memory. He'd said I should be glad I didn't know any, that pookas were tiresomely cheerful and inclined to play pranks. And this was whom Lachlan had sent to guard me?

"Megan? Lass, are ye well? Yer scowling like an angry moggie."

"Sorry if I seem absentminded. Lachlan's dru—salt—makes me . . . confused. I forget things. And I *see* things sometimes, which is a bit frightening." I was still feeling a bit discombobulated by what I had seen on the beach with the seals the previous day, though today all was calm and beautiful, if rather cold. Of my other thought I made no mention; there was no need to be impolite.

"Aye, weel, MacCodrums hae always had the Sight. Ye joost tell me if there's aught that frightens ye and I shall force it away." He said this all quite comfortably. Apparently nothing upset or surprised him.

"Did the seals come and find you?" I asked.

"The seals? Nay. Why waud they?"

"Oh, I thought that perhaps . . ." I stopped, unwilling to admit that I had been talking to animals in hope of getting a message to Lachlan. "You know about the finman?" I asked abruptly.

"Aye. That is also why I am here. Lachlan feels that ye need protecting."

"Does he?" I tried to keep my voice even. If he thought I was in danger, what the devil was he doing going off to visit relatives? Surely my pregnancy was not so urgent a matter. Not yet.

"Aye. He says yer a wee bit reckless and impulsive, and might not stay indoors where ye'd be safe. Tae be honest, he maun be very worried, because he usually says I'm the ficklest being he knows and nowt tae be trusted."

This seemed honesty indeed. I wasn't sure how to react. Finally I decided upon: "Well, fair enough. I'm glad to know he cares at least *that* much."

Eonan turned his head to study me, catching the annoyance beneath my mild tone. "Yer a bit like a tricky tide. Calm aen the surface, but running rough beneath. I've angered thee?"

I smiled wryly. "Hm, I suppose that is true—the surface calm, I mean. Be glad of it. Otherwise I might express my annoyance at you instead of at Lachlan."

"Then ye *are* annoyed."

"Lachlan seduces me . . ." This was perhaps slight exaggeration, since I had been far from unwilling. ". . . tells me I'm pregnant, gives me a drug that addles my brain and then leaves without so much as a note of farewell or thanks, all when there is a killer finman loose in the village, who has come to this very cottage more than once . . . Of course I'm annoyed!" I stopped. Jekyll was being taking over by Hyde, and none of this was Eonan's fault.

"A note. Ah, weel, selkies arenae accustomed tae writing. We've never needed it much, ye ken? Though I believe Lachlan has the knack. He learned whilst on land."

This stopped my peevishness. Of course selkies didn't need to write. They lived in the ocean. As seals. Which reminded me: "Oh my God—what have I done?" I asked, feeling suddenly cold as reality again asserted itself. "What's going to happen to me? I'm *pregnant.*"

"There noo. Ye just need a cup of tea and a bit of sit-down. Ye've exhausted yerself. All shall be well." Eonan's arm came around me. I was grateful for the warmth, though very aware that he was not Lachlan.

"Eonan, the finman has killed someone in the village. A monger called Bertie Stornmont. They're saying it was suicide, but I don't think so. The creature is getting desperate. And bold. Maybe he's gone after Lachlan as well."

"The finman was always these things," Eonan answered, reaching for the latch at the garden gate and shoving it open. The yard looked sad and dead. It seemed impossible that anything would ever grow there again. "And it waud simplify things a deal if he went after Lachlan directly. The finman might be able tae kill me, but he'll nowt escape Lachlan. My cousin is a verra dangerous man."

"Lachlan told you what the finman was after?" I asked.

"His heart, aye."

"Did he tell you that—?" But here I stopped dead; the words simply would not leave my mouth. I tried again to say that the heart was buried in the cottage floor, but all to no avail. I tried so hard to shape the syllables that my eyes watered. I could feel a prohibition to speak of this like a weight on my tongue that I couldn't shift. This was some kind of spell. "Damn it, Lachlan! Let go!"

"I beg yer pardon?" Eonan was puzzled. "Megan,

what ails ye? Can ye nowt see that it is I wham holds thee?"

"Of course I can see. It is just that Lachlan did something to me. He doesn't want me to talk about . . . *something*, and he . . . he bespelled me. That bastard! He didn't say he could do this to me! How dare he? I'll . . . I'll . . . *ooh!*" I shook off Eonan's arm. Rage had warmed me and given my weak knees strength.

"Lass, if Lachlan has silenced ye, there is a guid reason fer it. Ye maun be calm." Eonan actually sounded slightly alarmed.

"I don't care! He has no right to do things to me without asking!" I charged up to the cottage door and threw it open, not caring that it banged against the wall. I could not express sufficient rage with words alone. I spun about, ready to describe in detail what I thought of Lachlan's high-handedness, when I felt a small flutter that I knew came from the babe in my womb. The child was distressed, maybe even in pain. That stopped me dead in my tracks.

"There noo. It's the babes. Ye've upset the bairns. This is why we use the salt on ye lassies. Ye maun be calm while the babes are sae wee." Eonan had followed me inside. He closed the door softly, setting down the pail and spade. He did not take Lachlan's charm off of the door.

I made my way to the nearest chair and sat down. I was only a few feet from the finman's repulsive heart, but I felt dizzy and disinclined to move.

"So, I am to be a slave to the baby's wants as well as Lachlan's."

Eonan knelt before me. He took my hands in his, and I realized that I was very cold and again frightened. "Is that not always the way?" he asked gently. "A mither must think first of her bairns."

He was correct, but I doubt that a human baby would be able to cause so much bother so early on. How quickly did selkie children develop? "So, for nine months I will be kept drugged and coddled like a halfwit who can't be trusted with her own care?"

Eonan didn't answer.

"Eonan? The truth, please."

"Weel, the truth depends on the bairns."

"How so?"

"Let me make ye some tea." He made to rise.

"Later." I clamped down on his hands and those long, long fingers. He was far stronger than I, but allowed himself to be held in place. "What do you mean, it depends on the bairn?"

"Mayhap Lachlan had best—"

"Lachlan isn't here."

"Nay—and I'm wishing noo that I had gone tae Avocamor instead of coming here. It couldna be any more difficult." He said this with great feeling.

"You have my sympathy. Answer the question. You don't want me getting upset again. It's bad for the baby."

He stared at me, and I knew the thought that he could drug me into quiet flitted across his mind.

"Try it and I'll pound a yew stake through your heart," I warned. It was an idle threat, but the anger that made me utter it was not.

"If the bairn is a lassie, then ye'll be three seasons—

nine months—perhaps a bittock less. But that is un-likely, ye ken?"

"And if it's a boy?"

"Then ye might be carrying him longer."

"How much longer?"

"Six seasons." He said this reluctantly.

I thought it through. Twice. Then I said: "Are you saying that I may be pregnant for eighteen months?"

"Aye."

I dropped his hands. "Perhaps I had better have some tea. With whisky." My voice was hollow enough to have an echo.

"Nay. Ye cannae be drinking that poison while yer wi' child. The pups waud nae like it."

"The *what?*" I felt the blood leave my head. "What did you say?"

"The babes—er, babe," he corrected himself. "Noo, put yer head doon," he instructed, taking hold of my neck and pushing my face toward my knees. "Yer lookin' swoonish, and Lachlan willnae be pleased if he returns tae find ye sick."

I did not fight him. I was indeed feeling swoonish. I could barely contemplate the idea of giving birth to a human child; what if the baby looked like a seal?

"I hope Lachlan is bluidy grateful," I heard Eonan mutter as he headed for the kitchen. "I'd nae be doin' this if I didnae owe him my life."

The boat has left the stormy land,
Stormy sea before her—
When, O! too strong for human hand
The tempest gathered o'er her.
—Thomas Campbell,
"Lord Ullin's Daughter"

Chapter Nineteen

"Where's the cat?" I asked, almost dropping my mug as alarm overran me. I had succumbed to Eonan's coaxing and was sitting by the fire with a cup of rather weak tea. He was obviously less experienced with brewing the universal British panacea than Lachlan, but I didn't complain. "I can't leave him outside. It isn't safe. And he hates rain." It had started to pour again.

"There is nae need to fret o'er the moggie. He is weel."

"But the finman—"

"Cannae harm yer puss. He'll nowt even see him."

"He can't?" Lachlan had said this too. I began to calm. My fuzziness of thought was leaving, just as it had the time Lachlan "anesthetized" me, but I still felt distracted, as though a good portion of my mind was busy listening to something that my ears couldn't quite hear.

"Nay."

"Why not?" I asked. "Why can't he hurt the cat?"

Eonan took a breath and reached for the teapot with fingers so long they nearly could have surrounded it. He topped off my mug. "Yer moggie . . . weel, ye've heard that a cat has nine lives? It is so. It is just that, fer some cats, some lives are a wee bit different from the ones before."

"Why? How is Herman different?"

"Herman was a familiar. Ye ken this? Fergus Culbin inherited him frae the witch wha lived here before. She was a kindly creature and gentle wi' the animals and didnae deserve wha happened tae her." He didn't pause long enough for me to ask about her fate. "Weel, yer moggie was . . ." Eonan faltered. "He was sacrificed by Fergus Culbin. The idiot mage didnae realize that ye cannae kill a witch's cat sae simply."

"Sacrificed?" I recalled Fergus's journal. He had planned to kill the cat and mummify him so that he could use the corpse to hunt for the lost Spanish gold. But, in spite of the bag of gold in the desk, I had assumed that Fergus died before he got around to completion. It was a good thing the bastard was dead, or I would have had to do something terribly unpleasant to him, probably involving the iron shackles and the yew beater.

"Yer moggie was slain by a mage. But he wasnae a verra competent mage, and since yer moggie wasnae joost a cat, he's come back." Eonan thought for a moment and spoke mostly to himself. "Think ye that Fergus Culbin was trying tae steal the finman's powers wi' a blood sacrifice? Was that why he killed the moggie? The man was a vile sneak-thief."

"I don't care about Fergus," I snapped. This was a lie, of course; I cared, but in that moment I cared about Herman more. "Herman is not a ghost. Or a mummy. And he isn't out for revenge or anything nasty," I insisted.

"Nay. He isnae," Eonan agreed.

"Then what is he, and why would he come back?" I swallowed hard, thinking of the finman. How many undead things had come back here looking for Fergus?

Lachlan's cousin sighed, apparently feeling that the more he explained, the more he would have to explain. And he was correct, which was probably why his cousin had opted for silence on so many subjects.

"Yer moggie is an imp. Ye can only kill them in verra specific ways."

"An imp?" I was spending a great deal of time repeating Eonan's words, but my brain seemed unwilling or unable to take them in on the first try. "I haven't read about imps. What are they?"

"Aye, weel . . . imps can be many things: cats, rats, sometimes sma dogs or hares or birds. They live a lang time, a verra lang time. And they need . . ." Another pause as he picked his words carefully. "They prefer a certain kind of companion. Like a witch or a mage."

A witch? Did he mean me? I started to ask, but decided I didn't want to hear the answer. Instead I said: "So, in summation, our situation is as follows: Fergus, in need of magic, probably to find buried Spanish treasure, first tried to kill his cat. When that didn't work, he talked my husband into waylaying and stealing a heart from a finman. But not just any finman. They chose the wickedest and most powerful monster around—one who had already buried this village once."

"Aye," Eonan agreed. "Mayhap Fergus thought it best tae stick wi the devil he knew. Perhaps he had a spell tae contact this finman too. They are nowt sae easy to meet, ye ken?"

"I ken that Fergus wasn't merely an incompetent mage. He could have qualified as the village idiot!" I gulped some tea, glad that it wasn't hot enough to burn. "And Duncan was one too, if he helped."

"He was o'erqualified as an idiot," Eonan suggested. I didn't ask if he meant Duncan or Fergus. "Even a fool waud know better. 'Tis the sheer insanity o' the act that has had Lachlan sae baffled and wondering if there is mair going on."

There was a silence and I eventually asked, "Why didn't Lachlan tell me this? Does he not trust me? I thought surely after . . . well, all that has passed between us, that he would be willing to confide more."

Eonan actually looked uncomfortable. "Lass, ye must understand aboot the auld king."

"Yes? Understand what?" I got up and poked at the fire with more force than was necessary. "That he's stubborn, secretive and untrusting?" Like my family. Like Duncan. Like me—though I hadn't ever thought of myself that way before. Still, the shoe fit a bit too well. As was the habit in my family, I had come home from Duncan's funeral and brushed the unhappy and rather dirty memory of my strange marriage under the parlor rug and tried my best to do the out-of-sight-out-of-mind trick. But squint as I would, the bulge never got any smaller or any easier to look at. And even having fled to Scotland I could not escape it, since one can never outrun one's memory.

Well, I'd had enough of sweeping unpleasant things under the rug. There wasn't any more room under there. I vowed that from here on out I would face the unpleasant things rather than hiding from them.

"Lachlan . . . he is verra old," Eonan was saying. "The eldest of all of us. He was born intae an age when there were great wars and our males were ca'ed tae bloody battle at an early age. He'd very little gentleness as a pup, and was given young tae a wizard fer training when he was only nine seasons auld. He learned tae keep his secrets or suffer."

These words made my heart clutch a little. I could only barely imagine Lachlan as a child, but the thought of any young boy being taken from his mother and given to someone for training was horrifying. Particularly someone who would make a child suffer.

"His first wife . . . weel, she was of a guid family. Her clansmen were strong allies and she made a decent consort fer a king. But there was little love there. It was tae his second wife that he gave his heart. And she didnae live long after giving birth tae their son. I think for a time he was a bit mad wi' the loss. The family wasnae verra understanding. It was then he renounced his clan and disappeared."

"But why? Was he ashamed of loving her? Did he actually agree with the rest of his clan that she wasn't good enough for him?" There was a bit of self-interest in this question, I have to admit.

"Nay, nowt a bit of it. Understand, wi' oor people yer king 'til ye die. Lachlan didnae want the honor, and he kenned that anither should lead us when he was sae weakened wi' grief and anger at his own clan. Weel, lead *them*. I wasnae even born yet." This was said with the typical smugness of a human youth, and I had to smile at the similarity.

"How did you meet Lachlan?"

"In happened in the year of the Great Inundation. I was still a pup and couldnae change at will. I'd been caught in a fisherman's net when the boat capsized and was dragged down tae the bottom of the sea. Lachlan rescued me. He got me tae shore and then left at once. I didnae guess wham he was then."

I thought of how horrible a death this could have been, and tried not to show my horror at what had nearly been his fate. "You were very fortunate."

Eonan nodded and went on: "Fer a long while he traveled the warld. It isnae oor way tae leave the clan, but Lachlan went and lived wi' the merrows and mermen and other sea folk. I found him only by chance many seasons later and he swore me tae secrecy. The clan was thriving and he didnae want tae be king again. He still missed his wife and couldnae forgive them fer their treatment of her. They didnae ken at the beginning that soon the selkie women waud die out forever and we waud all be seeking wives among the humans and especially the fey. They didnae want tae believe this horrible thing."

"Poor man," I whispered, staring into the flames. I hadn't loved Duncan that way, but I could easily imagine the huge hole the death of Lachlan's wife had torn in his life. Certainly I understood the anger at his unsympathetic family.

"Ladies were different then tae. They were . . . mair biddable. He isnae yet accustomed tae the modern lassies. And he hasne been thinking of finding anither wife. Ye've surprised him. Ye'll need patience."

"Let us hope that this old dog can learn a new trick," I muttered, resisting the urge to snort. "Duncan rather used up my patience."

"Pardon?" Eonan sounded startled.

"It's just an expression." I put up the poker and returned to my chair. I'd had enough of hearing about Lachlan's unhappy past and felt that to speak any more of it without his presence was to indulge in gossip. "So, what now? You stay here playing guard dog until Lachlan returns?"

"Aye—but I want tae be clear. I am nowt a dog. I am selkie wi' a bit of pooka thrown in." He gave me a look.

"I understand," I said gravely. "Shall we continue to search for the finman during the day?"

Eonan looked shocked. "Are ye daft? Lachlan waud skin me. Yer tae stay inside and keep safe. We leave the searching tae Lachlan."

"You don't think I make good bait to draw the finman out?"

"Aye, excellent bait. And Lachlan willnae stand fer it."

I did snort that time, but didn't argue. Even young dogs needed a little while to learn new behaviors. I got up and headed for the kitchen.

"What are ye aboot?" This was said with some alarm, as though I might find a way to end my benign confinement by crawling out a window barely wide enough to accommodate a cat.

"Looking for the last of the honey. I'm going to eat those cockles I dug up."

"Wi'out cooking them?" He sounded hopeful.

"Definitely. But I need honey." I added: "Lachlan better hurry. I need . . . something. Sweets. Maybe they have a sweetshop in Keil. I am so hungry all the time, and nothing I eat helps!" It was driving me mad.

"He shallna linger unnecessarily," Eonan promised, though he sounded uneasy for the first time. "Yer very important tae him."

"I hope so. Because I don't think I can do this alone." This I said softly. Leaning over a much-scarred work table, I cracked open a shutter and whistled for the cat. When he didn't appear, I asked, "Will Herman come back while you're here?" In spite of reassurances that he would come to no harm, I did not feel easy with the feline absent.

"Mayhap he will. Pookas and imps are close kin. And, after all, what's not tae like?"

Eonan proved correct. Herman did appear when we sat down to eat, and he assisted us with the remaining raw cockles. He didn't want them cooked, either, but permitted me to pry open the shells.

The cat kept his distance from Eonan, but he

showed none of the hostility or shyness that he had with Lachlan or the finman. Though neither of the two males got close to the other, I noticed that each scented the other from time to time. Their flaring nostrils made them look enough alike that I couldn't help but chuckle.

"Why did ye marry a Culbin?" Eonan asked suddenly, after a longish silence. "I hae thought on it and can see nae reason why ye'd be sae daft."

The words were rude but the tone was not. Lachlan's cousin reminded me of a precocious child who did not quite have the knack of good manners yet. He also reminded me, even more so than my lover, that these creatures were profoundly estranged from the concerns and motivators of my world.

"It was hope, mostly." Then I thought for a moment about what I had said. "My world was a very small one—a rather secretive one, it now seems—and I never felt I belonged."

When Eonan nodded encouragingly, I continued. "I hoped that by marrying Duncan my world would enlarge. And so it has." I laughed wryly. "Also, let us not forget the power of flattery to turn a young woman's head. Duncan courted me diligently, relentlessly even. And now I know why. He wanted someone to fight off the finman."

"Ye shouldna blame yerself, lass. It was wrong of yer people tae move away frae the place they belonged. Yer clan belongs here, near the sea. The way ye felt was yer true nature, trying tae get ye back home. Duncan took advantage of ye in yer weakness. It is the way of vile men to use kind women."

I nodded, finally feeling comforted after all the blame that had been heaped on me by my friends and family. "Eonan, I've been thinking," I said, trying without much success to wipe honey off of my fingers. Herman and Eonan had declined to try my new recipe of raw cockles in honey, and were consequently a deal more tidy. "Could there be more than one finman at work here?"

He stared at me. "Why are ye asking? Fer that matter, why are ye thinking? Ye should be fast asleep after that enormous meal."

I gave him what I hoped was a withering look. Though willing to discuss many more things than Lachlan, he certainly was mistrustful of my cooperation with his and Lachlan's plan for my safety.

"This finman seems to be everywhere, and he is managing to evade both Lachlan and me. One day he was in the vaults of the church, but he also seemed to be in sea caves up the coast where Lachlan was hunting. I know that he's a powerful magical being, but he can't be omnipresent. *Can* he? It just occurred to me that 'he' might appear more all-pervading if there were more than one of him."

Eonan was thoughtful. "All finmen are born twins," he admitted slowly. "In that they are like . . ." He stopped, looking guilty.

"Like what?" I asked.

"Nithing. It is just common in sea folk. Like with water kelpies."

"So there could indeed be two of them at work. Our finman might not be doing everything on his own. He might actually be holed up in a sea cave somewhere, nursing his injuries and sending his brother ashore to search while he makes mischief with the tides and weather."

"I am doubtful. In finmen, the stronger twin always eats the brother. If they both live, then the power is halved between them." I was speechless with disgust at this casual pronouncement, but Eonan continued: "They hae anither nasty trick, however. They can enslave any weaker mind that comes too close to their sphere of influence. And this one is a powerful sorcerer. It might be that he found someone else wi' magical abilities and has been using them. Animals too are at his call."

"Like sharks," I said, remembering how Lachlan had been attacked. Thinking of him made my heart contract a little. I prayed again that he was well, even if he was stubborn and pigheaded and bossy.

"Aye, like sharks—and also ither weaker finmen." A pause. "Or humans. Though this requires greater effort and is not often done."

"So there could be more than two enemies working together. Is there any way to find out if this is true?" I took a breath as I considered something else. "Never mind *that;* is there any way to get word to Lachlan about what we suspect? I don't want him walking into a trap, and I fear he may be, since the finman—either the finman or his slave—isn't here now, and could be off lying in wait for him."

"How dae ye ken the finman is not aboot?"

"The weather. The cat." I thought about it. "And I don't see or feel him. I could sense the last time he was near. He smelled bad." It was just something I knew, a conviction made more certain by my increased sensitivity.

Eonan didn't dispute this pronouncement. Instead, he ruminated in a surprisingly serious manner. "Mayhap I could gae oot at twilight and try tae send a message. It waud be useless tae gae now."

I noticed that he didn't tell me how he was going to do this or why he couldn't do anything during daylight hours. I was very curious about this matter, but didn't press him for details of selkie communication; it was one more thing for Lachlan to explain—if he were willing.

"Herman and I will be fine while you're gone," I assured him quickly. "We have Lachlan's talisman for the door. And Herman is a very good guard cat."

Eonan nodded. "Ye'd have tae bar the door against everyone, though. Yer neighbors, strangers—everyone. Ye couldna make a single exception."

"I know." It was frightening to think that any of my neighbors could be overshadowed by this monster, but after what had happened to Bertie Stornmont, I did not try to deny the possibility. No sane person would drink a bottle of lye, and it would take great power and magic to force a person to do it.

When night came silently lay
Dead on Culloden Field
—Alexander Cowan

Chapter Twenty

How could wind blow from every direction? Somehow it did, and the storm carried the taint of damnation in the form of brimstone and rot on its every eddying current. But I had no sense of the finman nearby, so I remained convinced of the necessity of carrying out our plan.

I could tell that Eonan was uneasy about leaving me unprotected, and I almost stopped him a few times, since there was danger for him as well. But then I thought of Lachlan, and the fear that clutched me was greater than any dread caused by the smell of the wind. "Why does it always storm?" I muttered.

Perhaps to him the answer was obvious, for Eonan sounded nearly prosaic. "The finman needs the lightning tae beat his stolen heart."

I didn't like this, but it made horrifying sense. I had once seen a demonstration where current was passed through a dead frog, making his legs kick. And was it not lightning that brought Frankenstein's monster to life?

"Be very careful," I said quietly, checking the talisman on the door. "And maybe you should bring your skin to the cottage when you return. There is a secret room. We could hide it there."

Eonan nodded once, and I felt honored that he trusted me. It was more than Lachlan had done, I thought with some bitterness.

"Aye, and ye have a care yerself as well. Bar the door ahind me, and dae not open it unless yer moggie says it is safe." Eonan smiled at Herman, and I swear the cat nodded in response. Then Eonan was gone, into the twilit storm, and Herman and I were alone.

"Go with God," I whispered belatedly, aware that perhaps this was not the right thing to say to a selkie but needing to say something. I didn't know any other blessing, except, "May the wind rise up to greet you," and that didn't seem appropriate, given the breath of Hell being exhaled that night.

I barred the door, made up the fire and then sat down with another of Fergus's books. This time I did not read closely but skimmed until I found a section on selkies. This I read diligently, translating slowly and perhaps inaccurately what I could out of the old Gaelic. Herman took up a position on the table beside me, careful not to block the lamplight but close enough to reach out a paw and touch me if he needed to get my attention. He didn't mind that I occasionally scratched him under the chin. In spite of Eonan's belief that Herman was an imp, I could not in any way detect that he was different from other cats. And yet I knew he had to be.

"I'm glad you're my kitty," I told him once, and he obliged me with a few rough purrs.

I read all night and into the dawn, and Eonan did not return. Once an hour had passed, the tiniest tendrils of unease began to curl around my heart. Dread's touch was light, as soft as the moonlight that found its way through the clouds and past my open shutters to crawl up my arms, but I felt it all the same. And though I wanted to deny it, I could not repudiate the growing alarm that came with Eonan's prolonged absence. Certainty that something had gone awry grew with every passing hour until I was near panic.

After the sun was well up, we gave in to our fears; a weary Herman and I fetched the yew beater and iron shackles from my bedroom, then unbolted the door and went to find Lachlan's missing cousin. It was a desperate act, yet I felt I had no choice. At the edge of the dizzying path that ran along the cliff edge, common sense—a commodity I had been lacking for some time—briefly asserted itself and I slowed my steps. But fear for Eonan could overcome every emotion, and even sensibleness, and I found my footsteps quickening again almost immediately.

The cat led the way. It never occurred to me not to follow him. My belief in his supernatural makeup was by now absolute. I was afraid of our task, of course, but guilt spurred me on. Lachlan's cousin had gone out into the night as a favor to me. If he had been killed or captured, the fault was mine. The thought of this was unacceptable, something I could not live with. And there was other guilt besides. I had hidden emotionally from my husband when he needed me and—though I didn't know it at the time—left him to be eaten alive by fear of this monster who stalked Findloss village. Maybe the fear was earned if Duncan had helped Fergus steal the finman's heart, but the creature was evil and had been for a very long time. At the beast's door lay the deaths of everyone buried in Findloss: Bertie Stornmont, some poor nameless merman, and probably countless others besides. He wasn't going to get the chance to harm anyone else important to me. He was not going to harm Eonan.

Hunger rode me but I ignored it as best I could. Fear helped suppress my worst cravings. I did my best to remain calm and not upset the baby, but I know the child was frequently disturbed and I found myself stroking my belly in an attempt to calm it. In concession to my new state, I stayed far from the cliff edge where the blustery wind was apt to kick up suddenly. The fog was thick and eddying in strange and most likely unnatural ways, first parting and then closing in a swirling dance whose rhythms I could not discern but was still disconcertingly aware of.

Herman seemed to know where he was going. Whether he followed the beast's spoor or Eonan's footsteps, I could not say, but he led me to the narrow stretch of beach I had traversed on my last walk and then to the faerie mound. We went slowly, the cat having no love of wet feet and I being in no haste to return to the cave where I had nearly drowned, especially if the monster were waiting within.

Perched atop a large flat stone, waiting for the tide

to pull back from the last sandbar, I caught my first glimpse of the finman. I knew immediately what he was. Perhaps once he had been able to pass for human, but not anymore. We were perched up high, perhaps a dozen feet above his molding head as he stalked out of the surf. The wound around the creature's stolen heart was covered in what looked like dead ticks and leeches. These parasites had supped heavily of the evil flesh, and it had killed them. Now they were beginning to rot. With my heightened senses I could smell them too. They were an odor distinct from his vile scent that made me silently gag.

Herman was doing his best to flatten himself onto the rock. His ears were laid back and his lips curled in a frozen snarl. It might be that the finman couldn't hurt him because he was nimble enough to escape, but I knew Herman would not desert me and that this protective loyalty placed him in danger.

Once fully ashore, the finman dropped to his tentacles and knees and began convulsing. His skin was leprous. Iridescent slime began running out of every orifice—he had a couple of extra orifices that I assumed were gills—and turning black in the air. He let out a roar that sounded like no animal on earth and I saw the rows of sharklike teeth. Then, the fit past, he rose back onto his bowed but muscular legs and continued toward the dreaded cave.

This creature had Eonan? The awful answer was yes. Had Eonan been elsewhere, I felt sure Herman would not have brought me here.

Our enemy glanced up at us only once. As he did, I looked into the finman's face and it was insanity made flesh. A terrible evil animated this creature, and it seemed to me that his body was stretched to its limit, trying to contain a multitude of kidnapped souls that seemed to kick at the flesh. At last fog folded itself around the figure, hiding the horror from my sight.

Such things were not part of the natural world! Not my natural world. And yet, here it was: A genuine monster more horrible than anything in Grimm's. I scooped up Herman, turned the other way and fled up the cliff, in spite of my blindness in the putrid mist and the danger of falling. I thought I heard stealthy noises behind me, but it might well have only been blood racing in terrified circles as it tried to outrun the horror in my brain.

I did not slow or look back to see if I was being chased until we broke free of the fog and Herman had calmed, but then I paused and took stock. I knew now where the finman was hiding. What I needed was a plan and some weapon more fearsome than a carpet beater. What could kill a being that survived with no heart? With nothing else, I found myself recoursing to prayer.

Though their chords like thunder roll,
When at Beltane brims the bowl
Thou'rt the music of my soul.
——"The Maiden of Morven"

Chapter Twenty-one

I had not gone far when I found a selkie footprint filled with rainwater. My nose was not keen enough to tell me whether it belonged to Eonan or Lachlan—or some other—but the print was enough to re-engage my logic and return a degree of calm . . . and cause me to take an action suggested by my reading in Fergus's library. Not stopping to consider what might happen if this print belonged to someone other than Lachlan or Eonan, I dropped to my knees and leaned over the mark, so like a human's but with the blur of webbing between the toes; and then, though the act was bestial, I drank from that small puddle until I was lapping earth. All my instincts demanded it.

I tasted blood and knew that the mark was not Lachlan's. It had to be from Eonan or some other. I sat back on my heels and waited for the dizziness and interference with cognitive function I had experienced after tasting Lachlan's salt, but it never came—perhaps because this selkie was younger and perhaps he was not all selkie? Either way, instead of dazed I felt stronger and more energized, though perhaps less capable of removing emotion from reason as I tried to think my way through my growing worry about the finman's presence. I was filled with a new instinct that overrode human logic, and suddenly I knew what I needed to do, even if the idea of engaging in an ancient magical ritual was both strangely thrilling and terrifying.

I can swim tolerably well in a calm lake or pond; the heaving sea I faced was another matter entirely. Whipped into a rage by wind and lightning—and possibly by the finman himself—there was danger both above and below, and the storm and tide were coming nearer all the time. Still, I knew that I could not run away from this enemy if there were any chance that Eonan was in danger; nor could I wait there on the beach with the tide on the turn. Options were a bit limited. Still, I would never again retreat into a sea cave with the tide chasing me to wait and die; if I were to drown, let it be in the open, performing heroic deeds and not cowering in the dark.

Was I insane then? Perhaps. My courage was bolstered by rage, which put steel in my spine and in my quaking knees. This finman had come into my village and was moving about with the arrogance of a bully who has never been defeated in a fair fight. I didn't believe that all alone I was strong enough to defeat the creature; no indeed, the entire village probably could not kill him. But cower or clash, the result would be the same: a war. And innocents were not being spared in this struggle because they hid or refused to take sides. If I did not die now, there was every chance that I—and everyone in the village—would die later. But if I acted swiftly, perhaps I could summon help.

Abandoning the shackles and beater, and Herman, leaving them all on their safe perch on some rocks, I climbed down a short way into the churning surf. The water stung and was unpleasantly cold, but this only helped me fill the ocean with my ready tears. The sea, already salty, didn't seem to notice or care, but I hoped with all my heart that Lachlan would. If the legends in Fergus's book were true, by the time my seventh tear hit the waves, my lover—and any other selkie who encountered them—would receive my summons and have to answer if he were at all capable of doing so. If Lachlan's salt bound me to him, so then did my tears—*my* salt—bind him to me. For once, I was on the other end of the leash. If the legends were true.

Message sent, I wiped my face and looked about in hopeful expectation. Indeed, I found immediately that part of my earlier prayer had been answered. Floating in the water beside me was some sort of javelin or gaff with its end broken off in a sharp point, probably lost from a fishing boat. Thanks to my increased sensitivity, I knew it was made of yew. I had been given a weapon. It would not be pleasant to hold, but I would manage.

Dresses are not made for swimming or climbing, so I removed mine and tossed it to where I could retrieve it later, up on a rock that I hoped would be above the highest tide. A last remnant of modesty had me hoping that I would not encounter any neighbor in this state of undress, but my unrestricted movement seemed imperative.

Herman waited for me on a tall rock. He was calmer but still looked rather feral and I did not try to pet him. He was also sandy and wet, and I had the feeling that he'd rolled in Eonan's footprint.

"We need to find another way into the finman's cave," I said to the cat. "If we go in the front, we will surely drown or be captured."

The feline turned and took a different path over the rocks. As before, I followed, and again Herman found an entrance among the boulders. That it belonged to the finman, I did not doubt for an instant. Even without the cat's certainty, there was a yellowed flapping husk—a human skin and loosely connected bones—flung over a nearby cleft boulder where a bloated grayish crab watched me with some alarm. Were these remains, perhaps of a neighbor, a prize, or some trophy on display? A warning to trespassers? Or were they simply a cast-off lunch, of no more importance than crumbs left behind at a picnic? At least the husk was not Eonan. This hapless corpse had red hair.

I shuddered, fighting another wave of hunger and also sudden bile. Horrible things had happened here. Often. The very walls sweated with fear at what they had witnessed, and thanks to the leftover salt and perhaps selkie blood I had ingested I was aware of it all. A heavy weight was pressing down on this part of the world, and the air was filled with the stench of rage and insanity. Here there be monsters. There was also a noise, liquid but terrible even at a distance: If leprosy could talk, if tumors had a voice, this was what they would sound like. I knew it was the finman, chanting. There would be no waving the white flag of surrender if he caught me in his lair.

I took a deep breath and straightened my slumped spine. Losing my life was not what I wanted, but so much worse would it be to lose my soul to this creature. I would not allow it to happen. I would kill myself first. And the babe.

This last thought made me livid, and a new maternal ferocity arose in me. This creature would not get my child.

Tired of waiting, Herman growled softly and disappeared among the rocks. I ventured after him into the narrow darkness, this time untroubled by the fading light because my eyesight had been enhanced along with all my other senses.

Heaps of rotting sea wrack were jumbled together with uprooted gorse and what looked like human finger bones that crunched unpleasantly whenever underfoot. Every inch of putrescent flotsam was covered with gray misshapen crabs as yet too small and bloodless to compete with their shell-covered brethren out in the tide pools along the shore. The cavern was like a monster's stomach as it digested a foul meal, and somewhere in these tunnels was the finman, lodged there as a parasite, a tumor growing inside the stony caves and eating away at its host. I feared that Lachlan and the village had left it too long: One way or another, Findloss was doomed and possibly damned. Our only hope seemed flight before disaster struck again.

A green darkness surrounded me as I descended into the cave. The relentless tides, or perhaps the finman's magic, had by millennia of grit-laced torrent cloven out a passage from the heart of the stone, but the channel I traversed was not made for those who went about on two legs. I was soon forced to my hands and knees, my freezing fingers and bare limbs making reluctant contact with the green phosphorescence of the walls, which was my only light. The near darkness was Plutonian, and cold as the grave, and the tunnel soon doubled back on itself and headed away from the land and down toward the roaring sea. I was terribly grateful that Herman remained at my side. Anger could carry me a long way, but the cat's presence was a huge comfort.

The horrible chanting ceased, and I knew from Herman's more relaxed posture that the finman had again departed his cave by some other exit. Emboldened, I crawled faster, uncaring of the damage being done to my body by the rough stone. Every instinct was shouting that Eonan was near. I was also certain that he was wounded.

On I crawled, rounding a corner that required me to turn on my side and squeeze through the smallest of gaps—leaving some of my chemise behind—and then I was in my enemy's lair. I got to my feet at once. The floor was covered in bones: some human, most not. I did not look at them in any detail or try to count the remains.

Herman yowled and sprang on top of what I think was a shark's carcass. Hurrying over to the rotting body with steps that showed no respect for the scattered dead, I rushed to the pile where the cat waited and immediately found a seal skin under the decayed remains. Only, it wasn't a seal skin; it belonged to a selkie and my nose told me that it was Eonan's.

I examined the skin carefully, inspecting it for wounds with my eyes and nose. There were none that I could see, and the inside was not bloody, as I had half expected. It was wondrously soft and smelled of Eonan. It was also warm, a living thing even without its owner.

"But why is it here?" I asked Herman. "Surely he needed it to swim to wherever he was going."

The cat moaned angrily and thrashed his tail. He remained with me but was hating every moment.

"Did the finman steal it? Perhaps Eonan didn't need his skin and left it on the beach while . . ." I stopped. I had finally found a wound. It wasn't large. In fact, it was no bigger than an arrow hole, but it was very near where a human heart would be.

I dropped to my hands and knees, heedless of the slime. I searched with eyes and nose and fingertips, but found none of Eonan's blood on the floor. The injury had not happened here.

"Herman, we have to find Eonan. He's hurt." Not dead. I refused to believe that he was dead. Far better to believe that he had been attacked in the water and shed his skin so that he could escape on land. The finman had captured the skin and brought it here, perhaps to perform magic upon it later. Or perhaps only to deprive Eonan of it. Or maybe to attempt to wear it . . . ?

The last thought was blasphemous. Herman and I exited the cave with more speed than I had used in entering, even burdened with Eonan's skin settled on my shoulders as if it had been tailored for my use.

Outside, the storm had closed in. The clouds were so charged with electricity that it made my teeth hurt, and the color that limned them was a strange shade of green that was exceedingly unnatural. My blood thrummed with terror-driven excitement and beat at my brain with a roar louder even than the sea breaking on the rocks and likely flooding the cave I had just vacated. I did not feel the cold, though. Eonan's fur kept me warm.

"Too late, you evil bastard," I muttered. "We're out and we have the skin."

The wind snatched all smell away as quickly as my nose could grab it, but Herman's senses were better. Ignoring the rain and wind that threatened to blow him bodily away, we traveled toward the faerie mound where I had seen the corpse candle. I had done my level best to forget about that terrifying day, but that isn't the sort of memory that fades quickly, and I knew that a corpse candle could not only mark where a body had been, but also where a body was going to be. Nothing had suggested particularly that it would be Eonan's body I found, but I had to look.

We forded a sea-bound stream that ran dangerously fast between sea-tumbled boulders with surfaces gritty and abrasive to the skin. Or, I did the fording; Herman was held in my arms as I crossed the frothing water. I should have been debilitated with cold, but was not. Whatever changes had come over my body, they allowed me to ignore the freezing water despite being all too aware of its power.

Our path turned inland and we had to pass next through a valley of eerie shell dunes. It was not so much an avian midden as a graveyard, a place where many birds through many centuries had made their meals, and the bank of abandoned mussel and oyster shells rose up to nearly twice my height and hid us completely from the furious sea that whipped the shore. The way through the bleached shell hills was slippery, and the sharp-edged shells grabbed at my shoes. Fearing that he would injure the pads of his paws, I continued to carry Herman. I went slowly, but in spite of my best efforts I often found myself off balance and on the verge of falling. This meant slowing the pace even more, though urgency beat at me with every beat of my quickened heart, and I felt the desire of the skin I carried to be reunited with its owner.

Disaster was avoided until Herman and I emerged on the sea side of the mound. Perhaps the wind's constant battering had had an effect, or maybe it was a deliberate trap laid by the finman. Whichever, the more solid earth gave way to slick sand. The soil beneath my boot-shod feet became unsound, my weight shifted the fragile crust of sand and I suddenly found the shell-strewn earth rushing at me with upthrust blades of white and gray.

"Christ on a crutch!" I gasped. I managed to toss Herman onto a rock before I fell. Startled birds that had been sheltering silently suddenly screamed back at me and fled into the air as I toppled, hands outstretched. The impact was hard, and it forced painful shards of broken shell into my palms and knees with enough force to slice through my wrinkled skin and draw blood.

Tears started to my eyes as the pain invaded my body, but I did not cry out again or even try to roll away from the shells. Before me lay a quaking seal pup, trapped under a pile of displaced stones. My breath washed over it, brushing its delicate fur. It was wrapped in sea wrack from neck to flippers. The pup was hiding its tiny face in terror. There was a small amount of blood.

Moved by a new compassion for this creature—for all creatures, but especially this one, who was doubtless being hunted by the finman and who had fled inland looking for shelter—I tore off the hem of my tattered chemise. This pup was not my pup, but it was someone's child, and I felt protective of it.

"It's all right," I whispered softly, pitching my voice like a gentle sigh. "I'm sorry I frightened you. We'll get that flipper out straightaway. Please don't be frightened."

Slowly, I removed the rocks with my bleeding hands and carefully freed the pup's flipper, which did not seem broken, if bruised and a little bloodied. With infinite care, I cleaned the tiny wound. The pup did not fight me. It seemed frozen with fear, its trembling body unable to move and the soft panting breaths through its tiny nose the only sign that it still lived.

"There now," I said gently to the terror-stricken seal as I slowly backed away. "We are all done. You can be off now, if that's what you want. There is some smoother sand just a ways up the beach. You can rest there."

The seal slowly turned its head and looked first at its flipper and then to me. Its eyes were wide and black and unblinking, but it stopped shivering. Making a small noise, which I chose to think of as thanks, it turned toward the sea and began to hump away.

"Good-bye. Be careful!"

Abandoned except for Herman and feeling suddenly more alone than I ever had in my life, I scrambled to my feet and inspected the damage to my person. Fortunately, this turned out to be minimal. I had apparently imagined the wounds to be more serious than they were, hallucinating the white knives piercing my hands and knees. The shells *had* cut me, but only shallowly, and the cuts were already closed and had stopped stinging. A few dabs of my ruined chemise removed the last of the damp blood from my left palm, which was the worse afflicted.

Herman mewed and patted my leg, reminding me of our task. Looking down I noticed that I had no shadow. This was because the sun was hidden by the storm, I assured myself.

"Yes. I'm ready now."

With extra caution, Herman and I worked our way slowly to the edge of the shell dunes, where flocks of alarmed birds impatiently awaited our departure from their feeding grounds. Of the young seal there was no sign. I prayed that he was safe away from the violent sea and the vicious finman. The birds continued to circle and screech, so I muttered an apology for disturbing them before Herman and I continued on our way. The need to find Eonan was stronger than ever.

Did the little mermaids ride
Through the ocean's foamy tide . . .
Do the little mermaids weep
In their sea caves, fathoms deep . . .
—A. S. Hardy

Chapter Twenty-two

Worried as I was, my body eventually insisted that I stop for food—the condemned required a last meal, I thought grimly. Herman looked on in admiration as I raided a tide pool and ate almost everything in it, crunching through shells when they were too stubborn to open. The rain had eased some and the unnatural tide was again on the wane, but Herman kept his distance from the turbulent water as I dined, suspicious of the stray waves that sometimes snatched at us.

My appearance was probably horrible. What I could see of my hair was snarled, and I could not have been attractive, stuffing what I had previously considered inedible creatures into my mouth and eating them raw. It was a meal that would turn the strongest stomach, but I ate it anyway.

As I studied a sea urchin, wondering mercilessly how to get past its spines, I thought about the people in Findloss village and how none had shown their faces the last couple of days. The fishermen, spending all their lives on the sea, had surely noticed the un-natural patterns of the tides. Given their religious in-clinations, they probably blamed it on the Devil and not a finman, but one did have to wonder why they hadn't left Findloss if their belief in evil was so strong. Could the finman somehow be influencing them to stay—perhaps because he knew that one of them had his heart and he would not be content until he had systematically questioned everyone? Or might it be Lachlan using some form of selkie magic to lull people's suspicions so they wouldn't flee and in turn lead the finman away? If the finman were responsible, I feared that all witnesses to his crimes would only be found with a shovel. Or not found at all because they were in the belly of a shark.

"Lachlan, where are you?" I asked, putting the ur-chin aside as I began to feel a bit nauseated. It was less my meal than disgust with my murderous glut-tony: I had in the space of only a few hours devolved into an animal. And it was at least partly Lachlan's fault.

I don't enjoy facing uncomfortable truths about myself, but I will do it when forced. The truth of the day was that I had a bad habit of being attracted to men who were secretive and incomprehensible and who probably did not have my best interests at heart. Men who disappeared. My consolation prize was hav-ing a child at last, and I was glad for this, if also worried about how very odd such a child might be, and if I were fit to care for it.

These insights rated a sigh and then a word or two of blasphemy, though I did apologize to the Lord afterward because it wasn't He who had gotten me pregnant and then disappeared.

It seemed I was heard and forgiven. The clouds parted—perhaps forcibly, if Lachlan were nearing— and weak sun shone through. But this only brought the illusion of warmth; the day remained cold. It was winter, the dying time of year: Life-giving daylight lessened with every cycle of the sun.

The fear that had propelled me into barely thought-out action was all at once like an indigestible lump in my gut. Or perhaps it was only my lunch taking revenge. I knew that I could not dwell on my anxiety or I would be enfeebled. If I weakened, Eonan might die. Lachlan too. And yet . . .

Herman climbed in my lap and began to purr.

"I appreciate the gesture and that you have stayed with me," I said, stroking his warm fur and feeling almost normal for the first time in hours. It is perhaps the greatest virtue of cats that they can radiate calm under even the most trying of circumstances.

As I squatted on the slick rock, petting Herman, a man walked out of the receding tide, pulling off a mask and some kind of cloak. For a moment I saw him not as a whole being but as a series of isolated and foreign features—dark eyes, midnight hair, lips pressed thin by worry. Then the seal skin slipped off completely and he was my familiar Lachlan again.

He saw me and stopped, still as a statue and just as

beautiful—and, in that moment, as inanimate and inhuman. My emotions made certain that my body missed no clichéd reaction: I got faint, forgot to breathe and even put a hand to my heart. I forgot to be angry. My only comfort is that I managed to stop myself before I devolved into an actress in a farce and swooned or threw myself on his naked chest and reenacted the death aria from *Tosca*.

Herman, less impressed with our would-be rescuer, tensed and went hard-eyed.

"Hello," I said, and then paused. My voice was almost unrecognizable. Salome seducing the King Herod couldn't have sounded sultrier. "You look well, and obviously you got my message." I was trying for dry wit but am not sure I succeeded. What I really wanted was to cry and throw myself into his arms.

"Aye." He resumed walking, now carrying his fur over his arm like a cape.

"I'm very glad to see you," I added unnecessarily, setting Herman aside and rising to my feet. Assorted shells, remains of my lunch, scattered noisily. I tried smoothing my hair.

"You look pale. Ye'll be needing tae come wi' me soon. Tae Avocamor. Ye'll find proper nourishment there. I swear I'd not hae left ye if I'd kenned the hunger waud set in sae fast." He was frowning. "Where is Eonan?"

These weren't really the words I wanted to hear, and probably not the ones he wanted to speak. His posture, especially evident in his nudity, wasn't completely rigid but it was braced. I wanted to look inside his mind for the truth of his feelings about me, but his stubbornness and perhaps lingering distrust were blocking the door. And his eyes, those windows to the soul, were veiled.

Of course, I could not swear that they had ever been transparent. Had I been so busy looking at the outside that I failed to ever look within? The exterior was handsome but what was in my lover's heart? By his own words, he was a hunter, a killer. At the moment there was no give in him. I could go willingly or with a struggle, but he was determined that I was going.

"First you abandon and then you bully me. It would serve you right if I had hysterics and cried all over you." I made my voice light. My own capacity for indignation over this matter—and I had cause for it—was long overrun by fear, first for Lachlan and then for Eonan.

My lover smiled fleetingly and with little genuine amusement. Lachlan was not enjoying himself, and he was going to like the most recent news I brought even less. I wished that he would hold me. I was cold and frightened and wanted to be reassured, but I could not bring myself to approach him or even ask for what I wanted. It seemed rather that my lover was not a lover anymore.

This didn't seem to matter to my body. *It* was glad to see him.

"But ye willnae cry." He inhaled deeply, taking my scent.

"No, I won't. But that is only because I believe in fair play," I said, as I reached for my emotional bootstraps and found them. It required some hauling, but

I managed to not whine or be tearful and accusing. Time enough for that later. If we lived.

This time, Lachlan's smile was more natural. You can hide most anger, and you can hide a great deal of fear, but it is almost impossible to hide elemental sexual attraction. It is particularly difficult when you are happy to see a person and feeling lighthearted for the first time in what seems years. Lachlan read this in me—though he did not know the true cause of my giddiness—and finally relaxed.

"*Tapadh leat*, lass. I am grateful." He took a step toward me, beginning to smile in earnest. I hated that I was going to have to darken his mood.

"I will go to Avocamor, but we can't go yet. I fear that the finman has taken Eonan." I pointed at Eonan's skin where it lay on a high rock. "There's a wound. Near the heart. Herman and I have been tracking him."

That stopped Lachlan. "Yer what?" He sounded incredulous. His view of my activities was clearly illiberal. I reminded myself that he was a product of the Dark Ages, and to his credit, he didn't say anything more. Perhaps the fact that I looked like Medusa and he had found me eating out of a tide pool helped him stay any incautious words while he awaited further information. I thought my own reactions were quite restrained under the circumstances. Most women would be crying or having vapors.

"Tracking him. I found his skin in the finman's cave. It isn't far from here. I can show you where it is. Eonan isn't there, though."

"Alone? Yer tracking him alone?" The voice was

gentle and calm but I wasn't deceived; Lachlan was horrified and furious and perhaps even a bit awed. By my stupidity.

"Not anymore. You're here now. And I'm armed." I pointed. Lachlan looked at my beater, javelin and shackles, and I could see he was not impressed. In fact, it was worse than that. He had a short internal debate, which I somehow felt. Reason triumphed over ire. Again. I was sure he would lecture later, though. It seemed that we were both saving serious discussions for a less dire moment.

"When was Eonan taken?"

"I don't know. Hours ago. Perhaps at dusk last night. He went to send you a message—we thought there might be two finmen at work in the village and wanted you to be warned so you didn't get caught in a trap." This was a simplification of events, I admit. I was more culpable than that, but saw no need to mention it at the moment.

"Aye. The suspicion occurred tae me after I left ye. It is also possible he has a confederate in the village. There is a fisherman who has not been fishing in a fortnight. His brother has supposedly 'left the village,' but is likely a hostage."

"Is he dead, the fisherman?"

"I don't think so. Not yet." Lachlan didn't elaborate. "Yer moggie can find the finman . . . or men?" His eyes fixed on Herman, who for once had not disappeared. The cat stood guard over Eonan's skin.

"Yes. And I can smell Eonan."

Lachlan's dark gaze turned my way. "How?"

"My senses are stronger now. I think it's the baby."

I shied away quickly from this topic, sensing Lachlan's paternal protectiveness and perhaps, I hoped, a bit of jealousy. "And I drank from his footprint. There must have been some blood." I said the last in a whisper. "I am . . . in some kind of sympathy with him."

"Blood." Lachlan went to Eonan's skin and picked it up. He found the hole right away. His face was tight, but I could feel the rage radiating off his naked body. "I think we'd best pay a call on Niall McLaughlin."

"He is the fisherman?" The people I knew from my old life got angry within predictable parameters. I had no notion of the things of which Lachlan might be capable. I was not worried for myself, but someone was going to pay for hurting Eonan, and it might be the unfortunate Niall.

"Aye. Though I doubt he's a fisherman anymore, poor soulless bastard. And the brother too. Dead or held hostage. Either way, the finman will hae taken their souls. They are both dead men walking."

Dead men walking. A shudder tore through me, nearly bringing me to my knees, and finally Lachlan took me in his arms. I huddled in the heat of his body, suddenly aware of my own state of almost complete undress.

"Ye daft, brave lass," he murmured into my hair. One hand slid down my body and rested against my belly. "Yer nae match fer this evil creature. What possessed thee tae leave the cottage?"

"I don't know. I couldn't abandon Eonan. I . . . I just couldn't. It's my fault he went out." As always, I had ended up confessing the truth to Lachlan, whether I wanted to or not. Just thinking of the finman brought back my terror and loathing. I wanted to reduce him to his basic component parts, stomp on and then burn them. Surely that would kill the evil creature.

"Hush. Eonan isnae dead. I waud ken were he no longer living. We've a bond, he and I." Lachlan inhaled again and closed his eyes. His hold loosened as he turned and faced north. When he spoke, his voice was distant. "He was wounded and couldna swim, sae he abandoned his skin and crossed over land. The finman found his fur and took it tae the cave. He's likely tracking him now."

"Is this true?" I asked, feeling hopeful. I had told myself that it was, but wanted confirmation. "Eonan is really alive? It's what I've been feeling but didn't know if it was true. And if—"

"Aye, he's alive." Lachlan opened his eyes. "But injured. He maun be put back in his skin at once."

"Then we must hurry. Where is he going?"

"Tae the faerie mound, most likely. He'd try tae seek shelter there, being part faerie himself." This was what I expected to hear, but wasn't happy to be right.

"Then we have to rush. That is where I saw the corpse candle."

Lachlan nodded. I thought that he would put me from him, and he did, but not until after he had kissed me hard on the mouth: He was not as unmoved by our reunion as he seemed.

"If I order ye tae the cottage, will ye gae?" he asked. I could still feel the heat of his hands on my shoulders.

"No. What if the finman is waiting there? I'm safest with you," I pointed out. "And if there is more than one finman, or he has a human confederate, then you might need me. And I am much stronger now. Angrier. I can fight."

Lachlan looked as though he wanted to argue, but instead nodded his head. In my first relationship, I had in the beginning loved, honored and obeyed in silence, as a meek wife should. In the end, I had not even obeyed. Over the course of that marriage I had lost the knack of doing what I was told, and had yet to regain it. My depravity, had it been known, would have made me even more notorious among family and friends. But here it might serve.

As though hearing my thoughts, Lachlan nodded again. His gaze and voice were firm as he said: "I've niver raised a hand tae a woman, and I shan't begin noo, but I can compel yer cooperation and will an ye fail tae dae as I ask. Oor lives are being risked and I'll nowt allow ye to endanger yerself or the babe. Ye'll *nowt* gae looking fer a fight wi' this evil creature."

"Fair enough," I said lightly, wondering if he meant it. Not that he *could* compel me—we already knew he could—but whether he actually would.

The bird of dawning singeth all night long;
And then, they say, no spirit
dare stir abroad;
The nights are wholesome;
then no planets strike,
No fairy takes, nor witch hath
power to charm,
So hallow'd and so gracious is that time.'
—William Shakespeare, *Hamlet*

Chapter Twenty-three

Niall McLaughlin's cottage was on the way to the faerie mound. I had never noticed it. It was a black
house, barely a hovel, with no windows and only a
door that stood open. It was located in the shadow of
a cliff and the twilight gloom was dark enough to pass
for early evening. As we drew closer, the beater and
gaff began to burn against my skin. This was an evil
place.

A shape appeared in the doorway: the likely ensor-
celled fisherman. He proved to be a lean scarecrow of
a figure, and it wasn't until he spoke and revealed his
stutter that I realized we had met once before, though

not for some time. I didn't say anything about his drastic weight loss or silvered hair, and even if some of the shock showed on my face, the poor man never noticed. Perhaps he was distracted by Lachlan's nudity and my state of half undress. Or maybe the cataract wrapping his eyes completely blinded him. Herman would not come inside and I did not try to coax him. It was all I could do to cross the threshold myself. I had to leave my weapons outside.

Niall paced in front of the badly sooted hearth, which had not known a fire in days. This was an unfavorable sign for the fisherman, suggesting that he had so withdrawn from the normal world that he no longer was aware of the cold or the need to combat it. Where he would end, I could not guess; there was only a distant and irrational hope that he and his missing brother might finish their lives in some happy manner. I hated the smell of the cold damp ashes—yew, I sensed—but had no inclination to kindle a new fire, since all he had on hand was more of the same, and I found that the wood of my weapon had begun to make my hands sting. So had the iron shackles. I was becoming more sensitive with every hour and a fire would not deter the finman.

As Lachlan and the fisherman talked in some dialect of Gaelic that was too accented for me to follow, I wandered about the cottage. Near the front door were some drawings done in ash. The creature these depicted could only be the finman, though with an undamaged chest. The main picture was bordered with peculiar decorations that were similar and yet distinctly different from illuminations of the kind seen in

The Book of the Kells. Instead of the usual Celtic knots, however, there were complex twinings of sea grasses and mythical creatures, like a half-snake woman wreathed in seaweed until it almost disguised the undulations of her coiled and scaled lower body. The pictures were familiar, both from the books I had been reading and my own cottage hearth. The same artistic impulse had been at work here.

I turned to say something to Lachlan and found him holding the fisherman upright, his long fingers clasped around Niall's skull. The grip was not brutal. The fisherman did not fight, and he seemed to be answering Lachlan's questions.

Finally, the fisherman's cloudy gaze showed some awareness, and he looked directly into Lachlan's face. ". . . the isle of the chapel of the fisherman. I've told ye all I ken. Kill me noo," he begged in Scots, raising a hand badly knotted with arthritis that had not been there weeks before. "Please. I'm deid already."

"Gae hame tae yer God," Lachlan said—and then with a quick twist, he broke the fisherman's neck. I stood there too stunned to move, comprehending what had happened but distantly horrified. One instant the fisherman had been alive; the next he was dead.

Lachlan lowered the body to the floor and then looked at me. His voice was gentle.

"His soul was taken; his body was rotting wi'out it. The man waud hae taken his own life but the finman bespelled him, saving the puir bastard so he could take his heart later. We may yet find his soul and free it."

238   MELANIE JACKSON

I nodded numbly, holding Eonan and Lachlan's skins close. I had heard the fisherman ask Lachlan to take his life; it was just that I hadn't actually expected Lachlan to do it. Somehow I had hoped that we would find a way to put his soul back.

As I watched, Lachlan removed Niall's tartan and wrapped it about himself. I wasn't sure that this was actually looting the dead, but it somehow underlined how matter-of-fact and callous Lachlan could be. Next he went to the table and selected a needle from the jumble of dusty nets that someone had been repairing. I did not ask him why, fearing that I might not like the answer.

"We'd best be off," he said. "The mound has a way of slowing time for those it shelters. It is why Eonan has gone there, but it cannae keep him alive forever. It is nowt the refuge of sea creatures."

"Yes, let's go," I agreed, finding the cottage suddenly intolerable. It occurred to me that if I survived the coming hours I might need a head doctor. But then so would everyone else in the village, if they had fallen under the finman's influence.

Of course, to consult anyone about what we had seen would be to invite a stay in an asylum. As always, the evil attacking Findloss would stay in Findloss.

Tell me where is fancy bred,
In the heart or in the head?
—William Shakespeare, *Merchant of Venice*

Chapter Twenty-four

The narrow strip of sand that should have been submerged at that hour of the day remained clear, and Lachlan and I were able to hasten toward the mound. The ground was wrack strewn and stony, worse than on my previous visit, but Lachlan was able to traverse it without difficulty, and with his aid I was able to follow without injury or the indignity of falling into the water. I accepted his help, but every time his hands touched me I saw them breaking that poor wretch of a fisherman's neck. I was not repulsed, exactly, but I had trouble shaking off the vision and with every step I felt that I was losing control of myself and coming closer to being lost in some silent hysteria.

Birds followed us part of the way, their cries of warning shrill and grating to the nerves, and it was not as if I were unaware that we were courting danger. I didn't mean to whimper, but the small sound escaped before I could throttle it. Lachlan stopped immediately and looked me over. Not saying anything, he bent down and bit me on the shoulder. He immediately laved the skin and I felt the familiar narcotic surge through my blood.

I do not often care to surrender my will, but in that moment I was grateful to feel cold and worry recede from my body and mind. I pulled Eonan's skin closer and huddled in his fur, which was as warm as the cat. A part of me wished that I was naked and could just wear the skin.

Another part of me—doubtless an insane part—wanted to stop and make love to Lachlan, despite knowing Eonan was in danger and the finman nearby. The feeling was stronger than what I had known before, yet not unfamiliar. The salt, as Eonan called it, made me libidinous.

We soon passed the familiar miniature quagmire of moss and bog myrtle, now a somber brown as it huddled in the tiny and cold oasis of fresh water in the sand. Next came the curved beaches where the cliffs had been carved out into a disordered succession of arches and caves. Most were shallow, but a few seemed deeper and more ominous than I remembered. I was not tempted to explore them now that I knew for certain that the finman was close, probably ahead of us. And if not ahead, then not far behind.

I didn't carry Herman but kept a close eye upon him, both to warn us if the finman neared but also to see that he was not surprised by any stray waves. Perhaps he could swim, but Herman had no liking for the water.

We passed a group of seals and Lachlan went to

speak with them. What he said I do not know, but they turned as a group and waded into the surf, swimming in formation until they disappeared.

A moment later we rounded the headland and came face to cliff face with the *Sithean Mor*. Drugged as I was, the sight still shook me all the way to my quaking bones and caused my nerves to shrill with awed alarm. Of the corpse candle there was no sign, but an opening had appeared in the side of the mound, a man-sized hole seemingly cut right into the giant stone.

My feet stopped moving, but Lachlan had other ideas and since he had taken my arm, I accompanied him willy-nilly. Herman followed, his steps cautious but steady. Though it seemed impossible and I dismissed it as a trick of the light, he appeared to have gotten a bit larger and was now the size of small dog.

The interior of the mound was not what I expected. I had anticipated some sort of crypt, a cold tomb. But such was not the case. To begin with, the inside appeared immensely larger than the exterior suggested. The floor was glassy, a sort of aurora borealis of colors where the sunlight struck it. The light traveled through the crystalline ground and glowed a soft amber. There was a shallow pool of water in the distance and a fountain of fire-colored water rose up out of it, twirling gaily like a harmless garden cyclone, though this had no leaves or grass in it. Somewhere, perhaps below the level of normal hearing, there was the sound of inhuman but contagious laughter. I wanted to wade out into the water and let it caress my skin.

"I shall hunt for Eonan," Lachlan said. "You maun stitch up his skin."

"What?" My voice was blank, but I believe I had cause. "Can I do that? Just sew it up?"

"Aye. If ye've feelings enough for him."

"Feelings?" I said the word slowly, testing it for meaning. "What sort of feelings are you talking about?"

"Ye care for Eonan?" Lachlan asked.

"Well, yes, of course. But I don't . . . I'm not in love with him, if that is what you mean by 'having feelings.'" I could feel a flush mount in my cheeks. I was not comfortable talking about my emotions, which were in turmoil. A week ago I would have sworn that I would never again care for anyone, that Duncan had left me too badly damaged.

"But ye care enough to endanger yer own life by hunting the finman. Ye've shed tears on his fur."

This sounded like something very intimate in the selkie world, and I felt myself blushing more, as if caught doing something intimate and inappropriate with Lachlan's cousin. "Yes," I said, trying to think of a way to explain. "I like him a lot. But it is mainly guilt that brought me out. I was worried about you and I asked him to go out searching for—"

He waved a hand. "Yer in love wi' me then?" Lachlan asked, leaning down slightly, peering at me through my tangled hair. "Ye want me?"

I stared up at him, indignant that he should ask me this when I'd had little time to examine my feelings and no word from him to indicate his own emotional state. Also, some thoughts are as intimate and personal as the act of making love, and should be kept just as private. In that moment, Lachlan was a stranger to me, and I was unable to answer him straight.

There was also the matter of defining the word *want*. I wanted him for sexual purposes. Was that what he was asking? Or did he mean that I wanted him in my life forever? The answer, I thought, was yes. To both.

Lachlan stared at me. "Think on it, and on if ye have feelings fer me. If ye love me and can love my kin, then take a strand of yer hair and this needle and sew up Eonan's skin. He'll die wi'out it," Lachlan added, "and only a woman who loves may close the wound. This is a magical wound, lass. Only magic may close it." He straightened. "I'm sae sorry to lay this burden upon ye, but yer sewing will determine the scars he bears for the rest of his life—or if he shall even have one at all."

This felt like more than a mere challenge to do my best. I'd known too many people who were generous with their criticism; there had been an overabundance in my life and I wanted no more, especially not then and not from the man with whom I was having a child.

But when I looked into Lachlan's eyes, I saw no censure there. He was stating a fact. If I loved Lachlan enough to encompass his kin in those feelings—or could love Eonan himself—then Eonan would live. I also knew that if I could not do it, he wouldn't blame me. Probably he would blame himself for not being more lovable, for not having enthralled me sufficiently when he could have overcome my will. He was alien to me, but only in his kindness.

I accepted the needle without a word and sank down on the floor, which I found to be pleasantly warm. I didn't watch Lachlan as he moved deeper into the mound. The cave was lovely but so alien, and looking into its shadows made me slightly dizzy. Instead I stared at Eonan's skin and tried to sort through my emotions, fearing that if I touched the skin in the improper frame of mind, I might actually do more harm than good.

Lachlan's voice floated back to me. "Ye needna fear the finman here. He may not enter, for the verra earth and stone of this place finds him abhorrent."

"That's awfully sensible for something made of dirt and rocks," I muttered, and thought I heard Lachlan chuckle. The sound relaxed me. Maybe things were not so dire if he could still laugh.

Exhaling, I took emotional stock. The inventory was bizarre. I had passed into the realm of fairy tales, and like any stupid heroine of fiction I had blundered into something strange and wonderful and probably dangerous, but undoubtedly where a whole new set of rules applied. I had also fallen in love. What remained to be seen was whether Lachlan was a monster or a prince, the hero or the beast. My last visit to this insane state had been with a man I hadn't known well and whom I had soon liked only well enough to be tolerant of his company—when he was sober—and eventually disliked enough to be heartily glad when he was gone. Death had kindly intervened, saving me from my initial bad judgment, but my nerves had been tormented for months afterward and I had sworn never again to love anyone on earth. This wasn't an oath I had made lightly.

Of course, Lachlan wasn't exactly of the earth. He was a creature of the sea. I was not sure that this technicality released me, however, and now I was being asked to look about at a strange new world and admit, at least to myself, that my vow had been made hollow and that I was indeed again smitten—at the very least physically—with a man I did not know well. I had once said that Duncan was inhuman and meant it. The same could be said of Lachlan, in both the literal and metaphorical sense. I couldn't remember if things had worked out for Beauty and her beast. There never seemed to be a happy ending to any of the selkie stories I'd read. That made me stupid as well as an oathbreaker, didn't it, for I had known what he was from the beginning?

I exhaled a long low breath. My thoughts were tumultuous and the day's events disturbing, but the sound of the dancing waters was soothing and I soon felt the last of the anger and fear die away and I calmed enough to consider the next matter at hand without bringing all my past expectations and guilt to bear. The question was a fairly simple one, stripped of all the rest of my thoughts and memories and expectations: Did I care for Eonan? Of course I did. I liked him a lot. In many ways he felt like what I imagined a brother to be. But was that lesser love—this brotherly love—enough to close a wound inflicted by an evil wizard?

Herman came and sat beside me. He meowed softly.

"I love *you*, Herman," I said, slightly surprised when I voiced this thought. The chamber brightened, as though happy with these words, and the floor danced with light that resembled fire laced through with lightning. The nearby water grew luminescent and wildly swirled, reaching higher into the chamber whose ceiling now seemed very far away and lit by strange stars.

My heart would never be as wide open as it had been when I was younger and innocent, but never again would it be entirely closed against the idea of passionate love. If Lachlan, a man who was not really a man, could make me—even against my will—rethink this moral certitude, then I could never say with complete certainty that I could not or would not find abiding love with another. Perhaps this was not an entirely bad thing. Why live if there is no hope of love? Perhaps that is enough for plants or fish, but I was human and required more than mere survival. The question was, would it be with Lachlan?

I thought then about my feelings for Lachlan— and my desire. And for the babe I carried. There were so many kinds of love, and many of them confusing and not easy to categorize. The honesty of the process left me naked in my heart, but I did not flinch from it and kept on until I had my answers laid out methodically and in full view. Romantic love, physical love, brotherly love—I had it all sorted. Then, at last feeling peaceful and focused, I accepted my task and my responsibility for saving Eonan's life. I chose to love him as best I could. Perhaps it would not be enough in the end, but either way he would not die because I was too much of an emotional coward to make the attempt.

Herman stayed beside me, a warm and comforting weight pressed against my leg, letting me love him as well. The hole was small but I sewed for what seemed an eternity, pausing in my careful stitches only to pluck another hair from my head when the previous one ran out. My eyes shed a few tears, protesting the strain of work that I did by the honeyed light of the phosphorescent water and flickering floor. But I did not stop working, even after I considered the effect my still-falling tears and lingering arousal might have on the skin I stitched so diligently. Now open to my feelings, my heart ached when I thought of a world without Eonan. How much poorer the world would be. I could no longer imagine such a thing, and I felt his pain as if it were my own, which allowed me to stitch hope for all of us into the fur I mended. Tears were part of it: a part of life. So was desire, requited or not. If I could stand this, so could he. So could Lachlan, though I hoped he would not be jealous of the memories of our shared passion that I lent to Eonan as I closed this wound so tightly that no water or blood would ever leak through.

When Lachlan returned with Eonan's pale and limp body, which must have been retrieved from the water since both he and Lachlan were wet, I had his skin ready. Using gentle hands, I helped Lachlan dress Eonan in his skin and marveled at the transformation: He went silently from man to beast.

"Yer stitches are holding. Ye feel something," Lachlan said. There was relief and a good measure of satisfaction in his voice. "The lad shall live."

I nodded but was unable to speak. Though I had admitted my feelings to myself, I was not ready to tell either Lachlan or Eonan what was in my stupid,

stupid heart. I suspected though that Eonan would know. He would feel my love for Lachlan and my fear that it would never be entirely returned.

Though I was not ready to speak of my thoughts, I did not care for the careworn look on Lachlan's face and hoped that talking of something else might alleviate some of his pain. "Things are well with your family? You enjoyed your visit?" I asked tentatively. I had no idea what to expect. This seemed a safe question, but with Lachlan's strange situation it was hard to know what was normal.

"Enjoyed? Hardly. This isnae something you enjoy." Lachlan paused and then added: "My heart is gladdened that they are weel and sae many of them live yet."

I nodded. His feelings were roughly my own when it came to seeing my kin. Except my relations didn't make my heart glad and I could not have cared any less if they were well or even still walking on the planet. My true family was now the cat and the two men with me in this magic cave. Duty would never again take me back to my aunt and uncle.

"Aye. They were most surprised tae find me alive. Shocked, even. And they said sae. At length and repetitively."

His mobile features expressed bedevilment. I knew the expression well; I had worn it often enough when my relatives came to visit. The thought of this bond between us made me laugh, though I was very tired and had little else to be amused at. I pointed out, "Isn't it odd, how our nearest and dearest have often turned out to not be our kin?"

Lachlan's face relaxed. "Indeed."

After a pause I asked, "Do they know about me? About . . . the baby?"

"They know of you. I had not yet mentioned the child when your summons arrived. Every male in and around Avocamor felt it. It caused . . . a reaction. A fervor, I should say. Naebody has summoned a selkie in this manner for many a year. That made yer magic especially strong. Had I nowt warned them away, ye would be besieged wi' suitors!"

That was unnerving.

"Oh. Should I apologize?"

"Nay. The situation was dire, and ye were right tae call me. And I believe that I have seen enough of my kin fer a time. I am not sorry tae be away."

He frowned, reaching out a hand to touch my belly. I stayed very still. He was not touching me but rather communing with the tiny life inside me. "I will need tae swim oot fer some cheese soon."

"Cheese?" I repeated when his hand was withdrawn. A part of me was disappointed that the contact was broken; I still desired him, though there could not be a more inappropriate moment to feel aroused. "But . . . do selkies eat cheese?"

"Aye, at times. The seals help us make it, of course, noo that our women are gone. Bags of seal milk are mixed wi' brine and sea fruit and then taken out at high tide and anchored in the kelp. The sea stirs them. After, the whey is taken out and fed to the young ones who are tae old tae nurse any longer." He added: "We eat the curd ourselves sometimes, when we tire of sea fruit and fish."

"Seal milk . . ." Of course. Where would they get goat or sheep or cow milk, and besides, why would they prefer it?

I would have asked more, but Eonan gave a sigh and our attention returned to him. His breathing deepened for a moment and then seemed to stop while he stretched the rest of the way into his skin, looking rather like someone wiggling his fingers to reach the depths of his gloves. Then something utterly disconcerting happened. For a moment, it seemed as if Eonan were becoming aroused.

Lachlan and I were both relieved when Eonan's eyes opened, and I was especially happy when his nascent tumescence subsided, since what he was feeling was probably not his own emotion but mine. Though he was unable to speak in selkie form, his gaze said that he knew it was I who had stitched up his wounds, and that he cared for me in an equal manner, probably even wanted me sexually. Though shaken and slightly embarrassed by this revelation, I managed a smile for him and stroked him once on his head.

They were different, these two. Eonan was simpler, more animal in impulse, playful, shameless and accepting. Lachlan was much more a creature of calculation and reason.

Lachlan's gaze was weighty as he considered our silent exchange, but I did not face him. I could not. It wasn't really that I was still irritated by his forcing me to confront my feelings for him, but I still felt too raw and naked inside to risk any discussion of the matter. I knew the truth. The baby knew. Eonan knew, since I had probably stitched some of my turmoil as well as desire into his fur. Probably even the faerie mound and Herman knew. If Lachlan did not, he would have to content himself with guesswork and supposition until I was stronger.

"Rise up, ye lazy pooka," Lachlan said at last, offering his hand to his cousin. "Ye've slept enough and there is work tae be done. We must leave the mound."

Eonan chuffed and rolled onto his stomach without aid. He stretched again and yawned hugely.

"Be glad yer half pooka and more sex than reason," Lachlan muttered. "It let my Megan stitch thee up."

> *Blunt my spear and slack my bow,*
> *Like an empty ghost I go,*
> *Death the only hope I know.*
> *—"The Maiden of Morven"*

Chapter Twenty-five

We stood on the shore, looking toward where the isle of the fisherman's chapel was supposed to be. Or, rather, Lachlan and I stood. Eonan, still in selkie form, was lying on the sand.

We could see nothing through the fog that had pushed all the way to the narrow beach. The sea was oddly calm, as if Triton himself had frozen the tides, horrified by the finman and his acts. Or was it our temerity that amazed him? Wasn't it King Lear who said *upon such sacrifices the gods themselves throw incense*? Or perhaps it was just that the powers of the finman and Lachlan were deadlocked, and the sea itself taken prisoner.

Lachlan turned to me as he pulled his skin around himself. "I shall breathe for ye, lass, when ye can't manage on yer own. Hae no fear of the sea whilst I am with ye. Ye'll come tae nae harm."

He pulled the seal skin over his head. Drawing me down to the surf with him, he changed form and fastened his mouth over mine as we plunged into the slack black water. After the first shock of the cold, I opened my eyes and saw a phalanx of strange and very large seals close in around us. Were these Lachlan's kin? I wasn't sure. They seemed like the seals on the beach and not so large or clawed as Lachlan and Eonan.

I knew the reputation of the island where we were going. I had never attempted a visit because the bit of stone and cruel beach that made up the isle was surrounded by a forest of upthrust vicious gray rocks shaped like a shark's teeth that could rip the bottom from a boat, and it was guarded by a constant offshore wind that only the strongest oarsman could overcome. Why it was called the isle of the chapel of the fisherman I did not know, but the place was considered haunted and shunned by the current inhabitants of Findloss because of these strange winds that blew day and night.

I did not close my eyes, since the water did not bother them at first, and I felt the need to watch for the finman, who might not be far behind us. It was difficult to judge from beneath the waves what was happening above the surface, but it seemed that we passed under a band of pure black clouds where lightning danced. These clouds hurled an unpleasant dark rain down upon the water's surface, a painful downpour that did not dissolve when it hit the sea; and while Lachlan was somehow breathing for me, I could tell that this unnatural rain smelled strongly of sulfur and rotting things. So bitter and caustic was it, I was finally forced to close my eyes. After a moment, my skin began to sting as though bitten by a million ants. Lachlan's arms about me tightened, and he jerked us deeper into the ocean where the water was yet pure, if dark and cold.

I thought that I might cry out from the pain and pressure against my ears, but finally we moved into a place of eerie calm and clean water, and our pace slowed to one less frantic. We drifted back to the surface, and realizing that I had not inhaled on my own for some impossibly long time, I took a great gasp of air. Beside me, Lachlan and Eonan's breathing was also fast and labored. Though we breathed hard, it did us little good. It seemed the air was slowly being robbed of oxygen, and made me think of the deep shafts of the tin mines back home, or, far worse, of an enclosed tomb.

"He's tainted the very oceans," Eonan said, as he pushed his seal skin back and revealed his face. This was pale and sickly, but then so was Lachlan's. I stared at my hands. They looked as though they belonged to a corpse. The light here was unnatural and anathema to all healthy things.

The air split with a protesting yowl, and I realized that Eonan had carried Herman. Warned, Lachlan's cousin promptly set the wet cat on the gritty sand and let him get on with the business of restoring his sodden fur. It was not my imagination; the cat was growing larger.

Lachlan continued to carry me. I looked up at the sky as I wrung out my hair. Though surrounded by storm on all sides, the heavens overhead were clear, as though we were in the eye of a hurricane. But though the sun shone, it seemed as though something dark had been drawn over its face to blot out its vigorous light; an unhealthy veil separated us from the rest of the world. There was illumination in this foreign monochromatic land, but no heat and nothing green would grow.

Around us, the water was completely clear and calm. Too calm. It was dead, as sterile as water boiled for laundry. I thought then of the Dead Sea and understood how it could have a name like that. I wondered if other humans would perceive it this way, or was I seeing this evil because of my new senses?

Lachlan released me once my feet could touch bottom, and I walked gingerly onto the sterile sand littered with gray humps of rock. "Beware the crabs, lass," Lachlan warned, his voice hard. This was still the stranger Lachlan—the hunter. I did not fear that he would offer me any violence, or even be neglectful of my well-being, but I doubted there was any comfort to be had from him at that moment.

"They pinch viciously and will eat ye if they get a chance, for they are trapped here forever and always hungry fer living flesh," Eonan added, and I realized then that it was not stones that littered the beach, but rather crabs similar to the ones that had been in the finman's cave. The sound of their clicking claws was the only thing that disturbed the silence.

One approached, pincers waving. Though I am not in the habit of offering harm to fellow creatures, I speared it with my javelin and watched with satisfaction as it writhed and then withered. The effect on the evil beast was the same as pouring salt on a snail, and it pleased me despite my now-blistered hands. Perhaps I had not been carrying these toxic items for no purpose. Maybe here they would lend greater power over our foe.

"'Tis time we starved this beast." Lachlan said. I did not know what he meant, but followed him and Eonan as they walked up the shore and headed purposefully for the only structure on the isle.

They did not approach the door of the stone building, but instead went to the slitted windows and began prying off boards. They used only their bare fingers, apparently impervious to the pain that humans would feel if we abused our hands in that manner. Finally, after they had pried off all the boards, when the maximum light reached inside, they pulled the shattered remains of a rusted gate off the door and entered the chapel.

I followed slowly, carrying Herman, who was terribly heavy but whose heat I found comforting. From the doorway it was easy to discern the interior. The chapel was austere, even with the boards pulled off of the windows, but that did not come as any great surprise since we were in Scotland. The building was not a normal church, whatever may have been intended by the men who had built it centuries ago. It had no decorative belfry. It had no bell. There was no cross or statues, no communion tokens, nor wafers, nor chalices for wine. All it had were crypts. They all said: UNKNOWN. I realized sadly that these were temporary graves for drowned sailors and fishermen who waited for someone to claim them.

There were also dozens of pots and jars, all turned upside down, and I realized with a thrill of horror what they must contain. My reading had told me that when a finman stole a soul, if he did not consume it at once, he put it in an upside-down pot where he could dine on it later. Lachlan and Eonan began righting pots, and I put down the cat to join them in their efforts. I had not forgotten the poor fisherman and wanted to set his soul free.

My panting exhalations condensed into vapor and refused to dissipate. It was the same with Lachlan and Eonan. Our breath slowly gathered around the pots, surrounding them in a light fog. My lungs protested that they were drowning in a cold sea. I ignored them as best I could; we were on land—however strange and poisoned—and I tried my best to convince myself that this meant that we were safe and nothing could happen.

I tipped upright the first pot I reached. It was a teapot with a broken spout that had been stopped up with wax. The moment the obstruction broke, something rushed out into the growing fog, an entity formless but visible for the moment that it passed through my frozen breaths. It blew by me in a short stream with a sigh that was like a mournful hymn—*chyrme*, was what the locals called seal death songs, the ones they sang when their young were killed and their skins taken.

A soul! I thought, fresh tears starting in my eyes as I watched the faint silver trail that marked its passing. Perhaps drawn to the light, it fled through the door. Around me, other souls were likewise escaping.

Crying quietly at this awful proof of all the stories of the finman's evil, I crawled to the next pot, quickly turning it over. I went to another and another, myself made frantic by the terror of these trapped souls who knew we were nearby and sensed hope of escape. But each soul I freed was weaker and colder than the last, and I realized it was because the oldest and most depleted souls—some human, some not quite—were at the back of the church. For a moment I knew their names and stories, a bit of them brushing my mind as they fled past, racing for the freedom of the open air. But the contact also weakened and bewildered me, part of their fear and horror clinging like burs.

Each also stole a little warmth from my body, a little life. It was a horrible and draining assault, but I did not blame the thieving and sometimes insane souls. I forced myself on, no matter how tiring, until at last the tiny new life inside of me protested. Only then, reminded of my child's existence, I froze in place. Lachlan and Eonan would have to finish this task. I would not risk my baby.

As though hearing me, Herman came close and again pressed himself against my body. Immediately, I warmed. Feeling stronger, I left the chapel with the cat, he on his paws and I on my hands and knees. I looked back from the doorway. Eonan and Lachlan had nearly all of the pots overturned. Their faces were alike, masks of themselves, distorted by disgust and loathing for the finman. I understood. Doubtless some souls had been kin or friends. They were entitled to their rage.

I did not watch them finish. Instead, Herman and I just slumped against the building, trying to breathe normally of the horrible air and to warm ourselves in the gray-green light offered by the veiled sun.

A devil, a born devil. On whose nature
Nurture can never stick.
—William Shakespeare, *The Tempest*

Chapter Twenty-six

"Here," Lachlan said. "Try this."

"What is it?"

"Cheese. Eat a bit before we leave. It will make ye stronger."

I accepted the wet, yellowish lump without interest, but the babe inside me apparently recognized it as some high treat and I found myself eating it with growing enthusiasm. I was also enjoying watching the water roll down Lachlan's body, though I made an effort to keep my scrutiny discreet. I probably failed, but neither Lachlan nor Eonan seemed at all self-conscious. They probably expected me to be completely enthralled, now that my mate was near. Or perhaps it is just the way of the selkies to feel no more concern with nudity than a seal might.

"I believe that fer the trip back ye should carry the moggie and I'll take Megan," Eonan said to Lachlan, coming to sit beside me. I didn't mind his closeness, even though he was naked; a part of me was with him now and always would be. And I just liked being near a warm naked body. It seemed *normal*. I would have preferred Lachlan's, but Eonan would do. He was my family now.

"Was Herman ill-mannered enough to claw you?" I asked, after I swallowed some more cheese. For the first time in days I was feeling content and sated.

"Nay. As I said afore, pookas and imps hae much in common. But I waud still prefer to carry ye. Yer moggie's fat and getting fatter. Look at the beastie. He'll be as big as a coo afore long."

"Nonsense. And you are just being lazy."

"Lazy, aye. But verra handsome." Eonan grinned.

He was indeed handsome, if not in the same league as Lachlan.

My child's father shook his head at us, as though we were fractious children. And to him, perhaps we were. I think he was amused at our play even if he was not inclined, or capable, of joining in. I thought about blowing Lachlan a kiss just because it was undignified and fun, but I couldn't count on him understanding the playful act. It was just as likely that he would be confused as delighted. I thought, not for the first time, that it would be helpful if he came with some sort of translator that could explain his expressions and silences.

"Well, I would go with you," I said, turning back to Eonan. "Except for the fish breath." I waved a hand in front of my face.

"What have ye agin' fish?" the young selkie demanded. His tone was light, but he and Lachlan both looked as exhausted and haggard as it was possible for those fine physical specimens to look. Intense anger does that to you. The difference between them was that Eonan was incapable of remaining serious and subdued. Not even grief could suspend his humor for long, not even when it might be in his best interest to be calm and reflective.

I, on the other hand, was feeling better after my rest and food. Perhaps I was becoming accustomed to the stale air, or maybe the atmosphere was improving. Whichever it was, I was breathing more easily. I noticed that several of the misshapen crabs had died, withered by a brightening sun.

"There's nothing wrong with fish—so long as it's on a plate and not on your breath." I looked over at Lachlan. "Why *is* Herman getting bigger?"

"The beast is a mystery tae me," Lachlan answered. "But if I was tae make a guess, I waud say that he is growing larger sae he may protect ye."

"Are you getting big to help me?" I asked the cat, who was now the size of a large water spaniel. He blinked lazily but did not answer. This wasn't remarkable, except, in that moment, I had the feeling that he could have spoken if he chose. "What a good kitty, so brave and handsome," I added.

This time, both Eonan and Lachlan snorted. Herman came closer to me, assumed an expression of benign idiocy and began pawing my lap. His claws—his now very oversized claws—were carefully sheathed.

I noted that he could shed like a real cat in spite of his larger size. I gathered up his stray hairs and rubbed them into a ball, which I tucked in my shattered chemise. It is a testament of how far my thinking had come that I was actually concerned about leaving any of his hair behind, lest the finman could somehow use it against him.

"Wherever we're going when we leave Findloss, we're taking the cat," I said quietly. When Lachlan remained quiet I added: "Embrace the concept. We have a pet." It was bold, using the plural in that statement.

Lachlan raised a brow but still said nothing. Herman began making a noise that seemed a bit aggressive for a purr now that he was so large, and his expression was perhaps a little smug as he stared at my lover, but I stroked him anyway. Good, bad or really big, Herman was family. I wouldn't let him go.

"Lachlan, can the finman bespell me?" I asked, changing the subject. "I think he tried once and failed. That might be something we can use to our advantage."

Eonan and Lachlan both stared hard at me, and I began to wish that I hadn't spoken. I didn't relish being lectured again about how I was to stay at home and keep the hearth fires burning.

"Ye've felt the finman in yer mind?" Lachlan demanded.

"No, I saw him on the beach when I was searching for Eonan. I think he tried to put a spell on me but was too sick. I was also up a cliff so he couldn't reach me. And I ran away at once," I said to palliate them.

"Can a MacCodrum be eye-bitten?" Eonan asked. *Eye-bitten*. He meant bespelled.

"Apparently nowt. At least, nowt when she has her

familiar wi' her. Lass, ye say that the finman was sick? Ye mean ill, not merely repulsive."

I touched Herman's head. *My familiar?* I had evolved enough in my thinking to like this concept.

"Yes—sick, not sickening. He was throwing up his insides and he . . ." I trailed off as I thought about what I had seen. Perhaps he had felt no need to hide his true form, but I had suspected that the thing on the beach could no longer pass as human. Its head had been large and bloated, and covered in gray-green patches of mold or scaled flesh that had replaced most of its hair—assuming he'd ever had any. He had a shark's mouth, the individual teeth covered in coarse bony bristles. The legs, such as they were, were shorter and more powerful than a man's, and the arms were not arms at all but rather tentacular appendages of an inappropriate length and covered in large suckers that belonged to a squid. Then there was the gaping hole in his chest where the parasites had fed and died. Above all that, there had been the spiritual miasma; the evil cloud surrounding it was beyond anything I had ever imagined.

"He could not pass for human now, not even on a dark night in a gale. No one would open a door to him—not unless he could put a spell on them first."

"That is guid news indeed," Eonan said. "It seems the mage's soul didnae agree wi' him. Mayhap Fergus made a death wish and cursed the evil beast."

"And we've just emptied his larder." There was satisfaction in Lachlan's voice. "He can hide nae longer. He'll need tae come oot and fight."

"Ye've warned the ither finfolk?" Eonan asked.

"Aye. He'll surprise naebody else. His taking the merman's heart has angered many. He'll be given nae refuge frae the creatures aen the sea."

"Sae he's as guid as deid already!" Eonan was cheerful.

"Sae long as he doesnae regain his heart."

"The crypt," I said abruptly. "Under the kirk." They looked at me again. "It's full of broken pots. Was that you?"

"Nae. Mayhap it was the merman freeing his folk. The finman has been feeding among them and the water kelpies. Perhaps that is when the finman attacked him."

"This is the merman at the circus whose heart was stolen?" I asked, just to make sure. Surprisingly, I was beginning to see connective lines between events that felt more like Sight than plain old insight, and while I had no clear picture yet, I felt that I could join enough points of information to anticipate the finman's next move.

"Aye, sae I believe." Lachlan took my hand, running a finger over my wrist. Perhaps he was checking my pulse. Or perhaps he was deliberately inflaming me, deliberately calling my mind to the present, to him and away from what he considered a dangerous puzzle. The latter would not work.

"I think I know why Herman can track the finman," I said. Now everyone was looking at me, even the cat. "You were right about Fergus. Part of his soul is still in the finman, and Herman can feel it. This piece must be unchained before Herman can be free as well."

The cat grinned at me, proud that I had figured it out. Had he been smaller, the expression might have been amusing. As he was, I think all of us were a bit disconcerted.

"Sae we've anither twa allies," Lachlan said softly. "A dead mage and an angry imp cat."

Our return trip through the sea was not as painful as the journey in. Again, it could have been because I was growing accustomed to our surroundings, or perhaps because the evil water was being mixed with ocean that was unpolluted and so stung less. Beyond the ring of black about the island, we were once more escorted by a group of seals, from time to time some swimming close enough that I could reach out and touch them.

The cat rode on Eonan's back, and under other circumstances I think I would have been amused at their mutual unhappiness. Eonan held up well, but his lack of complaint, when I suspected that normally he would have enjoyed voicing his objections to the long trip and the burden of my cat, made me certain that he was actually tired and in need of food and rest.

We returned to the cottage, watching for ambush and also for villagers who might question my tattered clothing and why I was in the company of two naked men and a black jaguar with one white sock. Though I half expected to find my home burned, the building sat, to all appearances unmolested.

Inside, I insisted on fixing a meal: fish that Lachlan had caught and carried up to the house and some tired carrots that steamed up reasonably well. After that Eonan curled up on my settee and went to sleep. It was probably unneeded, given the selkies' constant state of warmth, but I spread a blanket over him anyway and made no objection when Lachlan stirred up the ashes and started a new fire. Herman lay down on the floor near the hearth and sighed contentedly.

Lachlan and I were tired too, but we did not attempt to nap, though we did retire immediately to bed. Aware that we had company, we undressed in silence; then with the door shut, we set about our own kind of healing.

I laid my ear against his heart and tried to hear what it might be saying. My supposed gift of Sight had not showed me anything about Lachlan, just potential deaths and cataclysms—important omens, certainly. But what I wanted most to know was how he felt about me.

"Have ye learned anything frae yer listening?" Lachlan asked, and I realized I had spoken aloud.

"Just that it sounds like you have two hearts." I shook my head, not looking up.

"I dae." The amused reply brought my gaze up.

"Really?"

"Aye. And lungs of much greater size than most men."

"Most everything is of greater size," I said, wiggling against him.

"Like my hands."

I laced fingers with him. "Yes, like your hands."

His free hand reached around me, stripping away the remains of the slip I wore, and he laid me down on the bed and stared, as though he were a starving man confronted with a feast. I looked up, unafraid and unresisting as he lowered himself onto me. I would not die from a surfeit of pleasure, but it might be close.

"For us," he whispered. "That we may live." And I knew that he spoke of the selkies.

His kiss was hard, an immediate onslaught that was perhaps caused by a bit of jealousy regarding my time with and care of Eonan. I did not resist, though it seemed a bit uncivilized and something that in another life I might have protested. In a moment his lips softened and then parted, and our breath joined as it had in the ocean, while something that was essentially Lachlan—his magic or perhaps his soul—was coupled with me. I could feel it making me strong and healthy, healing my heart and body, my mind and spirit. It also filled me with a longing and need for completeness that was almost painful. Words would be nice, but this union was imperative.

His hands were on me then. There was no time for sweet words, even had I known what to say in that transcendent moment. My legs were pushed apart and I was aware of the rough blanket at my back, the abrasion of my skin another kind of sensation, another arousal. Softer emotions were not on his mind—or in mine either.

I made no sound as he pushed into me. My breath was gone, all words and thoughts taken roughly away, just as I was being taken, and I reveled in the focused carnality, surrendering to my animal self and what it longed for. The cords in Lachlan's long neck pulled tight, the muscles of his chest segmenting into ridges, and he began to glow as the sheen of sweat—that drugging sweet madness of his kind—swept upward and overcame him, making him a victim as much as I.

I arched up to meet him, to receive his warmth, his passion, his ocean of wordless desires. We floated in the same magical sea where the first selkies were born, and found happiness there.

I wanted to ask about all the strange and vivid impressions I'd had while making love, but got ambushed by a giant yawn. It shuddered out from my torso, shaking my entire body and Lachlan's as well.

"Sleep, lass," he commanded. "Fer the guid of the babes, ye maun be rested on the morrow."

"Babes? Two babes?" I was perhaps not as surprised as I should have been. Eonan was not the master of discretion and I had noticed his slip of tongue even though I had defensively ignored it.

"Aye, there are twa. Male children."

Twins? This would require some thought. And they were boys? How did he know?

"You won't leave again?" My lips barely formed the question and I was unable to pry my eyelids open. I could feel the moonlight sneaking through the shutters, so delicate, so light on my skin as it clothed me in silver. I had a groggy thought that, with such light, who would ever need any other clothing?

"Nay. I shall be here when ye awake."

As always, argument was impossible, and so I took him at his word and allowed myself to sleep, happy in the knowledge that this time, Lachlan would remain with me through the night. I would have been even more ecstatic if he had said that he loved me, but as I had said nothing either and was being overwhelmed by the tide of sleep, I let the matter go unchallenged. He wanted me and was with me—that was enough for the time being.

A man that doth violence to the blood of a person, if he flee even to the pit, no man will stay him.
—Proverbs 28:17

Chapter Twenty-seven

It was decided in the early morning that Eonan and Lachlan would go to the crypt and track the finman from there. I was, you'll be astonished to hear, to remain at the cottage with Herman and a pot of tea.

My mood that morning was strange, and I said almost nothing. I felt slightly ill, still influenced by physical exhaustion and a surfeit of salt we had exchanged during lovemaking, and I was mainly interested in ending the clamor in my skull by returning to sleep. I was not to realize that outside influences were being used upon me until it was far too late to do anything to stop them.

Lachlan was content to leave me dozing on the settee while he and Eonan went out to make war. He kissed me good-bye, but it was not the embrace of a warrior who went to his death. This was no last farewell. My lover was confident that he could kill the finman and return to me before nightfall. I felt no alarm.

I roused from a semisleep near noon, called to wakefulness and longing for I knew not what, by a voice that was not a voice, a song that was not a song, a thought that was not my own but felt very comfortable in my head. I thought at first that perhaps it was the babies telling me they were lonely and bored and needed food, but they were quiet.

Restless, I went to the window and, for an instant, I thought that I could hear Lachlan's voice calling to me from the beach, but it faded even as I opened the casement to listen. A quick glance showed me Herman was still asleep by the hearth. That was good. I wanted him to stay asleep. It was important that he be undisturbed.

I padded to the door without my shoes. Without clothes. I wanted—needed—to go out into the beautiful sea, which was calm and warm and inviting and so very nearby. It was time I did this. I had slept enough. Of course, Lachlan had been right to leave me earlier. I had needed to rest, the same as anyone would after a terrible ordeal, but I was awake now and wanted to be out in the open. I wanted to be in the deep blue water, not in this cottage where I was kept deaf and blind and all but dead to the world by the drugs Lachlan had given me.

I breathed deeply of the sea air. It seemed odd that I had ever dreaded the waters that surrounded the village. But I recalled that I *had* feared the ocean, as all supposedly sensible land-dwelling creatures did: It had appeared to me as a voracious thing, full of monsters that might swallow up ships and men and brought terrible storms to bury my village. It had even tried to drown me once, hadn't it? But I felt that morning that I could ignore that fear when a sort of supra-rational knowledge of my true self and my place in the world came to me. I had a destiny. The sea was not a lonely place, not a vast and empty desert dissimilar from the ones on land only by being covered in water; it was a place of mystery and wealth and excitement. There was even a buried treasure out there. Wouldn't that be convenient to find?

And the sea had given me Lachlan and Eonan, so I knew that it was not really *lonely* out there. I would soon meet others who lived in the ocean and they would be wonderful and kind, so I had no reason for these silly qualms. There was no need to remain hiding behind my warded door with my sleeping cat.

I looked back at Herman. I was not supposed to venture out of the cottage without Lachlan, and I understood his concern that I not go out alone because . . . Actually, I couldn't remember why I was supposed to stay indoors. And the thought of the long wait I might have to endure chafed at me. Who knew how many hours it would be before Lachlan returned to the cottage and was able to join me for a swim?

I went out into the dead garden and paced and sang in my head, and tried any number of things to keep myself from answering the strange siren call that ceaselessly whispered. But it was useless. The allure was too strong. Something powerful and magical was telling me to step beyond my garden gate and go into the sea. Lachlan was worrying needlessly. What could possibly hurt me on such a sunny calm day? There was nothing dangerous out there.

Unable to resist the strange compulsion any longer, I opened the gate—it had a talisman on it too, I saw—and left my cottage behind, door open to anyone who wanted to venture in.

I made it to the shore without difficulty and had begun wading into the surf when Herman screamed. The sound was distant, though, and I did not at first feel alarmed by it. I wasn't going to go past the breakwater, so there was no need for the cat to be upset about me being in the water. Anyway, water was good for my babies. They would like being in the ocean.

I went confidently onward but paused when the waves brushed at my thighs with dead cold fingers. I had reached the end of the rock pier, and beyond lay deep water. I hesitated a moment as the waves lapped against me, trying to recall why this might be a foolish thing to do. When no answer occurred to me, I arched my body into a steep dive and swam for the open water.

Once under the waves and amid a garden of obscuring sea grass, I hesitated again. Water surged over me, and I heard as it crashed against the sheltering stone on either side of the inlet. I could feel many currents waiting just ahead, weaving one into the other and making the sand swirl. The sea grass had in some places become a snarl that might net me if I wasn't careful.

I should have felt cold but didn't. I should have felt breathless but wasn't. I looked out contentedly through the jungle of kelp, swaying in time with surges that breathed in and out of the cave, and did not feel concerned that I was not rising up for air as I normally would.

Compelled by some last instinct for survival, I looked up at the surface, only a few feet overhead. It was bright with light and sparkled like crushed glass in the noontime sun. It had to be near midday for the waves to be so blindingly bright. Should I go up there?

No. What I really wanted to do was go back to the island of the fisherman's chapel and see that the monster had not returned. It would be so good to know that the isle was safe. Lachlan would want me to do this. And without the finman, the island would be an ideal place for sunning.

I shouldn't do this, part of my mind argued back, using two soft voices. Lachlan could come back at any moment, and he would be worried about me. He would probably even be angry that I had not waited to share this moment with him. And what if the finman had returned to the island after all?

But the finman *couldn't* come back; Eonan and Lachlan had tracked him down and he was probably dead already. So the islet would be deserted. There were no people there now, no spirits, no monsters. And I really wanted to go to that island. I needed to go. And it wasn't far. No, not far at all. I could go and be back in almost no time. And air? That was silly. I could cavort all day in the strongest current and never tire or need to breathe. I should come to the island . . . come at once . . .

I twitched, my muscles wanting something in spite of my mind's insistence that I didn't need air and that I wasn't cold.

What about sharks? There might be something large and dangerous lurking in the water.

Nonsense, the other voice answered impatiently. Lachlan had said that sharks did not come near the shoreline of the village. They did not like the turbulence of the sea when it met land. And they did not like the People who used the beaches, or the water when it was hot and bright. I would only be in open water for a very few minutes anyway. If I left right now I would have dazzling sun for my entire journey and be able to see any warning fins if they should come my way.

Rising up high enough for my eyes to look over the water but not to take a breath of air, I glanced over the delicate wavelets toward the fisherman's island. There was no fog and its pastel outline was reassuringly close. I *could* swim very fast and be there in only a moment. I would have a quick look to be sure that all was well, and then I would come right back. No one would ever know.

Herman screamed again, the sound much louder, but I still did not look back toward the cliff where the cottage stood. Instead I pivoted to look at the shore behind me, reassuring myself that there were no witnesses to see me leave. Then, turning back and taking one last look at the island, I dropped beneath the oily surface and made an exceptional effort to begin swimming toward the gray islet.

The assault came without warning, and in a flash I was myself again. The finman rushed at me, eyes in his molding face held wide in some form of magical rapture, but he was not as powerful in body or mind as he might have once been. He was fast, though, and he was enraged and I think insane, and I knew immediately that he was far stronger than I, even with his rotting body and missing heart.

I tried to dodge, but he snagged me in those long ropey arms covered with suckers that had vicious teeth and spun me around in his coils and started to drag me down. I managed to avoid his eyes, not certain that he could paralyze me with his gaze but unwilling to risk it, but I felt his presence prying at my mind in some mental crevice that Duncan or the faerie mound—or someone else, perhaps even Lachlan—had opened. It made me sick.

Earlier he had whispered sweetly, acting as a lure. Now he screamed. And the sick thoughts he battered me with were not solely his own; they belonged to all the wicked dead whose souls he had taken. I also saw that this had nothing to do with me—I was irrelevant. This was revenge on selkies, on the People: Lachlan's female and children were to die.

The finman's attention wavered. He searched the nearby boulders, which were shattered into knifelike sharpness, and then began towing me toward them. I knew he planned to thrust me onto these rocks after he had sucked out my soul. But the horrified thrall that had me struggling ineffectually ended. Fighting then not just for my own life, I planted my feet on the nearest outcropping, and thrust back with all my might. At the same time I ducked my head, getting as far away from the finman's mouth as I could.

With all my will I cried out to Lachlan, praying I could reach him and he would understand what was happening. The internal scream was loud enough to shake my oxygen-deprived brain. Hurt followed hurt: My feet were cut. Sharp pain stung my left shoulder and right hip as the finman tried to subdue my struggles and turn me about for an easy mouth-hold. As he could not trick his way back into my mind, he spent all his effort in trying to squeeze the air from my body and to latch his teeth over my nose. We battled all the way to the sea floor, where our thrashing sent up a mushrooming cloud of sand.

The finman tried a new grip, and though my neck was stronger than before, it was no match for the power of the finman's tentacled arms. It would be broken if he could get beneath my chin.

I tried clawing at the finman, but couldn't get a grip on his arms, and my small nails left only shallow wounds. It was all I could do to keep him from wrapping a limb about my throat as he dragged me over the sand and back toward the fissured rocks, there to again try to impale me. My world began to go dark around the edges. I had an indignant and wholly inappropriate thought that the sailors' stories had gotten the details all wrong; there was no anesthesia to ease the pain of the last moments of life. Drowning was not a pleasant death. It was not peaceful as your life passed before your eyes. There was plenty of time to think and feel as your skull and chest seemed to balloon with used air and your muscles began to twinge with agony. And I wasn't even to the part where my lungs exchanged cold seawater for depleted breath and I started the actual drowning!

Lachlan, I screamed again inside my head, beginning to despair that he would reach me in time. Then to my babies: *I'm sorry, loves.*

Regret at this potential loss was so strong that it pierced even my personal horror at the thought of annihilation. That was what came at the end of life: regret! I could see it all in terrifying starkness. My life—all the struggle and suffering I had done—was for nothing. My babies would die too, and it was all my fault for having been too stupid to realize that I was being lured by magic.

Sorry, Lachlan.

But then Herman was beside me. Water was not his natural element, but hunting and killing were. His giant claws pulled great chunks of flesh from the fin-man's back. And if Herman's attack was unexpected and vicious, then Lachlan's was even more so. I saw at once, and perfectly clearly, how selkies differed from normal seals. Lachlan's arms were strangely elongated and jointed oddly as they reached for his foe, and at the end of each flipper tip was some sort of retractable claw that jutted out into long, wicked hooks that belonged on a raptor. Selkies also have long hooked teeth, like in a skeleton of a prehistoric cat I once saw, and these fangs can shear flesh away from bone. My lover was fast and graceful and lethal, and I understood finally how ruthless he could be.

The shocked finman tried to untangle his arms from around my body to meet the new attack, but he was too slow to make an effective defense while holding me. Then Eonan was there as well. Claws slashed over the creature's face, rendering him first blind and then hemorrhagic as his throat was cut in four places. He finally released me, and Herman grabbed my hair in his mouth and pulled me to the surface where I at last could gulp in desperately needed air.

Something smacked me in the face as a wave cuffed

my head. It was my necklace—the one from Duncan.
My talisman. Herman snarled at me, and I understood. He wanted me to use it.

After a few more desperate breaths, I ducked my
head back under the water. Our wounded foe was
spasming, his convulsions so sharp that it seemed he
would be broken in half at the hips. His tentacles
lashed like whips, cutting fur and skin whenever they
touched Lachlan or Eonan. The water was full of
blood—both red and milky white. My world was still
dark at the margins, but I knew what I needed to do—
what might kill the finman or weaken him enough
that the others could finish him.

Lachlan and Eonan circled their opponent, coming
close enough to slash his flesh but doing their best to
stay away from the still-thrashing tentacles. I pulled
off my necklace and jackknifed downward. As I knew
would happen, the finman grabbed me and pulled me
close when I got within range. I didn't fight. Instead,
I thrust my fist into his chest and let go of the necklace. And I thought the word *Die,* hurling it at him
with all my will.

He released me at once, and Lachlan took my arm
and flung me away. I couldn't see much after that for
the turbulence in the water. But once I reached the
surface and had grabbed a few more breaths, I again
forced myself under the waves for another look at the
battle. As I had hoped, the finman appeared dead, his
chest sporting a hollow cavity that had imploded with
the entry of the talisman.

I didn't fight Herman as he again snapped my hair
in his teeth and began paddling for shore, towing me

like a fish on a line. A moment later I was joined by Lachlan, who took over the task of ferrying me to land. Over his shoulder I saw Eonan, dragging what was left of the finman's carcass. He did not look like a conquering hero, aglow with the satisfaction of having vanquished an enemy. His face was white, nearly bloodless, and he and Lachlan both had wounds.

Poor Eonan, I thought. He never gets to carry the girl.

But we were alive, all of us. And the finman was dead.

Houses live and die: there is a time for building . . . and a time for the wind to break the loosened panes.
—T. S. Eliot

Chapter Twenty-eight

We returned to the cottage and found another finman. He lay on the floor, surrounded by a pool of white ichor, and was a smaller version of the creature Eonan carried. He was also apparently weaker, at least magically, because Herman had been able to kill him without our assistance. I think perhaps the cat received some help, because there was a pair of familiar scissors on the floor, but of Fergus's shadow thieves we saw no other sign. Mayhap they had also been freed by the death of the finman. I had no love for them or of Fergus, but I hoped their souls had moved on.

The two bodies were loaded into the massive fireplace and set to burning. It required a lot of coal and peat and the rest of my driftwood to set them ablaze, but once started, the fire was hot and they burned satisfactorily. When the bodies were ashes and lumps of bone, Lachlan moved the giant table and retrieved the heart. It was by then a mass of goo, but he poured this into the fire and then smashed the crystal box and let it burn as well.

I don't know precisely when the change happened, but when I saw Herman next he had returned to house-cat size. He looked the same, but I sensed a difference, and I wondered if it was because Fergus's soul had departed from the finman and that this had in turn set him free. Or perhaps it was just that he no longer needed to be fierce and large.

I had more sewing to do that afternoon, but it was easier this time to close up the wounds on Eonan and Lachlan's skins. They were, after all, only physical and not magical injuries. It occurred to me, though, as I worked with surprisingly steady hands, that I had crossed a line—a big one that estranged me forever from my old life. I had killed . . . not a human, but still a sentient being, and not an animal raised for food. It had been necessary and in a good cause, but by the standards to which I had been raised, this would forever mark me as Cain. But what else could I have done? Nothing. And I felt no regret for fighting beside Eonan and Lachlan and saving my babies. In fact, I was better off for it. At that moment of decision, I had really begun living.

Yes, now I could live my life without looking back and regretting the choices I had failed to make because I was too timid. I had paid back any debt I owed Duncan for failing to protect him during our marriage, if indeed there had been one. I'd freed Fergus from a fate truly worse than death, and I had rid Findloss of its monster. All in all, this seemed to me a good day's work.

My own injuries were superficial. Lachlan laved the wounds on my feet so that they did not hurt so much, and then bound them up with clean linen. Eonan kept me supplied with tea and a strange selection of foods, which I ate without comment except to say thanks for his efforts.

I had hoped that Eonan would stay the night, but he elected to leave once the sun set; someone had to spread the word that the finmen were dead and that he and Lachlan had survived. It was decided that he would make no mention of the babies I carried. After some thought—probably brought about by his visit to Avocamor—Lachlan decided that perhaps we would like to spend some time with a clan of friendly sea kelpies; this would prepare me for the rest. Still too stunned by events to make any decisions of my own, I simply agreed to the plan. We would have to leave Findloss; that I knew.

"Wi' the finman gone the village will slowly be reburied. It was his will and magic that kept the sea and sand frae being called inland. Now there is nothing to stop the evil spell from taking back Findloss."

"I know. It makes me sad, but after all, it is only a house. We have our lives—all of our lives," I said, brushing my stomach. "That is far more important than property."

Lachlan knelt at my feet and offered me his hand. "This has been a time of surprise fer me. But sometimes life sets the terms of existence, and who am I tae quibble? Though I've said nowt of it afore, I want ye to ken that I appreciate wham you are—and am at peace wi' whatever roads ye traveled to arrive here. All of it, good and ill, went intae the making of ye. I couldnae ask fer anyone braver or mair bonny. Yer advent intae my life was unexpected but welcome."

"And I feel this way about you. How could I want you to have had any other life if it would change who you are?" If he could overlook my being a Mac-Codrum and married to a Culbin, then I could get over my envy of his dead wife. From what Eonan had said, it was his human wife who had taught Lachlan to love.

"Are ye nowt sorry we met then? Yer life waud be verra different if ye'd gone on yer way in ignorance of the other warld."

"No. I am not the least bit sorry—not for any of it." A moment's honest reflection told me that this was true. For all my concern about facing my unknown future, I would not want to go back to the days of ignorance. The state has been likened to bliss, but my supposed bliss was always overshadowed by smothering rules, bitterness and worry. It all seemed so petty now: A sad life that belonged to someone else who had allowed herself to be consumed with worry over petty things.

"I am offering ye a last chance. I've gold enough tae buy ye any sort of home ye might wish for. Ye can yet be free of me and make a new life among yer kind if ye desire."

I thought briefly of all the people I could be if I

stayed behind in the world of men. Of all the lives I could choose if I gave up Lachlan and my children. And then I put my hand in Lachlan's and smiled.

"Your life is also changed . . . if we stay together," I pointed out. "Do *you* regret meeting *me?*"

He did not hesitate. "Nowt a day or night of it."

"Well then."

He stared into my eyes. "And if I said that I worship ye?"

I laughed. "I should doubt your sincerity. I am too plain to be an idol."

Lachlan laughed as well, but more faintly. "Yer anything but plain." And to prove this, he kissed me.

"I love you, you know," I said, a short time later.

"Aye, I kenned this when ye sewed up Eonan's skin. For a moment I feared that it was him ye loved, but he did not behave as one besotted, which he waud hae been if ye'd stitched passion for him intae his fur."

I snorted. "We will have to work on your turn of phrase."

"As ye like. We've a' the time in the deep, wide warld."

For walking with his fey, her to the rock he brought,
On which he oft before his necromancies wrought.
And going in thereat, his magicks to have shown,
She stopt the cavern's mouth with an
enchanted stone,
Whose cunning strongly crost, amazed
while he did stand,
She captive him conveyed unto the Faerie-land.
—Melanie Jackson, *The Outsiders*

Epilogue

The sand has encroached steadily on the village, and Findloss has all but disappeared in the days it took to finish writing this document. The villagers, the ones not killed by the finman, have awoken from whatever thrall they were under and escaped to Keil or other villages in their boats. Lachlan, Herman and I will leave tonight. The seas are calm and cooperative.

What adventures await I can only guess, but I am excited to be off to see the magical realms I never knew existed. Worry not about my well-being. I am happy and I am at last living the life I was meant to have.

The End & The Beginning

Author's Note (the real one)

I shouldn't have to say this, but will for the sake of those who are confused. I do not have an aunt who married a selkie. This is a work of fiction—darn it!

It has been a long while since *The Selkie* and it was fun to revisit Scotland and all my finned and furred friends. Events of this book actually precede the story of *The Selkie*, so don't be confused if you don't see characters you remember from the first book.

A complete reference list of resource material for this novel would take up many pages, but I especially want to make mention of *The Buried Barony* by Alasdair Alpin MacGregor. This is the book you should read if you want to know more about Culbin Sands, the real Scottish town that was buried by a terrible storm and never seen again. Two other useful books were *A Field Guide To Demons, Fairies, Fallen Angels and Other Subversive Spirits* by Carol K. Mack and Dinah Mack, and my fey bible, *The World Guide to Gnomes, Fairies, Elves and Other Little People* by Thomas Keightley. Don't go elf hunting without them.

If you ever want to visit between books and see what stories are in progress, please feel free to drop in at my website www.melaniejackson.com or send a note to melaniejaxn@hotmail.com. I always look forward to hearing from you.

Melanie Jackson

Melanie Jackson

THE SELKIE

While the war to end all wars has changed the face of Europe, some things stay the same; the tempestuous Scottish coast remains a place of unquenchable magic and mystery. Sequestered at Fintry Castle by the whim of her mistress, Hexy Garrow spares seven tears for her past—all of which are swallowed by the waves.

By joining the water, those tears complete a ritual, and that ritual summons a prince. He is a man of myth whose eyes hold the dark secrets of the sea, and whose silken touch is the caress of the tide. His very nature goes against all Hexy has ever believed, but his love is everything she's ever desired.

ISBN 13: 978-0-505-52531-4

New York Times Bestselling Author

ANGIE FOX

"Fabulously fun." —*Chicago Tribune*

A Tale of Two Demon Slayers

Last month, I was a single preschool teacher whose greatest thrill consisted of color-coding my lesson plans. That was before I learned I was a slayer. Now, it's up to me to face curse-hurling imps, vengeful demons, and any other supernatural uglies that crop up. And, to top it off, a hunk of a shape-shifting griffin has invited me to Greece to meet his family.

But it's not all sun, sand, and ouzo. Someone has created a dark-magic version of me with my powers and my knowledge—and it wants to kill me and everyone I know. Of course, this evil twin doesn't have Grandma's gang of biker witches, a talking Jack Russell terrier, or an eccentric necromancer on her side. In the ultimate showdown for survival, may the best demon slayer win.

"This rollicking paranormal comedy will appeal to fans of Dakota Cassidy, MaryJanice Davidson, and Tate Hallaway."
—*Booklist*

ISBN 13: 978-0-505-52827-8

INTERACT WITH DORCHESTER ONLINE!

Want to learn more about your favorite
books and authors?
Want to talk with other readers that like
to read the same books as you?
Want to see up-to-the-minute Dorchester
news?

VISIT DORCHESTER AT:
DorchesterPub.com
Twitter.com/DorchesterPub
Facebook.com (Search Pages)

DISCUSS DORCHESTER'S NOVELS AT:
Dorchester Forums at DorchesterPub.com
GoodReads.com
LibraryThing.com
Myspace.com/books
Shelfari.com
WeRead.com

□ **YES!**

Sign me up for the Love Spell Book Club and send my FREE BOOKS! If I choose to stay in the club, I will pay only $8.50* each month, a savings of $6.48!

NAME: _____

ADDRESS: _____

TELEPHONE: _____

EMAIL: _____

□ I want to pay by credit card.

□ **VISA**   □ **MasterCard**   □ **DISCOVER**

ACCOUNT #: _____

EXPIRATION DATE: _____

SIGNATURE: _____

Mail this page along with $2.00 shipping and handling to:
Love Spell Book Club
PO Box 6640
Wayne, PA 19087
Or fax (must include credit card information) to:
610-995-9274
You can also sign up online at **www.dorchesterpub.com**.
*Plus $2.00 for shipping. Offer open to residents of the U.S. and Canada only.
Canadian residents please call 1-800-481-9191 for pricing information.
If under 18, a parent or guardian must sign. Terms, prices and conditions subject to change. Subscription subject to acceptance. Dorchester Publishing reserves the right to reject any order or cancel any subscription.